Josephus

Norman Bentwich

Contents

JOSEPHUS

Norman Bentwich

PREFACE

Josephus hardly merits a place on his own account in a series of Jewish Worthies, since neither as man of action nor as man of letters did he deserve particularly well of his nation. It is not his personal worthiness, but the worth of his work, that recommends him to the attention of the Jewish people. He was not a loyal general, and he was not a faithful chronicler of the struggle with Rome; but he had the merit of writing a number of books on the Jews and Judaism, which not only met the desire for knowledge of his nation in his own day, but which have been preserved through the ages and still remain one of the chief authorities for Jewish history. He lived at the great crisis of his people, when it stood at the parting of the ways. And while in his life he was patronized by those who had destroyed the national center, after his death he found favor with that larger religious community which was beginning to carry part of the Jewish mission to the Gentiles. For centuries Josephus was regarded by the Christians as the standard historian of the Jews, and, though for long he was forgotten and neglected by his own people, in modern times he has been carefully studied also by them, and his merits and demerits both as patriot and as writer have been critically examined.

It has been my especial aim in this book to consider Josephus from the Jewish point of view. I have made no attempt to extenuate his personal conduct or his literary faults. My judgment may appear somewhat severe, but it is when tried by the test of faithfulness to his nation that Josephus is found most wanting; and I hope that while extenuating nothing I have not set down aught in malice.

Of the extensive literature bearing on the subject, the books to which I am under the greatest obligation are Niese's text of the collected works and Schuerer's *History of the Jewish People in the Time of Jesus*. I have given in an Appendix a Bibliography, which contains the names of most of the works I have referred to.

I would mention in particular Schlatter's *Zur Topographie und Geschichte Palaestinas*, which is a remarkably stimulating and suggestive book, and which confirmed a view I had formed independently, that in the *Wars*, as in the *Antiquities*, Josephus is normally a compiler of other men's writings, and constantly expresses opinions not his own.

My greatest debt of thanks, however, is due to the spoken rather than the written word. Doctor Buechler, the Principal of Jews' College, London, has constantly assisted me with advice, directed me to sources of information, and let me draw plentifully from his own large stores of knowledge about Josephus; and Doctor Friedlaender, Sabato Morais Professor at the Jewish Theological Seminary of America, has done me the brotherly service of reading my manuscript and making many valuable suggestions on it. To their generous help this book owes more than I can acknowledge.

NORMAN BENTWICH.
Cairo, February, 1914.

I
THE JEWS AND THE ROMANS

The life and works of Flavius Josephus are bound up with the struggle of the Jews against the Romans, and in order to appreciate them it is necessary to summarize the relations of the two peoples that led up to that struggle. It is related in the Midrash that the city of Rome was founded on the day Solomon married an Egyptian princess. The Rabbis doubtless meant by this legend that the power of Rome was created to be a scourge for Israel's backslidings. They identified Rome with the Edom of the Bible, representing thus that the struggle between Esau and Jacob was carried on by their descendants, the Romans and the Jews, and would continue throughout history.[1] Yet the earliest relations of the two peoples were friendly and peaceful. They arose out of the war of independence that the Maccabean brothers waged against the Syrian Empire in the middle of the second century B.C.E., when the loyal among the people were roused to stand up for their faith. Antiochus Epiphanes, anxious to strengthen his tottering empire, which had been shaken by its struggles with Rome, sought to force violently on the Jews a pagan Hellenism that was already making its way among them. He succeeded only in evoking the latent force of their national consciousness. Rome was already the greatest power in the world: she had conquered the whole of Italy; she had destroyed her chief rival in the West, the Phoenician colony of Carthage; she had made her will supreme in Greece and Macedonia. Her senate was the arbiter of the destinies of kingdoms, and though for the time it refrained from extending Roman sway over Egypt and Asia, its word there was law. Its policy was "divide and rule," to hold supreme sway by encouraging small nationalities to maintain their independence against the unwieldy empires which the Hellenistic successors of Alexander had carved out for themselves in the Orient.

[1: Lev. R. xiii. (5), quoted in Schechter, Aspects of Rabbinic Theology, p. 100.]

At the bidding of the Roman envoy, Antiochus Epiphanes himself, immediately before his incursion into Jerusalem, had slunk away from Alexandria; and hence it was natural that Judas Maccabaeus, when he had vindicated the liberty of his nation, should look to Rome for support in maintaining that liberty. In the year 161 B.C.E. he sent Eupolemus the son of Johanan and Jason the son of Eleazar, "to make a league of amity and confederacy with the Romans"[1]: and the Jews were received as friends, and enrolled in the class of Socii. His brother Jonathan renewed the alliance in 146 B.C.E.; Simon renewed it again five years later, and John Hyrcanus, when he succeeded to the high priesthood, made a fresh treaty.[2] Supported by the friendship, and occasionally by the diplomatic interference, of the Western Power, the Jews did not require the intervention of her arms to uphold their independence against the Seleucid monarchs, whose power was rapidly falling into ruin. At the beginning of the first century B.C.E., however, Rome, having emerged triumphant from a series of civil struggles in her own dominions, found herself compelled to take an active part in the affairs of the East. During her temporary eclipse there had been violent upheavals in Asia. The semi-barbarous kings of Pontus and Armenia took advantage of the opportunity to overrun the Hellenized provinces and put all the Greek and Roman inhabitants to the sword. To avenge this outrage, Rome sent to the East, in 73 B.C.E., her most distinguished soldier, Pompeius, or Pompey, who, in two campaigns, laid the whole of Asia Minor and Syria at his feet.

[1: I Macc. viii. 7. It is interesting to note that the sons had Greek names, while their fathers had Hebrew names.]

[2: I Macc. xii. 3; xiv. 24.]

Unfortunately civil strife was waging in Palestine between the two Hasmonean brothers, Aristobulus and Hyrcanus, who fought for the throne on the death of the queen Alexandra Salome. Both in turn appealed to Pompey to come to their aid, on terms of becoming subject to the Roman overlord. At the same time, a deputation from the Jewish nation appeared before the general, to declare that they did not desire to be ruled by kings: "for what was handed down to them from their fathers was that they should obey the priests of God; but these two princes, though the descendants of priests, sought to transfer the nation to another form of government, that it might he enslaved."

Pompey, who had resolved to establish a strong government immediately subject to Rome over the whole of the near Orient, finally interfered on behalf of Hyrcanus. Aristobulus resisted, at first somewhat half-heartedly, but afterwards, when the Roman armies laid siege to Jerusalem, with fierce determination. The struggle was in vain. On a Sabbath, it is recorded, when the Jews desisted from their defense, the Roman general forced his way into the city, and, regardless of Jewish feeling, entered the Holy of Holies. The intrigues of the Jewish royal house had brought about the subjection of the nation. As it is said in the apocryphal Psalms of Solomon, which were written about this time: "A powerful smiter has God brought from the ends of the earth. He decreed war upon the Jews and the land. The princes of the land went out with joy to meet him, and said to him, 'Blessed be thy way; draw near and enter in peace.'" Yet Pompey did not venture, or did not care, to destroy or rob the Temple, according to Cicero and Josephus,[1] because of his innate moderation, but really, one may suspect, from less noble motives. It was the custom of the Roman conquerors to demand the surrender, not only of the earthly possessions of the conquered, but of their gods, and to carry the vanquished images in the triumph which they celebrated. But Pompey may have recognized the difference between the Jewish religion and that of other peoples, or he realized the widespread power of the Jewish people, which would rise as a single body in defense of its religion; for he made no attempt to interfere either with Jewish religious liberties, or with a worship that Cicero declared to be "incompatible with the majesty of the Empire."

[1: Cicero, Pro Flacco, 69, and Ant. XVI. iv, 4.]

The Jews, however, were henceforth the clients, instead of the allies, of Rome. Though Hyrcanus was recognized by Pompey as the high priest and ethnarch of Judea, and his wily counselor, the Idumean Antipater, was given a general power of administering the country, they were alike subject to the governor of Syria, which was now constituted a Roman province. Moreover, the Hellenistic cities along the coast of Palestine and on the other side of Jordan, which had been subjugated by John Hyrcanus and Alexander Jannaeus, were restored to independence, and placed under special Roman protection, and the Jewish territory itself was shortly thereafter split by the Roman governor Gabinius into five toparchies, or provinces, each with a separate administration.

The guiding aim of the conqueror was to weaken the Oriental power (as the Jews were regarded) and strengthen the Hellenistic element in the country. The Jews were soon to feel the heavy hand and suffer the insatiate greed of Rome. National risings were put down with merciless cruelty, the Temple treasury was spoiled in 56 B.C.E. by the avaricious Crassus, one of the triumvirate that divided the Roman Empire, when he passed Jerusalem on his way to fight against the Parthians; even the annual offering contributed voluntarily by the Jews of the Diaspora to the Temple was seized by a profligate governor of Asia. The Roman aristocrats during the last years of the Republic were a degenerate body; they regarded a governorship as the opportunity of unlimited extortion, the means of recouping themselves for all the gross expenses incurred on attaining office, and of making themselves and their friends affluent for the rest of their lives. And Judea was a fresh quarry.

A happier era seemed to be dawning for the Jews when Julius Caesar became dictator. At the beginning of the civil war between him and Pompey, Hyrcanus, at the instance of Antipater, prepared to support the man to whom he owed his position; but when Pompey was murdered, Antipater led the Jewish forces to the help of Caesar, who was hard pressed at Alexandria. His timely help and his influence over the Egyptian Jews recommended him to Caesar's favor, and secured for him an extension of his authority in Palestine, and for Hyrcanus the confirmation of his ethnarchy. Joppa was restored to the Hasmonean domain, Judea was granted freedom from all tribute and taxes to Rome, and the independence of the internal administration was guaranteed. Caesar, too, whatever may have been his motive, showed favor to the Jews throughout his Empire. Mommsen thinks that he saw in them an effective leaven of cosmopolitanism and national decomposition, and to that intent gave them special privileges; but this seems a perverse reason to assign for the grant of the right to maintain in all its thoroughness their national life, and for their exemption from all Imperial or municipal burdens that would conflict with it. It is more reasonable to suppose that, taking in this as in many other things a broader view than that of his countrymen, Caesar recognized the weakness of a world-state whose members were so denationalized as to have no strong feeling for any common purpose, no passion of loyalty to any community, and he favored Judaism as a counteracting force to this peril.

His various enactments constituted, as it were, a Magna Charta of the Jews in the Empire; Judaism was a favored cult in the provinces, a ***licita religio*** in the capital. At Alexandria Caesar confirmed and extended the religious and political privileges of the Jews, and ordered his decree to be inscribed on pillars of brass and set up in a public place. At Rome, though the devotees of Bacchus were forbidden to meet, he permitted the Jews to hold their assemblies and celebrate their ceremonials. At his instance the Hellenistic cities of Asia passed similar favorable decrees for the benefit of the Jewish congregations in their midst, which invested them with a kind of local autonomy. The proclamation of the Sardians is typical. "This decree," it runs, "was made by the senate and people, upon the representation of the praetors:

"Whereas those Jews who are our fellow-citizens, and live with us in this city, have ever had great benefits heaped upon them by the people, and have come now into the senate, and desired of the people that, upon the restitution of their law and their liberty by the senate and people of Rome, they may assemble together according to their ancient legal custom, and that we will not bring any suit against them about it; and that a place may be given them where they may hold their congregations with their wives and children, and may offer, as did their forefathers, their prayers and sacrifices to God:--now the senate and people have decreed to permit them to assemble together on the days formerly appointed, and to act according to their own laws; and that such a place be set apart for them by the praetors for the building and inhabiting the same as they shall esteem fit for that purpose, and that those who have control of the provisions of the city shall take care that such sorts of food as they esteem fit for their eating may be imported into the city."[1]

[1: Ant. XIV. x. 24.]

Caesar's decrees marked the culmination of Roman tolerance, and the Jews enjoyed their privileges for but a short time. It is related by the historian Suetonius that they lamented his death more bitterly than any other class.[1] And they had good reason. The Republicans, who had murdered him, and his ministers, who avenged him, vied with each other for the support of the Jewish princes; but the people in Palestine suffered from the burden that the rivals imposed on the provinces in their efforts to raise armies. Antipater and his ambitious sons Herod and Phasael contrived to maintain their tyranny amid the constant shifting of power; and when the hardy mountaineers of Galilee strove under the lead of one Hezekiah (Ezekias), the founder of the party of the Zealots, to shake off the Roman yoke, Herod ruthlessly put down the revolt. But when Antigonus, the son of that Aristobulus who had been deprived of his kingdom by Hyrcanus and Pompey, roused the Parthians to invade Syria and Palestine, the Jews eagerly rose in support of the scion of the Maccabean house, and drove out the hated Idumeans with their puppet Jewish king. The struggle between the people and the Romans had begun in earnest, and though Antigonus, when placed on the throne by the Parthians, proceeded to spoil and harry the Jews, rejoicing at the restoration of the Hasmonean line, thought a new era of independence had come.

[1: Suetonius, Caesar, lxxxiv. 7.]

The infatuation of Mark Antony for Cleopatra enabled Antigonus to hold his kingdom for three years (40-37 B.C.E.). Then Herod, who had escaped to Rome, returned to Syria to conquer the kingdom that Antony had bestowed on him. He brought with him the Roman legions, and for two years a fierce struggle was waged between the Idumeans, Romans, and Romanizing Jews on the one hand, and the national Jews and Parthian mercenaries of Antigonus on the other. The struggle culminated in a siege of Jerusalem. As happened in all the contests for the city, the power of trained force in the end prevailed over the enthusiasm of fervent patriots. Herod stormed the walls, put to death Antigonus and his party, and established a harsher tyranny than even the Roman conqueror had imposed. For over thirty years he held the people down with the aid of Rome and his body-guard of mercenary barbarians. His constitution was an autocracy, supplemented by assassination. In the civil war between Antony and Octavian, he was first on the losing side, as his father had been in the struggle between Pompey and Caesar; but, like his father, he knew when to go over to the victor. The master of the Roman Empire, henceforth known as Augustus, was so impressed with his carriage and resolution that he not only confirmed him in his kingdom, but added to it the territories of Chalcis and Perea to the north and east of the Jordan. Throughout his reign Herod contrived to preserve the friendship of Rome as effectually as he contrived to arouse the hatred of his Jewish subjects. "The Imperial Eagle and some distinguished Roman or other," says George Adam Smith,[1] "were always fixed in Herod's heaven." He ruled with a strong but merciless hand. He insured peace, and while he turned his own home into a slaughter-house, he glorified the Jewish dominion outwardly to a height and magnificence it had never before attained. Yet the Jewish deputation that went to plead before Augustus on his death declared that "Herod had put such abuses on them as a wild beast would not have done, and no calamity they had suffered was comparable with that which he had brought on the nation."[2] Beneath the fine show of peace, splendor, and expansion, the passions of the nation were being aroused to the breaking-point.

[1: Jerusalem, ii. 504.]

[2: Ant. XVII. xi. 2.]

Augustus himself, following the example of his uncle Julius Caesar, yet lacking the same large tolerance, held towards Judaism an ambiguous attitude of impartiality rather than of favor. He caused sacrifices to be offered for himself at the Temple at Jerusalem,[1] but he praised his nephew Gaius for having refrained from doing likewise during his Eastern travels.[2] He was anxious that the national laws and customs of each nation should be preserved, and he issued a decree in favor of the Jews of Cyrene; but he initiated the worship of the Emperors, which necessitated a conflict between the kingdom of God and the kingdom of Caesar, and in the end destroyed the religious liberty that Julius Caesar had given to the Empire. His aim was at once to foster the veneration of the Imperial power and establish an Imperial worship that should replace the effete paganism of his subjects. He made no attempt to force this worship on the Jews, but its existence fanned the prejudice against the one nation that refused to participate. And the Jews could not but look with distrust on a government that "derived its authority from the deification of might, whereof the Emperor was the incarnate principle."[3]

[1: Philo, De Leg. ii. 507.]

[2: Suetonius, Aug. 93.]

[3: Schechter, Aspects of Rabbinic Theology, p. 108.]

Marcus Agrippa, the trusted minister of Augustus, was also an intimate friend of Herod, and served to link the two courts. But on the death of Herod, in 4 C.E., the friendship of Rome for the Idumean royal house was modified. Archelaus, who claimed the whole succession, was appointed simply as ethnarch of Judea, while Herod's two other sons, Philip and Herod Antipas, divided the rest of his dominions. The Zealots, rid of the powerful tyrant who had held them down, sought again to throw off the hated yoke of Idumea, which, not without reason, they identified with the yoke of Rome. With their watchword, "No king but God," they attempted to make Judea independent, and a fierce struggle, known as the War of Varus, ensued. Jerusalem was stormed once again by Roman legions before the Zealots were subdued. Archelaus was deposed by his masters after a few years, and the province of Judea was placed under direct Roman administration. The Roman procurator was at first less detested than the Idumean tyrant, since he interfered less with the legal institutions, such as the Sanhedrin and the Bet Din; but his presence with the legionaries in the Holy City and his constant, though often involuntary, affronts to the religious sentiments of the people roused the hostility of the nationalist party, who looked forward to the day when Israel should "tread on the neck of the Eagle." The Pharisees, who were anxious for the spiritual rather than the political independence of the Jews, counseled submission to Rome, and were willing "to render unto Caesar the things that are Caesar's," so long as they were not compelled to give up the Torah. But the Zealots desired political as well as religious freedom, and they fomented rebellion. They have been compared by Merivale to the Montagnards of the French Revolution, driven by their own indomitable passion to assert the truths that possessed them with a ferocity that no possession could justify. They were continually rousing the people to expel the foreign rulers, and in the northern province of Galilee, where they found shelter amid the wild tracts of heath and mountain, they maintained a constant state of insurrection.[1]

[1: It is important to notice that much of our knowledge of the Zealots is derived from Josephus, who, as will be seen, set himself to misrepresent them, and repeated the calumnies of hostile Roman writers against them. The Talmud contains several references to them, describing them as Kannaim (the Hebrew equivalent of Zealots), and it would appear that they were in their outlook successors of the former Hasidim, distinguished as much for their religious rigidity as their patriotic fervor. See Jewish Encyclopedia, s.v. Zealots.]

The Romans, on their side, accustomed to the ready submission of all the peoples under their sway, could not understand or tolerate the Jews. To them this people with its dour manners, its refusal to participate in the religious ideas, the social life, and the pleasures of its neighbors, its eruptions of passion and violence on account of abstract ideas, and its rigid exclusion of the insignia of Roman majesty from the capital, seemed the enemies of the human race. In their own religion they had freely found a place for Greek and Egyptian deities, but the Jewish faith, in its uncompromising opposition to all pagan worship, seemed, in the words that Anatole France has put into the mouth of one of the Roman procurators, to be rather an *ab*ligion than a *re*ligion, an institution designed rather to sever the bond that united peoples, than bind them together. Every other civilized people had accepted their dominion; the Jews and the Parthians alone stood in the way of universal peace. The near-Eastern question, which, then as now, continually threatened war and violence, irritated the Romans beyond measure, and they came to feel towards Jerusalem as their ancestors had felt two hundred years before towards Carthage, the great Semitic power of the West, ***delenda est Hierosolyma***. As time went on they realized that this stubborn nation was resolved to dispute with them for the mastery, and every agitation was regarded as an outrage on the Roman power, which must be wiped out in blood. It was the inevitable conflict, not only between the Imperial and the national principle, but between the ideas of the kingdom of righteousness and the ideas of the kingdom of might.

During the reign of Tiberius, however, the Roman governors were held in check to some extent by strong central control from Rome, and their extortion was comparatively moderate. The worst of them was Pontius Pilate, and the ***odium theologicum*** has, perhaps, had its part in blackening his reputation. Nevertheless, the broad religious tolerance initiated by the first Caesar was being continually impaired. The Jewish public worship was prohibited in Rome, and the Jews were expelled from the city in 19 C.E.; while at Alexandria an anti-Jewish persecution was instigated by Sejanus, the upstart freedman, who became the chief minister of Tiberius. In Palestine, though we hear of no definite movement, it is clear from after-events that the bitterness of feeling between the Hellenized Syrians and the Jewish population was steadily fomented. The Romans were naturally on the side of the Greek-speaking people, whom they understood, and whose religion they could appreciate. The situation may best be paralleled by the condition of Ireland in the sixteenth and seventeenth centuries, when England supported the Protestant population of Ulster against the hated Roman Catholics, who formed the majority of the people.

It had been the aim of Tiberius to consolidate the unwieldy mass of the Empire by the gradual absorption of the independent kingdoms inclosed within its limits. In pursuance of this policy, Judea, Chalcis, and Abilene, all parts of Herod's kingdom, had been placed under Roman governors. But when Gaius Caligula succeeded Tiberius in 32 C.E., and brought to the Imperial throne a capricious irresponsibility, he reverted to the older policy of encouraging client-princes, and doled out territories to his Oriental favorites. Prominent among them was Agrippa, a grandson of Herod, who had passed his youth in the company of the Roman prince in Italy. He received as the reward of his loyal extravagance not only Judea but Galilee and Perea, together with the title of king. He was not, however, given permission to repair to his kingdom, since his patron desired his attentions at Rome. Later he was detained by a sterner call. Gaius, who had passed from folly to lunacy, was not content with the customary voluntary worship paid to the Emperors, but imagined himself the supreme deity, and demanded veneration from all his subjects. He ordered his image to be set up in all temples, and, irritated by the petition of the Jews to be exempted from what would be an offense against the first principle of their religion, he insisted upon their immediate submission. In Alexandria the Greek population made a violent attempt to carry out the Imperial order; a sharp conflict took place, and the Jews in their dire need sent a deputation, with Philo at its head, to supplicate the Emperor. In the East the governor of Syria, Petronius, was directed to march on Jerusalem and set up the Imperial statue in the Holy of Holies, whatever it might cost. Petronius understood, and it seems respected, the faithfulness of the Jews to their creed, and he hesitated to carry out the command. From East and West the Jews gathered to resist the decree; the multitude, says Philo, covered Phoenicia like a cloud. Meantime King Agrippa at Rome interceded with the Emperor for his people, and induced him to relent for a little. But the infatuation again came over Gaius; he ordered Petronius peremptorily to do his will, and, when the legate still dallied, sent to remove him from his office. But, as Philo says, God heard the prayer of His people: Gaius was assassinated by a Roman whom he had wantonly insulted, and the death-struggle with Rome, which had threatened in Judea, was postponed. The year of trial, however, had brought home to the whole of the Jewish people that the incessant moral conflict with Rome might at any moment be resolved into a desperate physical struggle for the preservation of their religion. And the warlike party gained in strength.

The date of the death of Gaius (Shebat 22) was appointed as a day of memorial in the Jewish calendar; and for a little time the Jews had a respite from tyranny. Agrippa, who, after the murder of Gaius, played a large part in securing for Claudius the succession to the Imperial throne, was confirmed in the grant of his kingdom, and, despite his antecedents and his upbringing, proved himself a model national king. Perhaps he had seen through the rottenness of Rome, perhaps the trial of Gaius' mad escapades had deepened his nature, and led him to honor the burning faith of the Jews. Whatever the reason, while remaining dutiful to Rome, he devoted himself to the care of his people, to the maintenance of their full religious and national life, and to the strengthening of the Holy City against the struggle he foresaw. To the Jews of the Diaspora, moreover, the succession of Claudius brought a renewal of privileges. An edict of tolerance was promulgated, first to the Alexandrians, and afterwards to the communities in all parts of the habitable globe, by which liberty of conscience and internal autonomy were restored, with a notable caution against Jewish missionary enterprise. "We think it fitting," runs the decree, "to permit the Jews everywhere under our sway to observe their ancient customs without hindrance; and we hereby charge them to use our graciousness with moderation and not to show contempt of the religious observances of other people, but to keep their own laws quietly."[1] Nevertheless the tolerant principle on which Caesar and Augustus had sought to found the Empire was surely giving way to a more tyrannical policy, which viewed with suspicion all bodies that fostered a corporate life separate from that of the State, whether Jewish synagogue, Stoic school, or religious college.

[1: Ant. XIX, v. 2.]

The conflict between Rome and Jerusalem entered on a bitterer stage when Agrippa died in 44 C.E. Influenced by his self-seeking band of freedmen-counselors, who saw in office in Palestine a golden opportunity for spoliation, Claudius placed the vacant kingdom again under the direct administration of Roman procurators, and appointed to the office a string of the basest creatures of the court, who revived the injustices of the worst days of the Republic.

From 48-52 C.E. Palestine was under the governorship of Ventidius Cumanus, who seemed deliberately to egg on the Jews to insurrection. When a Roman soldier outraged the Jewish conscience by indecent conduct in the Temple during the Passover, Cumanus refused all redress, called on the soldiers to put down the clamoring people, and slew thousands of them in the holy precincts.[1] A little later, when an Imperial officer was attacked on the road and robbed, Cumanus set loose the legionaries on the villages around, and ordered a general pillage. When a Galilean Jew was murdered in a Samaritan village, and the Jewish Zealots, failing to get redress, attacked Samaria, Cumanus fell on them and crucified whomever he captured. Then, indeed, the Roman governor of Syria, not so reckless as his subordinate, or, it may be, corrupted by the man anxious to step into the procurator's place, summoned Cumanus before him, and sent him to Rome to stand his trial for maladministration.

[1: Ant. XX. v. 3.]

But this act of belated justice brought the Jews small comfort; Cumanus was succeeded by Felix, an even worse creature. He was the brother of the Emperor's favorite Narcissus, "by badness raised to that proud eminence," and the husband of the Herodian princess Drusilia, who had become a pagan in order to marry him. Tacitus, the Roman historian, says[1] that "with all manner of cruelty he exercised royal functions in the spirit of a slave." Under his rapacious tyranny the people were goaded to fury. Bands of assassins, Sicarii (so called by both Romans and Jews because of the short dagger, sica, which they used), sprang up over the country. Now they struck down Romans and Romanizers, and now they were employed by the governor himself to put out of the way rich Jewish nobles whose possessions he coveted. From time to time there were more serious risings, some purely political, others led by a pseudo-Messiah, and all alike put down with cruelty. Roman governors were habitually corrupt, grasping, and cruel, but Mommsen declares that those of Judea in the reigns of Claudius and Nero, who were chosen from the upstart equestrians, exceeded the usual measure of worthlessness and oppressiveness. The Jews believed that they had drunk to the dregs the cup of misery, and that God must send them a Redeemer. There were no prophets to preach as at the time of the struggle with Babylon and Assyria, that the oppression was God's chastisement for their sins. And it was inconceivable to them that the power of wickedness should be allowed to triumph to the end.

[1: Hist. v. 9.]

Steadily the party that clamored for war gained in strength, and the apprehensions of the Pharisees who viewed the political struggle with misgiving, lest it should end in the loss of the national center and the destruction of religious independence, were overborne by the fury of the masses. The oppression by Roman governors and Romanizing high priests did not diminish when Nero succeeded Claudius. For the rest of the Empire the first five years of his reign (the *quinquennium Neronis*) were a period of peace and good government, but for the Jews they brought little or no relief. The harsh Roman policy toward the Jews may have been specially instigated by Seneca, the Stoic philosopher, who was Nero's counselor during his saner years, and who entertained a strong hatred of Judaism. But we need not look for such special causes. It had been the fixed habit of Republican Rome to crush out the national spirit of a subject people, "to war down the proud," as her greatest poet euphemistically expressed it; and now that spirit was adopted by the Imperial Caesars in dealing with the one and only people resolved to preserve inviolate its national life and its national religion. Nero indeed recalled Felix, and Festus, who was appointed in his place, made an attempt to mend affairs, but he died within a year, and was succeeded by two procurators that were worthy followers of Felix. The first of them was Albinus (62-64), of whom Josephus says that there was no sort of wickedness in which he had not a hand. The same authority says that compared with Gessius Florus, the governor under whom the Rebellion burst out, he was "most just." Florus owed his appointment to Poppaea, the profligate wife of Nero, and his conduct bears the interpretation that he was deliberately anxious to fill the measure of persecution to the brim and drive the nation to war.

The very forms of privilege which had been left to the Jews were turned to their hurt. The Herodian tetrarchs of Chalcis, to whom the Romans granted the power of appointing the high priests, true to the tradition of their house, appointed only such as were confirmed Romanizers, and the most unscrupulous at that. When Felix was governor, the high priest was the notorious Ananias, of whom the Talmud says, "Woe to the House of Ananias; woe for their cursings, woe for their serpent-like hissings."[1] Herod Agrippa II, the son of Agrippa, who held the principate from 50-100 C.E., and was the faithful creature of Rome throughout the period of his people's stress, proclaiming himself on his coins "lover of Caesar and lover of Rome," deposed and created high priests with unparalleled frequency as a means of extorting money and rewarding the leading informers. There were seven holders of the office during the last twenty years of Roman rule, and "he who carried furthest servility and national abnegation received the prize." The high priests thus formed a kind of anti-national oligarchy; they robbed the other priests of their dues, and reduced them to poverty, and were the willing tools of Roman tyranny. Together with the Herodian princes, who indulged every lust and wicked passion, they undermined the strength of the people like some fatal canker, much as the priests and nobles had done at the first fall of Jerusalem, or, again, in the days of the Seleucid Emperors. Apart from governors, tax-collectors, and high priests, the Romans had an instrument of oppression in the Greek-speaking population of Palestine and Syria, which maintained an inveterate hostility to the Jews. The immediate cause of the great Rebellion actually arose out of a feud between the Jewish and the Gentile inhabitants of Caesarea. The Hellenistic population outnumbered the Jews in the Herodian foundations of Caesarea, Sepphoris, Tiberias, Paneas, etc., as well as in the old Greek cities of Doris, Scythopolis, Gerasa, Gadara, and the rest of the Decapolis. This population regarded religion only as the pretext for public ceremonials and entertainments; it was scornful of the Jewish abstention from these things, and was aroused to the bitterest hatred by the social aloofness of their neighbors. Violent riots between Jew and Gentile were constantly taking place, and whether they were the aggressors or merely fighting in self-defense, the Jews were the scapegoats for the breaking of the peace. Stung by constant outrage on the part of their neighbors, the Jews turned upon them at Caesarea, and drove them out of the town. Thereupon Florus called them to reckoning, marched on Jerusalem, and plundered the Temple treasury. This event happened on the tenth day of Iyar in the year 66 C.E. The war-party determined to force the struggle to a final issue. Hitherto they had only been able to arouse a section to venture desperate sporadic insurrection against the might of Rome. Now they carried the people with them to engage in a national rebellion.

[1: Pesahim, 57a.]

Agrippa II, who was amusing himself at Alexandria when the first outbreak occurred, hurried back to Jerusalem, and sought to quiet the people by impressing upon them the invincible power of Rome. But he failed, and the Romanizing priests' party failed, and the peaceful leaders of the Pharisees failed, to shake their determination. Messianic hopes were rife among the masses, and were invested with a materialistic interpretation. The Zealots, it is alleged by the pagan as well as the Jewish authorities for the period, believed that the destined time was come when the Jews should rule the world. The people looked for the realization of the prophecy of Isaiah (41:2), "He shall raise up the righteous one from the East, give the nations before Israel, and make him rule over kings."

The belief in the approach of the Messianic kingdom was undoubtedly one of the mainsprings of the revolt. There had been a series of popular leaders claiming to be Messiahs, but in the final struggle it was not the claim of any individual, but the passionate faith of the whole people, that inspired a belief in the coming of a perfect deliverance. Some events appeared to favor the fulfilment of their hopes of temporal sovereignty, bred though they were of despair. Rome under the corrupting influence of Nero seemed to be passing her zenith; national movements were stirring

in the West, in Gaul and in Germany; in the East the Parthians were again threat-
ening the security of the Roman provinces. The Jewish cause, on the other hand,
seemed to be gaining ground everywhere. Its converts, numerous in the West, were
still more numerous and important in the East. Among those recently brought over
to the true faith as full proselytes were Helena, the queen of Adiabene, a kingdom
situate in Mesopotamia, and her son Izates, who built themselves splendid palaces
at Jerusalem. In Babylon the Jews had made themselves almost independent, and
waged open war on the Parthian satraps. A large section of the people cherished a
somewhat simple theodicy. How could God allow the wicked and dissolute Romans
to prosper and the chosen people to be oppressed? The Hellenistic writers of Sibylline oracles and the Hebrew writers of Apocalypses, imitating the doom-songs of
Isaiah and Ezekiel, announced the coming overthrow of evil and the triumph of
good. Evil had reached its acme in Nero, and the time had come when God would
break the "fourth horn" of Daniel's vision (ch. 8), and exalt his chosen people.

The fight for national independence was bound to have come, for nothing
could have prevented the Romans from their attempt to crush the spirit of the
Jews, and nothing could have held back the Jews from making a supreme effort to
obtain their freedom from the hated yoke. For one hundred and twenty years Palestine had been ground beneath the iron heel of Roman governors and Romanizing
tyrants. The conditions of the foreign rule had steadily grown more intolerable.
At first the oppression was mainly fiscal; then it had sought to crush all political
liberty, and finally it had come to outrage the deepest religious feeling and menace
the Temple-worship. As Graetz says, "The Jewish people was like a captive, who,
continually visited by his jailer, rattles at his fetters with the strength of despair, till
he wrenches them asunder." It was not only the freedom of the Jew, but the safety
of Judaism that was imperiled by the misrule of a Claudius and a Nero. The war
against the Romans was then not merely a struggle for national liberty, but, equally
with the wars of the Maccabees against the Seleucids, an episode in the more vital
conflict between Hebraism and paganism, between material force and the ardent
passion for religious freedom.

II
THE LIFE OF JOSEPHUS TO
THE FALL OF JOTAPATA

Josephus was essentially an apologist, and his writings include not only an apology for his people, but an apology for his own life. In contrast with the greater Jewish writers, he was given to vaunting his own deeds. We have therefore abundant, if not always reliable, information about the chief events of his career. It must always be borne in mind that he had to color the narrative of his own as well as his people's history to suit the tastes and prejudices of the Roman conqueror. He was born in 37 C.E., the first year of the reign of Gaius Caesar, the lunatic Emperor, who nearly provoked the Jews to the final struggle. Though he is known to history as Josephus Flavius, his proper name was Joseph ben Mattathias, Josephus being the Latinized form of the Hebrew [Hebrew: Yosef] and his patronymic being exchanged, when he went over to the Romans, for the family name of his patrons, Flavius. His father was a priest of the first of the twenty-four orders, named Jehoiarib, and on his mother's side he was connected with the royal house of the Hasmoneans. His genealogy, which he traces back to the time of the Maccabean princes, is a little vague, and we may suspect that he was not above improving it. But his family was without doubt among the priestly aristocracy of Jerusalem, and his father, he says, was "eminent not only on account of his nobility, but even more for his virtue."[1]

[1: Vita, 2.]

He was brought up with his brother Matthias to fit himself for the priestly office, and he received the regular course of Jewish education in the Torah and the tradition. He says in the ***Antiquities*** that "only those who know the laws and can interpret the practices of our ancestors, are called educated among the Jews;" and it is likely that he attended in his boyhood one of the numerous schools that existed in Jerusalem at the time. According to the Talmud there were four hundred and eighty synagogues each with a Bet Sefer for teaching the written law and a Bet Talmud for the study of the oral law.[1] From his silence we may infer that he did not study Greek at this period, and Aramaic was his natural tongue. He was never able to speak Greek fluently or with sufficient exactness, because, as he says in the ***Antiquities***, "Our own nation does not encourage those who learn the language of many peoples, and so color their discourses with the smoothness of their periods: for they look upon this sort of accomplishment as common, not only to freemen, but to any slave that pleases to learn it."[2] When, in his middle age, he set himself to write the history of his people in Greek, he was compelled to get the help of friends to correct his composition and syntax.

[1: Yer. Meg. iii. 1.]

[2: Ant. XX. xi. 2.]

As to his Hebrew accomplishments, he tells us, with his native immodesty, that he acquired marvelous proficiency in learning, and was famous for his great memory and understanding. When he was fourteen years of age, he continues, such was his fame that the high priests and principal men of the city frequently came to consult him about difficult points of the law. His mature works do not show any profound knowledge either of the Halakah or of the Haggadah, so that the statement is not to be taken strictly. It is probably nothing more than a grandiloquent way of saying that he was a precocious child, who impressed his elders. Paul, too, claimed that he was "a Pharisee of the Pharisees, and zealous beyond those of his own age in the Jews' religion," and yet he can hardly be regarded as an authority on the tradition. The autobiography of Josephus, it is pertinent to remember, was designed to impress the Romans with the greatness of the writer, and its readers were not equipped with the means of criticising his Jewish accomplishments. With the same object of impressing the Romans, Josephus recounts that, when about the age of sixteen, he had a mind to imbue himself with the tenets of the three Jewish parties, the Sadducees, the Pharisees, and the Essenes.

Elsewhere he describes the teaching of these sects for the benefit of his Roman readers according to a technical classification borrowed from his environment, i.e. he represents them as three philosophical schools of the Greek type, each holding different views about fate and Providence and the nature of the soul and its immortality. But just as this is demonstrably a misleading coloring of the difference between the sections of the Jewish people, so is his attempt to represent that he attended, as a cultured Greek or Roman of the time would have done, three philosophical colleges. He was compelled by the needs of his audience to present Jewish life in the form of Greco-Roman institutions, however ill it fits the mould, and his remarks about sects and schools must always be taken with caution. It is as though a modern writer should describe Judaism as a Church, and express its ideas and observances in the language of Christian theology.

There is, however, no reason to doubt that Josephus made himself acquainted with the tenets of the chief teachers of the time, and he may conceivably have sat at the feet of Rabbi Gamaliel, then the chief sage at Jerusalem. But, anxious to exhibit his catholicity, after professing himself a Pharisee, he says that, not content with these studies, he became for three years a faithful disciple of one Banus, who lived in the desert, and used no other clothing than grew upon trees, ate no other food than that which grew wild, and bathed frequently in cold water both night and day. [1] The extreme hermit form of the religious life was more fashionable in the first century of the Christian era among Gentiles than among Jews, and it is not unlikely that Josephus is embroidering his idea of life in an Essene community, rather than setting down his actual experience. An Essene he never became, but he remained throughout his life very partial to certain forms of the Essene belief, more especially those which coincided with the Greco-Roman superstitions of the time, such as the literal prediction of future events, the meaning of dreams, the significance of omens.[2] These ideas, handed down from primitive Israel, had lived on among the masses of the people, though discarded by the learned teachers, and Josephus, finding them in vogue among his masters, readily professed acceptance of them.

[1: Vita, 2.]

[2: Comp. B.J. II. viii. 12; III. viii. 3; VI. v. 4.]

Abandoning apparently the idea of being a hermit, Josephus at the age of nineteen returned to Jerusalem, and began to conduct himself according to the rules of the Pharisee sect, which is akin, he says, to the school of the Stoics. The comparison of the Pharisees with the Stoics is again misleading, and based on nothing more than the formal likeness of their doctrines about Providence. The Pharisees were essentially the party that upheld the whole tradition and the separateness of Israel. They numbered in their ranks the most popular teachers, and politically, though opposed to Rome and all its ways, they counseled submission so long as religious liberty was not infringed. It may be that Josephus only professed his attachment to them after his surrender, because, as pacifists and believers in moral as against physical force, they were favorably regarded by the Romans; but even if as a young and ambitious priest he attached himself to their body early in life in order to gain influence among the people, he was not a representative Pharisee. He obtained a certain acquaintance with the teaching of the Pharisees, and partly shared their political views, though not from the same motives as their true leaders. Yet the very next step in his life that he chronicles marks his outlook as fundamentally different.

At the age of twenty-six, after seven years in Jerusalem, during which he exercised his priestly functions, he journeyed to Rome. The cause of his voyage, on which he was picturesquely wrecked and had to swim for his life through the night, was the deliverance from prison of certain priests closely related to him, who had been sent there as prisoners by Felix, the tyrannical Roman governor. At Rome, through his acquaintance with Aliturius, an actor of plays, a favorite of Nero, and by birth a Jew, he came into touch with the profligate court. To the genuine Pharisee a Jewish play-actor would have been an abomination. Josephus used his acquaintance to obtain an introduction to Poppaea Sabina, the Emperor's wife for the time. Though a by-word for shamelessness of life, she was herself one of "the fearers of the Lord" ([Greek: sebomenoi]), who professed adherence to the Jewish creed without accepting the Jewish law. Josephus won her favor, and through it procured the liberation of the priests. The Imperial city was then at the height of its material magnificence, and must have made an immense impression of power upon the young Jewish aristocrat. Having acquired a lasting admiration for Rome and a desire to enter her society and a conviction of her invincibility, he returned to Palestine in triumph--and with the spirit of an opportunist. This at least is the picture he draws of himself, but a more kindly interpretation might see in the moment of his return the indication of a genuine patriotic feeling.

When he arrived in Jerusalem, in the year 65 C.E., he found his country seething with rebellion. The crisis soon came to a head. Gessius Florus, who owed his governorship, as Josephus owed the success of his errand, to the favor of the "God-fearing" Poppaea, roused the people to fury by his pillage of the Temple, and the moderates could no longer hold the masses in check. The Zealots seized the fortress of Antonia, which overlooked the Temple, and, having become masters of the city, murdered the high priest Ananias. Eleazar, whom Josephus, perhaps confusedly, describes as his son, an intense nationalist among the priests, became the leader in counsel, and sealed the rebellion by persuading the people to discontinue the daily sacrifice offered in the name of the Roman Emperor.

At the same time the extermination of the Jews in the Hellenistic cities, Caesarea, Scythopolis, and Damascus, by the infuriated Syrians, who organized a kind of Palestinian Vespers, convinced the people that they were engaged in a war to the death. The Herodian party, as the royal house and its supporters were called, endeavored to preserve peace, by dwelling on the overpowering might of Rome and the inevitable end of the insurrection, but in vain. In fear the priests withdrew to their duties in the Temple, and did not venture out till the Zealots were for a time dislodged. The Roman legate of Syria, Cestius Gallus, after the defeat of the Romanizing party by the Zealots, himself marched on Jerusalem in the autumn of 68 C.E. with two legions. But he failed ignominiously to quell the revolt. The Roman garrison in the city was put to the sword, and the legate, while beating a hasty retreat, was routed in the defiles of Beth-Horon, where two centuries before the Syrian hosts had been decimated by Judas the Maccabee. The two legions were cut to pieces. The fierce valor of the untrained national levies had broken the serried cohorts of the Roman veterans, and in the unexpectedness of this deliverance the party of rebellion for a time was triumphant among all sections of the Jewish people.

Even those who had been the most determined Romanizers, such as the high-priestly circle, were induced, either by a belief in the chances of success or from a desire to protect themselves by a seeming adherence to the national cause, to throw in their lot with the war party. It might have been better for their people, had they, like Agrippa, joined the Romans. Half-hearted at best in their support of the struggle, yet by their wealth and position able at first to obtain a commanding part in the conduct of the war, they used it to temporize with the foe and to dull the edge of the popular feeling. Josephus unfortunately does not enlighten us as to the inner movements in Judea at this crisis. He merely relates that the Sanhedrin became a council of war, and Palestine was divided into seven military districts, over most of which commanders of the Herodian faction were placed. Joseph the son of Gorion and Ananias the high priest, both members of the moderate party, were chosen as governors of Jerusalem, with a particular charge to repair the walls, and the Zealot leader Eleazar the son of Simon was passed over.

Josephus himself, though he possessed no military experience, and had apparently taken no part in the opening campaign, was made governor of Lower and Upper Galilee, the most important military post of all; for Galilee was the bulwark of Judea, and if the Romans could be successfully resisted there, the rebellion might hope for victory. It lay in a strategic position between the Roman outposts, Ptolemais (the modern Acre) on the coast and Agrippa's kingdom in the east. It was a country made for defense, a country of rugged mountains and natural fastnesses, and inhabited by a hardy and warlike population, which, for half a century, had been in constant insurrection. Thence had come the founders of the Zealots and the still more violent band of the Sicarii, and each town in the region had its popular leader. Josephus was expected to hold it with its own resources, for little help could be spared from the center of Palestine. Guerrilla fighting was the natural resource of an insurgent people, which had to win its freedom against well-trained and veteran armies. It had been the method of Judas Maccabaeus against Antiochus amid the hills of Judea. Josephus, however, made no attempt to practise it, and showed no vestige of appreciation of the needs of the case.

It is difficult to gather the reason of his appointment, unless it be that in his writings he deliberately kept back from the Romans the more enthusiastic part he had played at the outset of the struggle. So far as his own account goes, neither devotion to the national cause, nor experience, nor prestige, nor power of leadership, nor knowledge of the country recommended him. His distinguished birth and his friendship for Rome were hardly sufficient qualifications for the post. The influence of his friend, the ex-high priest Joshua ben Gamala, may have prevailed, and one is fain to surmise that those who sent him, as well as he himself, were anxious to pretend resistance to Rome, but really to work for resistance to the rebellion.

At all events, at the end of the autumn of 67, Josephus repaired to his command, taking with him two priests, Joazar and Judas, as representatives of the Sanhedrin at Jerusalem. In the record which he gives of his exploits in the *Wars*, he says that his first care was to gain the good-will of the people, drill his troops, and prepare the country to meet the threatened invasion. In the *Life*, which he wrote some twenty years later, when he had perforce to cultivate a more complete servility of mind, and was anxious to convince the Romans that he was a double-dealing traitor to his country, he represents that he set himself from the beginning to betray the province. The record of his actions points to the conclusion that he fell between the stools of covert treachery and half-hearted loyalty, that he was neither as villainous in design nor as heroic in action as he makes himself out to be. He made some show of preparation at the beginning, but from the moment the Roman army arrived under Vespasian, and he realized that Rome was in earnest, he abandoned all hope of success, and set himself to make his own position secure with the conqueror.

The chief cities of Galilee were Sepphoris, situated on the lower spurs of the hills near the plain of Esdraelon, which divides the country from Samaria and Judea; Tiberias, a city founded by Herod Antipas on the western borders of the Lake of Gennesareth, and Tarichea, also an Herodian foundation, situate probably at the southeast corner of the lake. All these Josephus fortified; and he strengthened with walls other smaller towns and natural fortresses, such as Jotapata, Salamis, and Gamala.[1] He says also that he appointed a Sanhedrin of seventy members for the province, and in each town established a court of seven judges, as though he were come to exercise a civil government. He did, however, get together an army of more than a hundred thousand young men, and armed them with the old weapons which he had collected. Though he despaired of their standing up against the Romans, he ordered them in the Roman style, appointing a large number of subordinate officers and teaching them the use of signals and a few elementary military movements. His army ultimately consisted of 60,000 footmen, 4,500 mercenaries, in whom he put greatest trust, and 600 picked men as his body-guard. He had little cavalry, but as Galilee was a country of hills, this deficiency need not have proved fatal, had he been a strategist or even a loyalist. During the eight months' respite that he enjoyed before the appearance of the Roman army, he spent most of his time in civil feud, and succeeded in dividing the population into two hostile parties. He boasts that, though he took up his command at an age when, if a man has happily escaped sin, he can scarcely guard himself against slander, he was perfectly honest, and refrained from stealing and peculation[2]; but he is at pains to prove that he threw every obstacle in the way of the patriotic party, and did all that an open enemy of the Jews could have done to undermine the defense of the province.

> [1: B.J. II. xx. 6. His account of his actions in Galilee is, however, from beginning to end, open to question; and the contemporary account of Justus has unfortunately disappeared entirely. It is likely that his rival's narrative would have shown him in a better light than his own.]

> [2: Vita, 15.]

Before his arrival in the north, the leader of the national party was John the son of Levi, a man of Gischala, which was one of the mountain fastnesses in Northern Galilee, now known as Jish, near the town of Safed.[1] Josephus heaps every variety of violent abuse upon him in order, no doubt, to please his patrons. When he introduces him on the scene, he describes him as "a very knavish and cunning rogue, outdoing all other rogues, and without his fellow for wicked practices. He was a ready liar, and yet very sharp in gaining credit for his fictions. He thought it a point of virtue to deceive, and would delude even those nearest to him. He had an aptitude for thieving," and so forth. Whenever the historian mentions the name of his rival, he rattles his box of abusive epithets until the reader is wearied by the image of the monster conjured up before him. But, unfortunately for his credit, Josephus also records John's deeds, and these reveal him as one who, if at times cruel and intriguing, yet lived and died for his country, while his enemy was thinking of saving himself.

[1: The Hebrew name of the fortress was [Hebrew: Nosh Halav], meaning "clot of cream"; the place was so called because of the fertility of the soil on which it stands.]

It is not surprising then that John, having eyes only for the defense of the land, was not blind to the double-dealing of the priestly governor, who had been sent by the Romanizing party to organize resistance. The first event that brought about a collision between them was the suspicious conduct of Josephus in the matter of some spoil seized from the steward of King Agrippa and brought to Tarichea. Agrippa had entirely turned his back on the national rising, and was the faithful ally of the Romans. He was therefore an open enemy, and Tiberias, which had been under his dominion, had revolted from him. Josephus upbraided the captors for the violence they had offered to the king, and declared his intention to return the spoil to the owner. A little later he prevented John from destroying the corn in the province stored by the Romans for themselves. The people were naturally indignant at this conduct, and led by John and another Zealot, Jesus the son of Sapphias, the governor of Tiberias, and by Justus of the same city, who was afterwards to be a rival historian, they rose against Josephus. With stratagems worthy of a better cause he evaded this onslaught.

More briefly in the *Wars*, and in the *Life* at wearisome length, Josephus tells a tale of intrigue and counter-intrigue, mutual attempts at assassination, wiles and stratagems to undermine the power of each other, which took place between him and John. The city of Tarichea was his stronghold, Tiberias the hot-bed of the movement against him. The part he professes to have played is so extraordinary in its meanness that we are fain to believe that it is largely fiction, composed to show that he was only driven in the end by danger of his life to fight against the sacred power of Rome. However that may be, John reported his doings to the Sanhedrin at Jerusalem, and that body, which was now, it seems, in the control of the Pharisees and Zealots, sent a deputation to recall him. Simon, the celebrated head of the Sanhedrin and leader of the national party, had pressed for the dismissal of Josephus. [1] Ananias, the ex-high priest and Sadducee, had at first been his champion, but he had been overborne. The deputation consisted of two Pharisees, Jonathan and Ananias, and two priests, Joazar and Simon. Warned by his friends in Jerusalem of their coming, Josephus had all the passes watched, seized the embassy, and recaptured the four cities that had revolted from him: Sepphoris, Gamala, Gischala, and Tiberias. According to the account in the **Wars**, the cities revolted again, and were recaptured by similar stratagems; and when the disturbances in Galilee were quieted in this way, the people, ceasing to prosecute their civil dissensions, betook themselves to make preparations for the war against the Romans. The invasion had begun in earnest, and Josephus, fortified, as he said, by a dream, which told him not to be afraid, because he was to fight with the Romans, and would live happily thereafter, decided for the time not to abandon his post.

> [1: It is notable that this is the only reference in the work of Josephus to the great Rabbi; the name of his successor in the headship of the Sanhedrin, Johanan ben Zakkai, does not occur even once.]

Josephus had displayed his administrative talents in these eight months of peaceful government by losing all that had been gained in the four months of the successful rebellion at Jerusalem. He now had an opportunity of displaying his military abilities. In the spring of 67 C.E., Flavius Vespasian, the veteran commander of the legions in Germany and Britain, who, on the defeat of Cestius Gallus, had been chosen by Nero to conduct the Jewish campaign, brought his army of four legions from Antioch to Ptolemais. He was met there by King Agrippa, who brought a large force of auxiliaries, and by a deputation of citizens from Sepphoris, the chief city of Galilee, who tendered their submission and invited him to send a garrison. Josephus, though he knew of the city's Romanizing leanings, had negligently or deliberately failed to occupy it, so that the place was lost without a blow. He made a feeble effort to recapture it, for appearance sake it would seem, and then, though he had an unlimited choice of favorable positions, and the Roman forces were not very large at the time, he abandoned the attempt of meeting the enemy in the field. Titus arrived from Alexandria, with two more legions, the fifth and the tenth, and then the Roman army, numbering with auxiliaries 60,000 men, set out from Ptolemais, and proceeded to occupy Galilee.

The Jewish forces were encamped on the hills above Sepphoris. Josephus describes the wonderful array and order of the Roman army on the march. The sight seems to have led a large part of his army to run away. He himself, when he saw that he had not an army sufficient to engage the enemy, despaired of the success of the war, and determined to place himself as far as he could out of danger. In this inspiring mood he abandoned the rest of the country, sent a dispatch to Jerusalem demanding help, and threw himself into the fortress of Jotapata, situated on the crest of a mountain in Northern Galilee, which he chose as the most fit for his security. Vespasian, hearing of this step, and, as Josephus modestly suggests, "supposing that, could he only get Josephus into his power, he would have conquered all Judea," straightway laid siege to the town (Iyar 16). For forty-two days the place was besieged, and during that period every resource that heroic resistance could suggest, according to the narrative of its commandant, was exhausted. The height of the wall was raised to meet the Roman embankments, provisions were brought in by soldiers disguised in sheep-skins, the Roman works were destroyed by fire, boiling oil was poured on the assailants, and finally the city was not stormed till the garrison was worn out with famine and fatigue. But, as has been pointed out, the details recorded are "the commonplaces of poliorcetics," and may have been borrowed by Josephus from some military text-book and neatly applied. Jotapata fell on the first day of Tammuz, and whatever the heroism of his army, the general did not shine in the last days of his command or in the manner of his surrender. Suspected by his men and threatened by them with death, he was unable to give himself up openly. He took refuge with some of his comrades in a deep pit, where they were discovered by an old woman, who informed the Romans. Vespasian, who, we are again told, believed that, if he captured Josephus, the greater part of the war would be over, sent one Nicanor, well known to the Jewish commandant, to take him. Josephus, professing prophetical powers, offered to surrender, and quieted his conscience by a secret prayer to God, which is a sad compound of cant and cowardice:

"Since it pleaseth Thee, who hast created the Jewish nation, now to bring them low, and since their good fortune is gone over to the Romans, and since Thou hast chosen my soul to foretell what is to come to pass hereafter, I willingly surrender, and am content to live. I solemnly protest that I do not go over to the Romans as a deserter, but as Thy minister."

It may be that Josephus really believed he had prophetic powers, and thought he was imitating the great prophets of Israel and Judah who had proclaimed the uselessness of resistance to Assyria and Babylon. But they, while denouncing the wickedness of the people, had shared their lot with them. And Josephus, who weakly sought a refuge for himself after defeat, resembles rather the prophets whom Jeremiah denounced: "They speak a vision of their own heart, and not out of the mouth of the Lord. They say still unto them that despise me, The Lord hath said, Ye shall have peace; and they say unto everyone that walketh after the imagination of his own heart, No evil shall come upon you."[1] His comrades however prevented him from giving himself up, and called on him to play a braver part and die with them, each by his own hand. He put them off by talking philosophically, as he has it, about the sin of suicide, a euphemism for a collection of commonplaces on the duty of preserving their lives. But when this enraged them, he bethought him of another device, and proposed that they should cast lots to kill each other. They assented, and by Divine Providence he was left to the last with one other, whom he persuaded to break his oath and live likewise.[2] Having thus escaped, he was led by Nicanor to Vespasian, the whole Roman army gathering around to gaze on the hero. Continuing his prophetical function, when he found that he was like to be sent to Nero, he announced to Vespasian, "Thou art Caesar and Emperor, thou, and this thy son.... thou art not only lord over me, but over the land and the sea and all mankind." The Roman general was incredulous, till, hearing that his prisoner had foretold the length of the siege of Jotapata--a prophecy which, of course, he had the ability to fulfil--and further, on the report of the death of Nero, having conceived the possibility of becoming Emperor, he had regard to the Jewish prophet, and, without setting him at liberty, bestowed favors on him, and made him easy about his future. Such was the end of the military career of Josephus.

[1: Jer. 23: 16-17.]

[2: A charitable explanation of this self-debasing account of Josephus is that he was driven to invent some story to extenuate his resistance to the Romans, and had to blacken his reputation as a patriot to save his skin. The fact that he was kept prisoner some time by Vespasian suggests that he was not so big a traitor as he pretends.]

The Talmud relates that Rabbi Johanan ben Zakkai, the head of the Pharisees, was carried in a coffin outside the walls of Jerusalem by his disciples, and was brought to the Roman camp, where he hailed Vespasian as Emperor and Caesar, and thereby gained his favor. If not apocryphal, the event must have happened in 69 C.E., when the Roman commander was generally expected to aim at the Imperial throne, then the object of strife between rival commanders. The rabbi belonged to the peace party, and from the beginning had opposed the war. And though his action was disapproved by the later generations, it was justified by his subsequent conduct; for it was he who, by founding the famous college at Jabneh, kept alive the Jewish spirit after the fall of the nation. For him surrender was a valid means to the preservation of the nation. The action of Josephus hardly bears the same justification. His desire for self-preservation was natural enough, but his manner of effecting it was not honorable. He was a general who, having taken a lead in the struggle for independence, had seen all his men fall, and had at the end invited the last of his comrades to kill each other, and he saved his life by sacrificing his honor. His mind was from the beginning of the struggle subjugated to Rome, but unhappily he accepted the most responsible post in the national defense and betrayed it. His address to Vespasian was mere flattery, designed to impose on a superstitious man's credulity; for the ear of Vespasian, says Merivale, "was always open to pretenders to supernatural knowledge." Lastly Josephus used his safety, not for the purpose of preserving the Jewish heritage, but for personal ends. He became a flunkey of the Flavian house, and straightway started on the transformation from a Jewish priest and soldier into a Roman courtier and literary hireling. Hard circumstances compelled him to choose between a noble and an ignoble part, between heroic action and weak submission. He was a mediocre man, and chose the way that was not heroic and glorious. Posterity gained something by his choice; his own reputation was fatally marred by it.

III
THE LIFE OF JOSEPHUS FROM
THE TIME OF HIS SURRENDER

Josephus was little more than thirty years old at the time of his surrender. At an age when men usually begin to realize their ambition and ideal, his whole life's course was changed: he had to abandon all his old associations, and accommodate himself to a different and indeed a hostile society. Henceforth he was a liege of the Roman conqueror, and had to submit to be Romanized not only in name but in spirit. His condition was indeed a thinly-disguised servitude. The Romans were an imperious as well as an Imperial people, and though in some circumstances they were ready to spare the lives of those who yielded, they required of them a surrender of opinion and an abasement of soul. For the rest of his years, which comprehended the whole of his literary activity, Josephus was not therefore a free man. He acted, spoke, and wrote to order, compelled, whenever called upon, to do the will of his masters. His legal condition was first that of a *libertus* (a freedman) of Vespasian, and as such he owed by law certain definite obligations to his patron's family. But the moral subservience of the favored prisoner of a subjugated people must have been a far profounder thing than the legal obligation arising from his status; and this enforced moral and mental subservience is a cardinal point to be remembered in forming a judgment upon Josephus. His expressed opinions are often not the revelation of his own mind, but the galling tribute which he was compelled to pay for his life. And apart from the involuntary and undeliberate adoption of Roman standards, which, living isolated from Jewish life in Rome, he could not escape, he had in writing, and no doubt in conversation, deliberately and consciously to assume the deepest-seated of the Roman prejudices towards his own people. Liberty has been defined as the power of a man to call his soul his own. And in that sense Josephus emphatically did not possess liberty. We must be on our guard, therefore, against regarding him as an independent historian, much less as writing from an independent Jewish point of view. From the time of his surrender till his death he lived and wrote as the client of the Flavian house, and all his works had to pass the Imperial censorship.

His domestic life is characteristic of his subservience. At the bidding of Vespasian, when in the Roman camp at Caesarea, he divorced his first wife, who was locked up in Jerusalem during the siege. Though by Jewish law it was forbidden to a priest to marry a captive woman, he took as his second wife a Jewess that had been brought into the Roman camp. Having no children by her, he divorced her after a year, and married again at Alexandria. By his third wife he had three sons, but with a Roman's carelessness of the marriage bond he divorced her late in life, and married finally a noble Jewess of Crete, by whom he had two more sons, Justus and Simon Agrippa. His last two wives, be it noted, came from Hellenistic-Jewish communities, and were doubtless able to assist him in acquiring Greek.

The public as well as the domestic life of Josephus was controlled by the Roman commander. Till the end of the Jewish struggle it followed the progress of the Roman arms. He continued to play an active part in the war, not, however, as a leader of the Jews, but as the adviser of their enemies. He was attached to the staff of Titus, and after witnessing the fall of the two fortresses of Galilee, Gamala and Gischala, which held out bravely under John after the capture of Jotapata, he accompanied the Roman at the end of the year 68 to Alexandria. There he spent a year, till a change of fortune came to him.

During the year 68, Vespasian captured the two chief cities which the Jewish national party held to the east side of the Jordan, Gadara and Gerasa. He then prepared to lay siege to Jerusalem. But hearing of the death of Nero and of the chaos at Rome that followed it, he stayed operations to await events in Italy. In the following year, largely by the aid of the Jewish apostate Tiberius Alexander, he secured the allegiance of all the Eastern legions, and was proclaimed Emperor. Three other generals laid claim to the same dignity, under the same title of armed force, but in the end Vespasian's friends in Italy made themselves masters of Rome, and he repaired himself to the capital and donned the purple. Josephus was rewarded with his complete freedom, and assumed henceforth the family name of his Imperial patrons. When, at the end of the year 69, Titus was appointed by his father to finish the war, he accompanied him back to Palestine. In the eighteen months' respite that had been vouchsafed to them, the Jews had spent their energy and undermined their powers of resistance by internecine strife. According to the account in the *Wars*, which unfortunately is the only full record we have of events, John of Gischala, fleeing to Jerusalem after the fall of the Galilean fortresses, roused the Zealots against the high priest Ananias, who was directing the Jewish policy towards submission to Rome. Ananias, who was of the same party as Josephus, seems to have come to the conclusion that resistance was hopeless, and he was anxious to make terms. John called in to his aid the half-savage Idumeans, who had joined the Jewish rebellion against Rome. They entered the city, and, possessing themselves of the Temple mount, spread havoc. The Temple itself ran with blood, and 8500 dead bodies, among them that of the high priest, defiled its precincts.[1] Josephus, who, to suit the Roman taste, identifies religion and ritual, declares that the fall of the city and the ruin of the nation are to be dated from that day, and upon Ananias he passes a eulogy that is likewise written with an eye to Roman predilections:

"He was a prodigious lover of liberty and of democracy; he ever preferred the public welfare before his own advantage, and he was thoroughly sensible that the Romans were invincible. And I cannot but think that it was because God had doomed the city to destruction on account of its pollution, and was resolved to purge His sanctuary with fire, that He cut off thus its great protector."

[1: B.J. IV. vi. 1.]

For the better part of a year, according to our historian, the Zealots maintained a reign of terror, and the various parties fought against one another in the Holy City as fiercely as the Girondists and Jacobins of the French Revolution. But on the approach of Titus they abandoned their strife and united to resist the foe. The Roman general brought with him four legions, the fifth, tenth, twelfth, and fifteenth, besides a large following of auxiliaries, and his whole force amounted to 80,000 men. As head of his staff came Tiberius Alexander, the renegade nephew of Philo and formerly procurator of Judea. Josephus also was on the besieger's staff--possibly he was an officer of the body-guard (***praefectus praetorio***)--and was employed to bring his countrymen to reason. Himself convinced, almost from the moment when he took up arms, of the certainty of Rome's ultimate victory, and doubly convinced now, partly from superstitious fatalism, partly from a need for extenuating his own submission, he wasted his eloquence in efforts to make them surrender. He knew that within the besieged city there was a considerable Romanizing faction (including his own father), and either he believed, or he had to pretend to believe, that he could bring over the mass to their way of thinking. On various occasions during the siege he was sent to the walls to summon the defenders to lay down their arms. He enlarged each time on the invincible power of Rome, on the hopelessness of resistance, on the clemency of Titus if they would yield, and on the terrible fate which would befall them and the Temple if they fought to the bitter end. What must have specially aroused the fury of the Zealots was his insistence that the Divine Providence was now on the side of the Romans, and that in resisting they were sinning against God. It is little wonder that on one occasion when making these harangues he was struck by a dart, and that his father was placed in prison by the Zealots. Indeed it says much for the tolerance of those whom he constantly reviles as the most abandoned scoundrels and the most cruel tyrants that they did not do him and his family greater hurt.

Titus, after beating back desperate attacks by the Jews, fixed his camp on Mount Scopas, by the side of the Mount of Olives, to the north of the city, and, abandoning the idea of taking the city fortress by storm, prepared to beleaguer it in regular form. The Jews were not prepared for a siege. Josephus and the Rabbis[1] agree that the supplies of corn had been burnt by the Zealots during the civil disturbances; and as the arrival of Titus coincided with the Passover, myriads of people, who had come up from all parts of the country and the Diaspora to celebrate the festival, were crowded within its walls. It is estimated that their number exceeded two and a half million. The capital was a hard place to capture. Josephus, following probably a Roman authority, gives an account of the fortifications of Jerusalem from the point of view of the besieger, which is confirmed in large part by modern research. [2] On the southeast and west the city was unapproachable by reason of the sheer ravines of Kedron and Hinnom, overlooked by almost perpendicular precipices, which surrounded it. It was vulnerable therefore only on the north, where the two heights on which it was built were connected with the main ridge of the Judean hills; and here it was fortified with three walls. The outermost, which was built by Agrippa I, encompassed the new quarter of Bezetha, which lay outside the Temple mount to the northeast. The second wall encompassed the part of the city on the Temple Mount and reached as far as the Tower of Antonia, which overlooked and protected the Temple. The third or innermost wall was the oldest, and encompassed the whole of the ancient city where it was open, including the hill Acra or Zion on the southeast, which was divided from Mount Moriah by the cleft known as the Tyropoeon, or cheese-market. Beyond this hill there was another eminence sloping gradually to the north, till it dropped into the valley of Jehoshaphat with an escarpment of two hundred feet.

[1: Comp. Abot de Rabbi Nathan, vi., ed. Schechter, p. 32.]

[2: B.J. V. iv. 1.]

Thus the rampart surrounded the two hills with a continuous line of defense, and the three quarters of the city were separated from each other by distinct walls, so that each could hold out when the other had fallen. The walls were strengthened with several towers, of which the most important were Psephinus, on the third wall at the northwest corner, Hippicus, on the old wall, which was opposite Phasaelus, and Mariamne. But the strongest, largest, and most beautiful fortress in Jerusalem was the Temple itself. It was not merely the visible center of Judaism, it was the citadel of Judea. As each successive court rose higher than the last, the "Mountain of the House" itself stood on the highest point of the inclosure. The Temple was guarded by the tower of Antonia, situated at the corner of the two cloisters, upon a rock fifty cubits high, overlooking a precipice. Like the other towers, Antonia was built by Herod, and manifested his love of largeness and strength. Within these fortifications there were eleven thousand men under Simon, and not more than thirty thousand trained soldiers under John, to pit against eighty thousand Roman veterans; but of the two and a half million people who, it is calculated, were shut up in the city, thousands were ready at any moment to sally upon the besiegers and lay down their lives for their beloved sanctuary.

Within the city, however, there were also a number of persons wavering in their desire for resistance and anxious to find a favorable opportunity of going over to the Romans. The leaders of the high-priestly party had been killed by the Zealots, but their followers remained to hamper the defense of the city. If Josephus is to be believed, during the respite of the Passover festival at the beginning of the siege, while the Romans were preparing their approaches and siege works, the party strife again broke out. Eleazar opened the gates of the Temple to admit the people for the festival, but John, taking treacherous advantage of the opportunity, led his men in with arms concealed beneath their garments, put his opponents to the sword, and seized the sanctuary. Josephus further represents that throughout the siege Simon and John, while resisting the Romans and defending different parts of the walls, were still engaged in their internecine strife, "and did everything that the besiegers could desire them to do."[1]

[1: B.J. V. vi.]

The story has not the stamp of probability, and it is more likely that Josephus is distorting the jealousies of the two commanders into the dimensions of civil strife. Anyhow, the resistance which the Jews offered to the Romans showed the stubbornness of despair, or what the historian calls "their natural endurance in misfortune." At every step the legionaries were checked; in pitching their camp, in making their earthworks, in bringing up their machines; and frequently desperate sallies were made by the defenders upon the Roman entrenchments. Nevertheless, after fifteen days the first wall was captured, and in five days more the second was taken. By a desperate sally the besieged recovered it for a little, but were again driven back by superior numbers and force. Josephus is fond of contrasting the different tempers of the two armies: on the one side power and skill, on the other boldness and the courage born of despair; here the habit of conquering, there intense national ardor.

After the capture of the second wall, he was sent to parley with the besieged, and urged, as he had done before, the invincible power of his masters.[1] "And evident it is," he added with his renegade's theology, "that fortune is on all hands gone over to them, and that God, who has shifted dominion from nation to nation, is now settled in Italy."[2] When his address was received with scorn, he proceeded, according to his account, to lecture the people from their ancient history, in order to prove that they had never been successful in aggressive warfare. "Arms were never given to our nation, but we are always given up to be fought against and taken." The Zealots' desecration of the Temple deprived them of Divine help, and it was madness to suppose that God would be well-disposed to the wicked. Had He not shown favor to Titus and performed miracles in his aid? Did not the springs of Siloam run more plentifully for the Roman general? All his appeals had no effect, and though some faint-hearted persons deserted, the multitude held firm, and the siege was pressed on more vigorously than ever. A wall of circumvallation was built round the city, and the horrors of starvation increased daily. Between the months of Nisan and Tammuz one hundred and fifty thousand corpses were carried out of the town.[3] Josephus expatiates on the terrible suffering, and again and again he denounces the iniquity of the Zealots, who continued the resistance. "No age had a generation more fruitful in wickedness; they confessed that they were the slaves, the scum, the spurious and abortive offspring of our nation." John committed the heinous sacrilege of using the oil preserved in the Temple vessels for the starving soldiers. "I suppose," says the ex-priest writing in the Roman palace, "that had the Romans made any longer delay in attacking these abandoned men, the city would either have been swallowed up by the ground opening on them, or been swept away by a deluge, or destroyed as Sodom was destroyed, since it had brought forth a generation even more godless than those that suffered such punishments."[4]

[1: B.J. V. ix. 3.]

[2: We are reminded of the saying of Rabbi Akiba some half-century later. When asked where God was to be sought now that the Temple was destroyed, he replied, "In the great city of Rome" (Yer. Taanit, 69a). But the Rabbinical utterance had a very different meaning from the plea of Josephus.]

[3: B.J. V. xiii. 7.]

[4: B.J. V. x. and xiii.]

Famine and weariness were breaking down the strength of the Jews, and, after fierce resistance, the tower of Antonia was captured and razed to the ground. Josephus adds another chapter to detail the horrors of the famine, in which he recounts the story of the mother eating her child, which occurs also in the Midrash.[1] The Romans, he tells us, were filled with a religious loathing of their foes on account of their sins in violating the Temple and eating forbidden food, and Titus excused himself for the sufferings he caused, on the ground that, as he had given the Jews the chance of securing peace and liberty, they had brought the evil on themselves. Slowly but surely the Romans gained a footing within the Temple precinct; inch by inch John was driven back, and on the Ninth of Ab the sanctuary was stormed. A torch, hurled probably by the hand of Titus (see below, p. 128), set the cloisters alight, and the fire spread till the whole house was involved. The crowning catastrophe, the burning of the Holy of Holies, happened on the following day.

[1: Ekah R. 65a.]

Josephus remained in the Roman camp throughout the siege, advising Titus at each step how he might proceed. After the fall of the Temple he witnessed the last desperate struggle, when a half-starved remnant of the defenders "looked straight into death without flinching." A great modern writer sees in this unquenchable passion of the Zealots for liberty a sublime type of steadfastness[1]; but Josephus, who after the fall of the Temple had made another unavailing effort to persuade them to lay down their arms, again pours forth his abuse upon those who fought against the sacred might of Rome. Over a million had perished in the siege, and less than one hundred thousand were captured, of whom only forty thousand were preserved. His favor with Titus enabled him to redeem from captivity his brother and a large number of his friends and acquaintances and one hundred and ninety women and children.[2] His own estates near Jerusalem having been taken for a military colony, he received liberal compensation in another part of Judea. From the victor he also obtained a scroll of the law.

[1: George Eliot, Impressions of Theophrastus Such.]

[2: Vita, 75.]

It is not certain whether he accompanied "the gentle Titus" through Syria after the fall of the city and the razing of its walls. The victor's progress was marked at each stopping-place by the celebration of games, where thousands of young Jewish captives were made to kill each other, "butchered to make a Roman holiday" and feast the eyes of the conqueror and the Herodian ally and his spouse. But he certainly witnessed at Rome the triumph of the Flavii, father and son, and gazed on the shame of his country, when its most holy monuments were carried by the noblest of the captives through the streets amid the applause and ribald jeers of a Roman crowd. Josephus enlarges with apparent apathy on the procession, which is commemorated and made vivid down to our own day by the arch in the Roman Forum, through which no Jew in the Middle Ages would pass. He records, too, that Vespasian built a Temple of Peace, in which he stored the golden vessels taken from the Jewish sanctuary, and put up the whole of Judea for sale as his private property. [1] Josephus himself was housed in the royal palace, and it does not appear that he ever returned to Palestine. The tenth legion had been left on the site of Jerusalem as a permanent Roman garrison, and a fortified camp was built for it on the northern hill. "The legions swallowed her up and idolaters possessed her." *A chacun selon ses oeuvres* is the comment of Salvador, the Franco-Jewish historian (fl. 1850), comparing the gilded servitude of Josephus with the fate of the patriots of Jerusalem; and another recent historian, Graetz, has contrasted the picture of Jeremiah uttering his touching laments over the ruins at the fall of the first Temple with the position of Josephus pouring out his fulsome adulation of the destroyer at the fall of the second.

[1: B.J. VII. vi. 6.]

Henceforth Josephus lived, an exile from his country and his countrymen, in the retinue of the Caesars, and entered on his career as his people's historian. But he was never allowed to forget his dependence. His first work was an account of the Roman war, in which he vilified the patriots to extenuate his own surrender and his master's cruelty. It is true that he afterwards composed an elaborate apology for his people in the form of a history in twenty volumes, which may be considered as a kind of palliation for the evil he had done them in action. It was more possible to refute the Roman prejudices based on utter ignorance of Jewish history, than the prejudices based on their narrowness of mind. But even here the writer has often to accommodate himself to a pagan standpoint, which could not appreciate Hebrew sublimity. When he wrote the ***Antiquities***, his mind was already molded in Greco-Roman form, and where he seeks to glorify, he not seldom contrives to degrade. His works are a striking example of inward slavery in outward freedom, for by dint of breathing the foreign atmosphere and imbibing foreign notions he had become incapable of presenting his people's history in its true light. He had been granted full Roman citizenship, and received a literary pension. Still he was not loved by other courtiers as worthy as himself, and he had frequently to defend himself against the charges of his enemies. In the reign of Vespasian, after the Zealot rising in Cyrene had been put down, the leader, Jonathan, who was brought as a prisoner to Rome, charged Josephus before the Emperor with having sent him both weapons and money. The story was not believed, and the informer was put to death. After that, Josephus relates, "when they that envied my good fortune did frequently bring censure against me, by God's Providence I escaped them all."

He remained in favor under Titus and Domitian, who in turn succeeded their father in the purple. Domitian indeed, though he persecuted the Jews, and laid new fiscal burdens upon them, punished the accusers of Josephus, and made his estate in Judea tax-free, and the Emperor's wife, Domitia, also showed him kindness. But perhaps the amazing and pathetic servility of the ***Life*** is to be explained by fear of the vainglorious despot, whose hand was heavy on all intellectual work. Historical writers suffered most under his oppression, and it may have been necessary to Josephus to make out that he had been a traitor. It may appear more to his credit as a courtier than as a Jew that the enemy of his people was friendly towards him. But his position must have been perilous during the black reign of the tyrant, who rivaled Nero for maniac cruelty. His chief patron was one Epaphroditus, by his name a Greek, perhaps to be identified with a celebrated librarian and scholar, to whom he dedicated his ***Antiquities*** and the books ***Against Apion***. He lived on probably[1] till the beginning of the second century, through the short but tranquil rule of Nerva, when there was a brief interlude of tolerance and intellectual freedom, into the reign of Trajan, who was to deal his people injuries as deep as those Titus had inflicted. It is uncertain whether he survived to witness the horrors of the desperate rising of the Jews, which sealed their national doom throughout the Diaspora.

At least he did not survive to describe it. His last work that has come down to us is the *Life*, which is an apologetic pamphlet, perversely self-vilifying, in which he sought to refute the accusation of his rival Justus of Tiberias, that he had taken a commanding part in the war against the Romans in Galilee, and had been the guiding spirit of the Rebellion.

> [1: It has, however, been suggested that the date of Agrippa's death, which is recorded in the *Life*, was really 95 C.E., instead of 103 C.E., as is usually accepted; if that is so, Josephus may not have outlived the black reign of Domitian, which lasted till 97 C.E. See J.H. Hart, s.v. Josephus, in Encycl. Brit. 11th ed.]

The *Life* is the least creditable of Josephus' works; but, as we have seen, it was wrung from him under duress, and cannot be taken as a genuine revelation of his mind. It is not a full autobiography; save for a short Prologue and a short Epilogue, it deals exclusively with the author's conduct in Galilee prior to the campaign of Vespasian, and it differs materially in political color as well as in the narrative of facts from the account of the same period in the *Wars*. In the earlier work his object had been to excuse his countrymen for their revolt, and at the same time to show the ability with which he had served their true interests, as the representative of the party that sought to preserve the nation at the sacrifice of its independence. But in the later work he is writing not a partisan but a personal apology, composed when his life was in danger, and when he no longer was anxious to save appearances with his countrymen. And he devoted his ingenuity to showing that throughout the events in Galilee he was the friend of Rome, seeking under the guise of resistance to smooth the way for the invaders and deliver the gates of Palestine into their hands. That he had so to demean himself is the most pathetic commentary on the bitter position which he was called on to endure after twenty years of servile life. The work was published or reissued after the death of King Agrippa, which took place in 103 C.E., and is recorded in it.[1] Agrippa was the last of the Herodians to rule, and with his death the last part of Palestine that had the outward show of independence was absorbed into the Roman Empire. But though the whole of the Jewish temporal sovereignty was shattered before his last days, Josephus may have consoled himself with the progressive march of Judaism in the capital city of the conqueror.

[1: See note above,]

It may be put down to the credit of Josephus that amid the court society at Rome he to the end professed loyalty to his religion, and that he did not complete his political desertion by religious apostasy. His loyalty indeed is less meritorious than might seem at first sight. The Romans generally were tolerant of creeds and cults, and the ceremonial of Judaism, especially its Sabbath, appealed to many of them. Within the ***pomoerium*** (limits), of the ancient city none but the city gods might be worshiped, but in Greater Rome there were numerous synagogues. In the time of Pompey, an important Jewish community existed in the cosmopolitan capital of the Empire, and later we have records of a number of congregations. Philo expressly mentions the religious privileges his brethren enjoyed at the heart of the Empire,[1] and save for an occasional expulsion the Jews appear to have been unmolested. The Flavian Emperors, satisfied with the destruction of the sanctuary and the razing of Jerusalem, did not attempt to persecute the communities of the Diaspora. For the old offering by all Jews to the Temple, they substituted a tax of two drachmas (the equivalent of the shekel voluntarily given hitherto to Jerusalem), which went towards the maintenance of the temple of Jupiter Capitolinus. Later the fiscus Judaicus, to which every Jew and proselyte had to pay, became an instrument of oppression, but in the reigns of Vespasian and Titus it was not harshly administered. Domitian indeed vented his indignation on the people which he had not had the honor of conquering, and instituted a kind of inquisition, to ferret out the early Maranos, who dissembled their Judaism and sought to evade the tax. But his gentle successor Nerva (96-98) restored the habit of tolerance, and struck special coins, with the legend calumnia Judaica sublata (on the abolition of information against the Jews), in order to mark his clemency. Save, therefore, for the short persecution under Domitian, Judaism remained a ***licita religio*** (legalized denomination) at Rome. More than that, it became a powerful missionary faith among the lower classes, and in small doses almost fashionable at the court. A near relative of the Emperor, Flavius Clemens, outraged Roman opinion by adopting its tenets. [2] It has been suggested, and it is likely, that the chief historical work of Josephus was written primarily for a group of fashionable proselytes to Judaism, to whom he ministered. He mentions members of the royal house that commended his work.[3] Some scholars have sought to associate him with the philosopher at Rome that was visited by the four rabbis of the Sanhedrin, the Patriarch Rabban Gamaliel, Rabbi Joshua, Rabbi Eleazar ben Arach, and Rabbi Akiba, when they came to Rome in the reign of Domitian.[4] But apart from the fact that he would hardly be described as a philosopher--a term usually reserved in the Talmud for a pagan scholar--it is as unlikely that the leaders of the Pharisaic national party would have had interviews with the renegade, as that the renegade would have befriended them. At Jotapata he deserted his people, and he passed thenceforth out of their life. It is significant that, while the history of the war was originally written in Aramaic for the benefit of the Eastern Jews, none of his later works was either written in his native language or translated into it, nor were they designed to be read by Jews.

[1: De Leg, 82.]

[2: It is interesting that the wife of the first Roman governor of Britain was accused, in 57 C.E., of "foreign superstition," and is said to have lived a melancholy life (Tac. Ann. xiii. 32), which may mean that she had adopted Jewish practices.]

[3: C. Ap. i. 5.]

[4: Sukkah, 22, quoted in Vogelstein and Rieger, Geschichte der Juden in Rom, pp. 28 and 29.]

In the palace of the Caesars Josephus became a reputable Greco-Roman chronicler, deliberately accommodating himself to the tastes of the conquerors of his people, and deliberately seeking, as Renan said, "to Hellenize his compatriots," i.e. to describe them from a Hellenized point of view. He achieved his ambition, if such it was, to be the classical authority upon the early history of the Jews. His record of his people survived through the ages, and his works were included in the public libraries of Rome, while among the Christians they had for centuries a place next the Bible.

As a writer, Josephus has, by the side of some glaring defects, considerable merits: immense industry, power of vivid narrative, an ability for using authorities, and at times a certain eloquence. But as a man he has few qualities to attract and nothing of the heroic. He was mediocre in character and mind, and for such there is no admiration. It may be admitted that he lived in hard times, when it required great strength of character for a Jew born, as he was, in the aristocratic Romanizing section of the nation, to stand true to the Jewish people and devote his energies to their desperate cause. He may have honestly believed that submission to Rome was the truest wisdom; but he placed himself in a false position by associating himself with the insurrection. And while his national feeling led him later to attempt to defend his people against calumny and ignorance, the conditions under which he labored made against the production of a true and spirited history. Yet if he does not appear worthy of admiration, we must beware of judging him harshly; and there is deep pathos in the fact that he was compelled in writing to be his own worst detractor. The combination, which the autobiographical account reveals, of egoism and self-seeking, of cowardice and vanity, of pious profession and cringing obsequiousness, of vaunted magnanimity and spiteful malice to his foes, of religious scruples and selfish cunning, points to a meanness of conduct which he was forced to assume by circumstances, but which, it is suggested, was not an expression of his true character. The document of shame was wrung from him by his past. He might have been a reliable historian had he not been called on to play a part in action. But the part he played was ignoble in itself, and it blasted the whole of his future life and his literary credit. It made his work take the form of apology, and part of it bear the stamp of deliberate falsehood. His besetting weakness of egoism led him as a general to betray his countrymen; as historian of their struggle with Rome, to misrepresent their patriotism and give a false picture of their ideals. Yet, though to the Jews of his own day he was a traitor in life and a traducer in letters, to the Jews of later generations he appears rather as a tragic figure, struggling to repair his fault of perfidy, and a victim to the forces of a hostile civilization, which in every age assail his people intellectually, and which in his day assailed them with crushing might physically as well as intellectually.

IV
THE WORKS OF JOSEPHUS AND HIS RELATION TO HIS PREDECESSORS

The Jews, though they are the most historical of peoples, and though they have always regarded history as the surest revelation of God's work, have produced remarkably few historians. It is true that a large part of their sacred literature consists of the national annals, from the earliest time to the restoration of the nation after its first destruction, i.e. a period of more than two thousand years. The Book of Chronicles, as its name suggests, is a systematic summary of the whole of that period and proves the existence of the historical spirit. But their very engrossment with the story of their ancestors checked in later generations the impulse to write about their own times. They saw contemporary affairs always in the light of the past, and they were more concerned with revealing the hand of God in events than in depicting the events themselves. Thus, during the whole Persian period, which extended over two hundred years, we have but one historical document, the Book of Esther, to acquaint us with the conditions of the main body of the Jewish people. The fortunate find, a few years back, of a hoard of Aramaic papyri at Elephantine has given us an unexpected acquaintance with the conditions of the Jewish colony in Upper Egypt during the fifth and fourth centuries, and furnished a new chapter in the history of the Diaspora. But this is an archeological substitute for literary history.

The conquest of the East by Alexander the Great and the consequent interchange of Hellenic and Oriental culture gave a great impulse to historical writing among all peoples. Moved by a cosmopolitan enthusiasm, each nation was anxious to make its past known to the others, to assert its antiquity, and to prove that, if its present was not very glorious, it had at one time played a brilliant part in civilization. The Greek people, too, with their intense love of knowledge, were eager to learn the ideas and experiences of the various nations and races who had now come into their ken.

Hence, on the one hand, there appeared works on universal history by Greek polymaths, such as Hecataeus of Abdera, Theophrastus, the pupil of Aristotle, and Ptolemy, the comrade of Alexander; and, on the other hand, a number of national histories were written, also in Greek, but by Hellenized natives, such as the Chaldaica of Berosus, the Aegyptiaca of Manetho, and the Phoenician chronicles of Dius and Menander. The people of Israel figured incidentally in several of these works, and Manetho went out of his way to include in the history of his country a lying account of the Exodus, which was designed to hold up the ancestors of the Jews to opprobrium. From the Hellenic and philosophical writers they received more justice. Their remarkable loyalty to their religion and their exalted conception of the Deity moved partly the admiration, partly the amazement of these early encyclopedists, who regarded them as a philosophical people devoted to a higher life. The Hellenistic Jews were led later by the sympathetic attitude of Hecataeus to add to his history spurious chapters, in which he was made to deal more eulogistically with their beliefs and history, and they circulated oracles and poems in the names of fabled seers of prehistoric times--Orpheus and the Sibyl--which conveyed some of the religious and moral teachings of Judaism. Nor were they slow to adapt their own chronicles for the Greek world or to take their part in the literary movement of the time. In Palestine, indeed, the Jews remained devoted to religious thought, and never made history a serious interest. But in Alexandria, after translating the Scriptures into Greek in the middle of the third century, they began, in imitation of their neighbors, to embellish their antiquities in the Greek style, and present them more thoroughly according to Greek standards of history.

A collection of extracts from the works of the Hellenistic Jews was made by a Gentile compiler of the first century B.C.E., Alexander, surnamed Polyhistor. Though his book has perished, portions of it with fragments of these extracts have been preserved in the chronicles of the ecclesiastical historian Eusebius, who wrote in the fourth century C.E. They prove the existence of a very considerable array of historical writers, who would seem to have been poor scholars of Greek, but ingenious chronologists and apologists. The earliest of the adapters, of whose work fragments have been thus preserved to us, is one Demetrius, who, in the reign of Ptolemy II, at the end of the third century B.C.E., wrote a book on the Jewish kings. It was rather a chronology than a connected narrative, and Demetrius amended the dates given in the Bible according to a system of his own. This does not appear to have been very exact, but such as it was it appealed to Josephus, who in places follows it without question. Chronology was a matter of deep import in that epoch, because it was one of the most galling and frequent charges against the Jews that their boasted antiquity was fictitious. To rebut this attack, the Jewish chroniclers elaborated the chronological indications of their long history, and brought them into relation with the annals of their neighbors.

Demetrius is followed by Eupolemus and Artapanus, who treated the Bible in a different fashion. They freely handled the Scripture narrative, and methodically embellished it with fictitious additions, for the greater glory, as they intended, of their people. They imitated the ways of their opponents, and as these sought to decry their ancestors by malicious invention, so they contrived to invest them with fictitious greatness. Eupolemus represents Abraham as the discoverer of Chaldean astrology, and identifies Enoch with the Greek hero Atlas, to whom the angel of God revealed the celestial lore. Elsewhere he inserts into the paraphrase of the Book of Kings a correspondence between Solomon and Hiram (king of Tyre), in order to show the Jewish hegemony over the Phoenicians. Artapanus, professing to be a pagan writer, shows how the Egyptians were indebted to the founders of Israel for their scientific knowledge and their most prized institutions: Abraham instructed King Pharethothis in astrology; Joseph taught the Egyptian priests hieroglyphics, and built the Pyramids; Moses (who is identified with the Greek seer Musaeus) not only conquered the Ethiopians, and invented ship-building and philosophy, but taught the Egyptian priests their deeper wisdom, and was called by them Hermes, because of his skill in interpreting ([Greek: Hermaeneia]) the holy documents. Fiction fostered fiction, and the inventions of pagan foes stimulated the exaggerations of Jewish apologists. The fictitious was mixed with the true, and the legendary material which Artapanus added to his history passed into the common stock of Jewish apologetics.

The great national revival that followed on the Maccabean victories induced both within and without Palestine the composition of works of contemporary national history. For a period the Jews were as proud of their present as of their past. It was not only that their princes, like the kings of other countries, desired to have their great deeds celebrated, but the whole people was conscious of another God-sent deliverance and of a clear manifestation of the Divine Power in their affairs, which must be recorded for the benefit of posterity. The First Book of the Maccabees, which was originally written in Hebrew, and the Chronicles of King John Hyrcanus[1] bear witness to this outburst of patriotic self-consciousness in Palestine; and the Talmud[2] contains a few fragments of history about the reign of Alexander Jannaeus, which may have formed part of a larger chronicle. The story of the Maccabean wars was recorded also at great length by a Hellenistic Jew, Jason of Cyrene, and it is generally assumed that an abridgment of it has come down to us in the Second Book of the Maccabees.

[1: They are referred to at the end of the book. Comp. I Macc. xvi. 23f.]

[2: Kiddushin, 66a.]

In Palestine, however, the historical spirit did not flourish for long. The interest in the universal lesson prevailed over that in the particular fact, and the tradition that was treasured was not of political events but of ethical and legal teachings. Moral rather than objective truth was the study of the schools, and when contemporary events are described, it is in a poetical, rhapsodical form, such as we find in the Psalms of Solomon, which recount Pompey's invasion of Jerusalem.[1] The only historical records that appear to have been regularly kept are the lists of the priests and their genealogy, and a calendar of fasts and of days on which fasting was prohibited because of some happy event to be commemorated.

[1: See above,]

In the Diaspora, on the other hand, and especially at Alexandria, which was the center of Hellenistic Jewry, history was made to serve a practical purpose. It was a weapon in the struggle the Jews were continually waging against their detractors, as well as in their missionary efforts to spread their religion. It became consciously and essentially apologetic, the end being persuasion rather than truth. Fact and fiction were inextricably combined, and the difference between them neglected.

The story of the translation of the Septuagint by the Jewish sages sent to Alexandria at the invitation of King Ptolemy, which is recounted in the Letter of Aristeas, is an excellent example of this kind of history. It is decked out with digressions about the topography of Jerusalem and the architecture of the Temple, and an imaginative display of Jewish wit and wisdom at a royal symposium. The Third Book of the Maccabees, which professes to describe a persecution of the Jews in Egypt under one of the Ptolemies, is another early example of didactic fiction that has been preserved to us. The one sober historical work produced by a Jewish writer between the composition of the two Books of the Maccabees and of the **Wars** of Josephus was the account given by Philo of Alexandria of the Jewish persecutions that took place in the reigns of Tiberius and Gaius. It was originally contained in five books, of which only the second and third have been preserved. They deal respectively with the riots at Alexandria that took place when Flaccus was governor, and with the Jewish embassy to Gaius when that Emperor issued his order that his image should be set up in the Temple at Jerusalem and in the great synagogue of Alexandria. Philo wrote a full account of the events in which he himself had been called upon to play a part. He is always at pains to point the moral and enforce the lesson, but his work has a definite historical value, and contains many valuable details about Jewish life in the Diaspora.

But if the Jews were somewhat careless of the exact record of their history, many of the Greek and Roman historians paid attention to it, some specifically for the purpose of attacking them, others incidentally in the course of their comprehensive works. The fashion of universal history continued for some centuries, and works of fifty volumes and over were more the rule than the exception. These "elephantine books" were rendered possible because it was the fashion for each succeeding historian to compile the results of his predecessor's labors, and adopt it as part of his own monumental work. Distinguished among this school of writers were Apollodorus of Athens, who in 150 B.C.E. wrote Chronicles containing the most important events of general history down to his own time, and Polybius, who was brought as a prisoner from Greece to Rome in 145 B.C.E., and in his exile wrote a history of the rise of the Roman Republic, in the course of which he dealt with the early Jewish relations with Rome. Then, in the first century, there flourished Posidonius of Apamea (90-50 B.C.E.), a Stoic and a bitter enemy of the Jews, who continued the work of Polybius down to the year 90, and, besides, wrote a separate diatribe against Judaism, which he regarded as a misanthropic atheism. The succession was carried on by Timagenes of Alexandria, who wrote a very full history of the second and the first part of the first century.

Among Roman writers of the period that dealt with general affairs were Asinius Pollio, the friend of Herod, and Titus Livius, who, under the name of Livy, has become the standard Latin historian for schoolboys. Josephus refers to both of them as well as to Timagenes, Posidonius, and Polybius; but as there is no reason to think that he ever tried to master the earlier authorities, it is probable that he knew them only so far as they were reproduced in his immediate sources and his immediate predecessors. The two writers whom he quotes repeatedly and must have studied are Strabo of Amasea (in Pontus) and Nicholas of Damascus. Strabo was an author of remarkable versatility and industry. Besides his geography, the standard work of ancient times on the subject, he wrote in forty-seven books a large historical work on the period between 150 (where Polybius ended) and 30 B.C.E. Nearly the whole of it has disappeared, but we can tell from Josephus' excerpts that he appreciated the Jews and their religion as did few other pagans of the time. He dealt, too, at considerable length with the wars of the Hasmonean kings against the Seleucids, and he is one of the authorities cited by Josephus for the period between the accession of John Hyrcanus and the overthrow of Antigonus II by Herod. The Jewish historian follows still more closely, and in many places probably reproduces, Nicholas, who was the court historian of Herod. Nicholas was a man of remarkable versatility. He played many parts at Herod's court, as diplomatist, advocate, and minister. He was a poet and philosopher of some repute, and he wrote a general history in forty-four books. In the first eight books he dealt with the early annals of the Assyrians, the Greeks, the Medes, and the Persians. Josephus, who took him for his chief guide after the Bible, often reproduces from him comparative passages to the Scripture story which he is paraphrasing. And for the later period of the *Antiquities*, from the time of Antiochus the Great (ab. 200 B.C.E.), he depends on him largely for the comparative Hellenistic history, which he brings into relation with the story of the Hasmoneans. When he comes to the epoch of Herod, the disproportionate fulness, the vivacity, and the dramatic power of the narrative in books XIV-XVI of the ***Antiquities*** are due in a large measure to the historical virtues of the court chronicler. We can tell how far this is the case by the immediate and marked deterioration of the narrative when Josephus proceeds to the reigns of Archelaus and Agrippa-- where Nicholas failed him.

Among Roman writers of his own day whom Josephus used was the Emperor Vespasian himself, who, to record his exploits, wrote ***Commentaries on the Jewish War***, which were placed at his client's disposal.[1] In the competition of flattery that greeted the new Flavian dynasty, various Roman writers described and celebrated the Jewish campaigns.[2] Among them were Antonius Julianus, who was on the staff of Vespasian and Titus throughout the war, and at the end of it was appointed procurator of Judea; Valerius Flaccus, who burst into ecstatic hexameters over the burning of the Temple; and Tacitus, the most brilliant of all Latin historians. Besides these writers' works, which have come down to us more or less complete, a number of memoirs and histories of the war appeared, some by those who wrote on hearsay, others by men who had taken some part in the campaigns. It was an age of literary dilettantism, when nearly everybody wrote books who knew how to write; and in the drab monotony of Roman supremacy, the triumph over the Jews, which had placed the Flavian house on the throne, was a happy opportunity for ambitious authors.

[1: Vita, 68.]

[2: C. Ap. 9-10.]

It has been suggested that the Roman point of view that pervades the ***Wars*** of Josephus, the frequent absence of sympathy with the Jewish cause, and the incongruous pagan ideas, which surprise us, can be explained by the fact that the Jewish writer founded his account on that of Antonius Julianus, which is referred to by the Christian apologist Minucius[1] as a standard authority on the destruction of Jerusalem. Antonius is mentioned by Josephus as one of the Roman staff who gave his opinion in favor of the burning of the Temple, and he has also been ingeniously identified with the Roman general (called [Hebrew: Otaninus] or [Hebrew: Ananitus]) who engaged in controversy with Rabbi Johanan ben Zakkai.[2] The evidence in favor of the theory is examined more fully later; but whether or not the history of Antonius was the main source of the *Wars*, it is certain that Josephus had before him Gentile accounts of the struggle, and he often slavishly adopted not only their record of facts but their expressions of opinion. In point of time Tacitus might have derived from Josephus his summary of the Jewish Wars, part of which has come down to us, and on some points the Jewish and the Roman authors agree; but the correspondence is to be explained more readily by the use of a common source by both writers. It is unlikely that the haughty patrician, who hated and despised the Jews, and who had no love of research, turned to a Jewish chronicle for his information, when he had a number of Roman and Greek authors to provide him with food for his epigrams.

[1: Epist. ad Octav. 33.]

[2: Yer. Sanhedrin, i. 4. Comp. Schlatter, Zur Topographie und Geschichte Palaestinas, pp. 97*ff*.]

One other writer on contemporary Jewish history to whom Josephus refers as an author, not indeed in the *Wars*, but in his *Life*, was Justus of Tiberias, Unfortunately we have to depend almost entirely on a hostile rival's spitefulness and malice for our knowledge of Justus. He did not produce his work on the wars till after Josephus had established his reputation, and part of his object, it is alleged, was to blacken the character and destroy the repute of his rival. The conduct of Justus in the Galilean campaign had been little more creditable than that of Josephus--that is, if the latter's account may be believed at all. He had been a leader of the Zealot party in Tiberias, and had roused the people of that city against the double-dealing commander; but on the breakdown of the revolt he entered the service of Agrippa II. He fell into disgrace, but was pardoned. Some twenty-four years after the war was over he wrote a History of the Jewish Kings and a History of the War. It is difficult to form any judgment of the work, because, apart from the abuse of Josephus, the criticism we have comes merely from ecclesiastical historians, who imbibed Josephus' personal enmity as though it were the pure milk of truth. Eusebius and

Jerome[1] accuse him of having distorted Jewish affairs to suit his personal ends and of having been convicted by Josephus of falsehood. His chief crime in their eyes and the reason for the disappearance of his work are that he did not mention any of the events connected with the foundation of the Christian Church, and had not the good fortune to be interpolated, as Josephus was, with a passage about Jesus.[2] Hence Photius says that he passed over many of the most important occurrences. [3] We know of him now only by the charges of Josephus and a few disconnected fragments.

[1: Hist. Eccl. III. x. 8; De Viris Illustr, 14.]

[2: See below]

[3: Bibl. Cod. 33.]

Coming now to the works of Josephus, his prefaces give a full account of his historical motives. He originally wrote seven books on the Wars with Rome in Aramaic for the benefit of his own countrymen. He was induced to translate them into Greek because his predecessors had given false accounts, either out of a desire to flatter the Romans or out of hatred to the Jews. He claims that his own work is a true and careful narrative of the events that he had witnessed with his own eyes and had special opportunities of studying accurately. "The writings of my predecessors contain sometimes slanders, sometimes eulogies, but nowhere the accurate truth of the facts." He goes on to complain of the way in which they belittle the action of the Jews in order to aggrandize the Romans, which defeats its own purpose; and he contrasts the merit of one who composes by his own industry a history of events not hitherto faithfully recorded, with the more popular and the easier fashion of writing a fresh history of a period already fully treated, by changing the order and disposition of other men's works. He iterates his determination to record only historical facts, and says, "It is superfluous for me to write about the Antiquities [i.e. the early history] of the Jews, because many before me, both among my own people and the Greeks, have composed the histories of our ancestors very exactly."[1] By the Antiquities he means the Bible narrative. He proposes therefore to begin where the Bible ends and, after a brief survey of the events before his own age, to give a full account of the great Rebellion. Josephus falls short of his promise. Many of the shortcomings he pointed to in his predecessors are glaringly present in his work. Nor is it probable that his profession of having taken notes on the spot is true. At the time of the siege of Jerusalem he had no literary pretensions, and it is unlikely that he contemplated the writing of a history. It has been pointed out that his account is much more accurate in regard to events in which he did not take part than in regard to those in which he assisted.

[1: B.J., Preface. The Greek name ***Archaeologia*** is regularly rendered by ***Antiquities***, but it means simply the early history.]

In the first book and the greater part of the second, where he is taken up with the preliminary introduction, he had ample sources before him, and his functions were only to abstract and compile; but when he comes to the final struggle with Rome, he would have us believe that he depended mainly on his independent knowledge. Recent investigation has thrown grave doubts on his claim, and has suggested that with Josephus it is true that "once a compiler, always a compiler." The habit of direct copying from the works of predecessors was fixed in the literary ethics of the day. In company with most of the historians of antiquity he introduces his general ideas upon the march of events in the form of addresses, which he puts into the mouth of the chief characters at critical moments. Here he is free to invent and intrude his own opinions, and here he almost unfailingly adopts a Roman attitude. The work, in fact, bears the character of official history, and has all the partiality of that form of literature. Titus, as the author proudly recalls, subscribed his own hand to it, and ordered that it should be published, and King Agrippa wrote a glowing testimonial to it in the most approved style.[1] It was accepted in Rome as the standard work upon the Jewish struggle. Patronage may have saved literature at certain epochs, but it always undermines the feeling of truth. It is not improbable that a juster appreciation of events was contained in the original writings of Josephus, but was corrected at the order of the royal traitor or the Imperial master, to whom he perforce submitted them.

[1: C. Ap. 8. See below,]

If in the **Wars** Josephus assumes the air of a scientific historian, in the **Antiquities** he is more openly the apologist. Despite his professions in the preface of the earlier work, he seems to have found it necessary or expedient to give to Greco-Roman society a fresh account of the ancestry and the early history of his people and of the constitution of their government. The Roman **Archaeologia** of Dionysius of Halicarnassus, who fifty years earlier had written in twenty books the early events of Rome, probably suggested the division and the name of the work. He issued it after the death of his protector, in the thirteenth year of the reign of Domitian and in the fifty-sixth year of his own life.[1] In the preface, inconsistently with the statement in the earlier work, he declares that he intended from the beginning to write this apology of his people, but was deterred for a time by the magnitude of the labor of translating the history into an unaccustomed tongue. He ascribes the impulse to carry out the task to the encouragement of his patron Epaphroditus and of his other friends at Rome. It probably came also from his circumstances at Rome and the necessity of refuting calumnies made against him on account of his race and religion. And with all his weaknesses and failings he was not lacking in a feeling of national pride, which must have moved him to defend his people.

[1: Ant. XX. xi. 3.]

Following on the destruction of Jerusalem, a passion of mixed hatred and contempt against the Jews moved the Roman nobility and the Roman masses. The Flavian court, representing the middle classes, by no means shared the feeling, and indeed the infatuation of Titus for the Jewish princess Berenice, the sister of Agrippa, was one of the scandals that most stirred the anger of the Romans. But the nobles hated those who had obstinately fought against the Roman armies for four years, and scorned those whose God had not saved them from ruin. At the same time Jewish persistence after defeat and the continuance of Jewish missionary activity offended the majesty of Rome, which, though tolerant of foreign religious ideas, was accustomed not merely to the physical submission of her enemies, but to their cultural and intellectual abasement. The hatred and scorn were fanned by a tribe of scribblers, who heaped distortion on the history and practices of the Jewish people. On the other hand, the proselytes to Judaism, "the fearers of God," who accepted part of its teaching--and in the utter collapse of pagan religion and morality they were many--desired to know something of the past grandeur of the nation, and doubtless were anxious to justify themselves to those who regarded their adoption of Jewish customs as an utter degradation. For those who mocked at him as a renegade member of a wretched people, which consisted of the scum of the earth, which harbored all kinds of low superstition, and which fostered inhumanity and misanthropy, and for those who looked to him as the accredited exponent of Judaism and the writer most able to set it in a favorable light, Josephus wrote the twenty books of his ***Antiquities***.

The work differed from all previous apologies for Judaism in its completeness and its historical character. Philo had sought to recommend Judaism as a philosophical religion, and had interpreted the Torah as the law of Nature. Josephus was concerned not so much with Judaism as with the Jews. He seeks to show, by his abstract of historical records, that his people had a long and honorable past, and that they had had intercourse with ancient empires, and had been esteemed even by the Romans. The ***Antiquities*** comprised a summary of the whole of Jewish history, as well that which was set out in the books of the Bible as that which had taken place in the post-Biblical period down to his own day. Some of his predecessors had elaborated only the former part of the story, and that, it is probable, not nearly so fully as Josephus. He claims not to have added to or diminished from the record of Scripture. Though neither part of the claim can be upheld, he does undoubtedly give a tolerable account of the Bible so far as it is an historical narrative. The finer spirit of the Bible, even in its narrative parts, its deep spiritual teaching, its simple grandeur, its arresting sincerity, he was utterly unable to impart. In style, too, his Greek falls immeasurably below the original. We feel as we read his abstract with its omissions and additions:

The little more and how much it is;   The little less and what miles away.

His is a mediocre transcription, which replaces the naivete, the rapidity, the unaffected beauty of the Hebrew, with the rhetoric, the sophistication, and the exaggerated overstatement of the Greek writing of his own time. Impressiveness for him is regularly enhanced by inaccuracy. His own or his assumed materialistic fatalism lowers the God of the Bible to a Power which materially rewards the righteous and punishes the wicked. In this immediate retribution he finds the surest sign of Divine Providence, and it is this lesson which he is most anxious to assert throughout his work. But he is at pains to dispel the idea of a special Providence for Israel. The material power of Rome made him desert in life the Jewish cause; the material thought of Rome made him dissimulate in literature the full creed of Judaism.

The second part of the ***Antiquities*** is a more ambitious piece of work. The compiler brings together all that he could find, in Jewish and Gentile sources, about Jewish history from the time of the Babylonian captivity to the outbreak of the war against Rome. And he was apparently the first of his people to utilize the Greek historians systematically in this fashion. There are long periods as to the incidents of which he was at a loss. Without possessing the ability or desire for research, he is not above confounding the chronology and perverting the succession of events to cover up a gap. But he does contrive to produce a connected narrative and to provide some kind of continuous chronicle. And for this service he is not lightly to be esteemed. Without him we should know scarcely anything of the external history of the Jewish people for three centuries. In style the last ten books vary remarkably. It depends almost entirely on his source whether the narrative is dull and monotonous or lively and dramatic. Where, for example, he is transcribing Nicholas and another historian of the period, he succeeds in presenting a picture of Herod that has a certain psychological value. Where, on the other hand, he has had to trust largely to scattered notes, as in the record of Herod's successors, his history is little better than a miscellany of disjointed passages. He lacks throughout a true sense of proportion, and for the deeper aspects of history he has no perception. He does not show in spite of his Jewish training the slightest appreciation of the spiritual power of Judaism or of the divine purpose illustrating itself in the rise and fall of nations. His conception of history is a biography of might, tempered by occasional manifestations of divine retribution. The concrete event is the important thing, and of culture and literature he says scarcely a word. His occasional moral reflections are on a mediocre plane and not true to the finer spirit of Judaism. He is consciously or unconsciously obsessed by the power of Rome, and makes little attempt to inculcate the higher moral outlook of his people. In soul, too, he is Romanized. He admires above all material power; he exhibits material conceptions of Providence; he looks always for material causes. Altogether the *Antiquities* is a work invaluable for its material, but a somewhat soulless book.

Josephus conveys more of the spirit of Judaism in his two books commonly entitled *Against Apion*, which are professedly apologetic. They were written after the *Antiquities*, and further emphasize two points on which he had dwelt in that work: the great age of the Jewish people and the excellence of the Jewish law. He was anxious to refute those detractors who, despite the publication of his history, still continued to spread grotesquely false accounts of Israel's origin and Israel's religious teachings; and he wrote here with more spirit and with more conviction than in his earlier elaborate works. He has no longer to accommodate himself to the vanity of a Roman Emperor, or to distort events so as to glorify his nation or to excuse his own conduct. He is able for once to set out his idea wholeheartedly, and he shows that, if he had few of the qualities required for a great historian, he had several of the talents of an apologist. His own calculated misrepresentation of his people in their last struggle would have afforded an opponent the best reply to his apology. In itself that apology was an effective summary of Judaism for his own times, and parts of it have a permanent value. For seventeen centuries it remained the sole direct answer from the Jewish side to the calumnies of the enemies of the Jews.

The last extant work of Josephus was the *Life*, of which we have already treated, and it were better to say little more. It was provoked by the publication of the History of Justus, which had accused Josephus and the Galileans of having been the authors of the sedition against the Romans.[1] Josephus retorts that, before he was appointed governor, Justus and the people of Tiberias had attacked the Greek cities of the Decapolis and the dominions of Agrippa, as was witnessed in the Commentaries of Vespasian. Not content with this crime, Justus had failed to surrender to the Romans till they appeared before Tiberias. Having charged his rival with being a better patriot than himself,[2] Josephus proceeds to argue that he was a worse historian: Justus could not describe the Galilean campaign, because during the war he was at Berytus; he took no part in the siege of Jerusalem, and, less privileged than his rival, he had not read the Commentaries of Caesar, and in fact often contradicted them. Conscious of this weakness, he had not ventured to publish his account till the chief actors in the story, Vespasian, Titus, and Agrippa, had died, though his books had been written some twenty years before they were issued. But in his pains to gainsay Justus and his own patriotism, such as it was, Josephus, as has been noticed, gives an account of his doings in Galilee that is often at complete variance with his statements in the *Wars*. The *Life*, in fact, is untrustworthy history and unsuccessful apology.

[1: Vita, 65.]

[2: Justus, no doubt, had done the converse, representing himself as a thorough Romanizer and Josephus as an ardent rebel.]

At the end of the *Antiquities* Josephus declares his intention to write three books concerning the Jewish doctrines "about God and His essence, and concerning the laws, why some things are permitted, and others are prohibited." In the preface to the same work, as well as in various passages in its course, he refers to his intention to write on the philosophical meaning of the Mosaic legislation. The books entitled *Against Apion* correspond neither in number nor in content to this plan, and we must therefore assume that he never carried it out. He may have intended to abstract the commentary of Philo upon the Law, which he had doubtless come to know. Certainly he shows no traces of deeper allegorical lore in the extant works, and his mind was hardly given to such speculations. But a humanitarian and universalistic explanation of the Mosaic code, such as his predecessor had composed, notably in his Life of Moses, would have been quite in his way, and would have rounded off his presentation of the past and present history of the Jews. The need of replying to his personal enemies and the detractors of his nation deterred him perhaps from achieving this part of his scheme. Or, if it was written, the Christian scribes, who preserved his other works, may have suppressed it because it did not harmonize with their ideas.

Photius ascribes to Josephus a work on *The Universe*, or *The Cause of the Universe* ([Greek: peri taes tou pantos aitias]), which is extant, but which is demonstrably of Christian origin, and was probably written by Hippolytus, an ecclesiastical writer of the third century and the author of ***Philosophumena***. Another work attributed to Josephus in the Dark and Middle Ages, and often attached to manuscripts of the ***Antiquities***, is the sermon on ***The Sovereignty of Reason***, which is commonly known as the Fourth Book of the Maccabees. The book is a remarkable example of the use of Greek philosophical ideas to confirm the Jewish religion. That the Mosaic law is the rule of written reason is the main theme, and it is illustrated by the story of the martyrs during the persecution of Antiochus Epiphanes, whence the book takes its title. In particular, the author points to the ethical significance underlying the dietary laws, of which he says in a remarkable passage:

When we long for fishes and fowls and fourfooted animals and every kind of food that is forbidden to us by the Law, it is through the mastery of pious reason that we abstain from them. For the affections and appetites are restrained and turned into another direction by the sobriety of the mind, and all the movements of the body are kept in check by pious reason.

Again, of the Law as a whole he says:

It teaches us temperance, so that we master our pleasures and desires, and it exercises us in fortitude, so that we willingly undergo every toil. And it instructs us in justice, so that in all our behavior we give what is due, and it teaches us to be pious, so that we worship the only living God in the manner becoming His greatness.

Freudenthal has conclusively disposed of the theory that Josephus was the author of this work.[1] Neither in language, nor in style, nor in thought, has it a resemblance to his authentic works. Nor was he the man to write anonymously. It reveals, indeed, a mastery of the arts of Greek rhetoric, such as the Palestinian soldier who learnt Greek only late in life, and who required the help of friends to correct his syntax, could never have acquired. It reveals, too, a knowledge of the technical terms of the Stoic philosophy and a general grasp of Greek philosophy quite beyond the writer of the ***Antiquities*** and the ***Wars***. Lastly, it breathes a wholehearted love for Judaism and a national ardor to which the double-dealing defender of Galilee and the client of the Roman court could hardly have aspired.

[1: Freudenthal, Die Flavius Josephus beigelegte Schrift ueber die Herrschaft der Vernunft, 1879.]

The genuine works of Josephus reveal him not as a philosopher or sturdy preacher of Judaism, but as an apologetic historian and apologist, distinguished in either field rather for his industry and his ingenuity in using others' works than by any original excellence. He learnt from the Greeks and Romans the external manner of systematic history, and in this he stood above his Jewish predecessors. He learnt from them also the arts of mixing false with true, of invention, of exaggeration, of the suggestion of the bad and the suppression of the good motive. He was a sophist rather than a sage, and circumstances compelled him to be a court chronicler rather than a national historian. And while he acquired something of the art of historical writing from his models, he lost the intuitive synthesis of the Jewish attitude, which saw the working of God's moral law in all human affairs. On the other hand, certain defects of his history may be ascribed to lack of training and to the spirit of the age. He had scant notion of accuracy, he made no independent research into past events, and he was unconscionable in chronology. In his larger works he is for the most part a translator and compiler of the work of others, but he has some claim to originality of design and independence of mind in the books against Apion. The times were out of joint for a writer of his caliber. For the greater part of his literary life, perhaps for the whole, he was not free to write what he thought and felt, and he wrote for an alien public, which could not rise to an understanding of the deeper ideas of his people's history. But this much at least may be put down to his credit, that he lived to atone for the misrepresentation of the heroic struggle of the Jews with the Romans by preserving some record of many dark pages in their history and by refuting the calumnies of the Hellenistic vituperators about their origin and their religious teachings.

V
THE JEWISH WARS

The first work of Josephus as man of letters was the history of the wars of the Jews against the Romans, for which, according to his own statement, he prepared from the time of his surrender by taking copious notes of the events which he witnessed. He completed it in the fortieth year of his life and dedicated it to Vespasian.[1] He seems originally to have designed the record of the struggle for the purpose of persuading his brethren in the East that it was useless to fight further against the Romans. He desired to prove to them that God was on the side of the big battalions, and that the Jews had forfeited His protection by their manifold transgressions. The Zealots were as wicked as they were misguided, and to follow them was to march to certain ruin. It is not unlikely that Josephus was commissioned by Titus to compose his version of the war for the "Upper Barbarians," whose rising in alliance with the Parthians might have troubled the conqueror of Jerusalem, as it afterwards troubled Trajan. But, save that it was written in Aramaic, we cannot tell the form of the original history, since it has entirely disappeared.

[1: B.J. VII. xv. 8.]

Josephus says in the preface to the extant Greek books that he translated into Greek the account he had already written. But he certainly did much more than translate. The whole trend of the narrative and the purpose must have been changed when he came to present the events for a Greco-Roman audience. He was concerned less to instill respect for Rome in his countrymen than to inspire regard for his countrymen in the Romans, and at the same time to show that the Rebellion was not the deliberate work of the whole people, but due to the instigation of a band of desperate, unscrupulous fanatics. He was concerned also to show that God, the vanquished Jewish God, as the Romans would regard Him, had allowed the ruin of His people, not because He was powerless to preserve them, but because they had sinned against His law. Lastly, he was anxious to emphasize the military virtue and the magnanimity of his patrons Vespasian and Titus. He intersperses frequent protests in various parts of the seven books, and repeats them in the preface, to the effect that while his predecessors had written "sophistically," he was aiming only at the exact record of events. But it is obvious that, in the *Wars* as in his other works, he has a definite purpose to serve, and he colors his account of events to suit this purpose and to please his patrons.

He sets out to establish, in fact, that it was "a sedition of our own that destroyed Jerusalem, and that the tyrants among the Jews brought upon us the Romans, who unwillingly attacked us, and occasioned the burning of our Temple."[1] And he apologizes for the passion he shows against the tyrants and Zealots, which, he admits, is not consistent with the character of an historian; it was provoked because the unparalleled calamities of the Jews were not caused by strangers but by themselves, and "this makes it impossible for me to contain my lamentations."[2] The historian, therefore, in the work which has come down to us, is dominated by the conviction, whether sincere or feigned, that the war with Rome was a huge error, that those who fomented it were wicked, self-seeking men, and that the Jews brought their ruin on themselves. This being his temper, it is necessary to look very closely at his representation of events and examine how far partisan feeling and prejudices, and how far servility and the courtier spirit, have colored it. We have also to consider how far his reflections represent his own judgment, and how far they are the slavish adoption of opinions expressed by the victorious enemies of his people.

[1: B.J., Preface.]

[2: B.J., Preface, 4.]

The alternative title of the work is *On the Destruction of the Temple*, but its scope is larger than either name suggests. It is conjectured by the German scholar Niese that the author called it *A History of the Jewish State in Its Relations with the Romans*. It is in fact a history of the Jews under the Romans, beginning, as Josephus says, "where the earlier writers on Jewish affairs and our prophets leave off." He proposes to deal briefly with the events that preceded his own age, but fully with the events of the wars of his time. The history starts, accordingly, with the persecution of Antiochus Epiphanes, and, save that he expatiates without any sense of proportion on the exploits of Herod the Great, Josephus is generally faithful to his program in the introductory portion of the work. For the Herodian period he found a very full source, and the temptation was too powerful for him, so that the greater part of the first book is taken up with the story of the court intrigues and family murders of the king. Very brief indeed is his treatment of the Maccabean brothers, and not very accurate. They are dismissed in two chapters, and it is probable that the historian had not before him either of the two good Jewish sources for the period, the First and the Second Book of the Maccabees. In his later work, in which he dealt with the same period at greater length, the account which he had abstracted from a Greek source, probably Nicholas of Damascus, is corrected by the Jewish work. The two records show a number of small discrepancies. Thus, in the *Wars* he states that Onias, the high priest who drove out the Tobiades from Jerusalem, fled to Ptolemy in Egypt, and founded a city resembling Jerusalem; whereas in the *Antiquities* he states that the Onias who fled to Egypt because Antiochus deprived him of office was the son of the high priest. Again, in the *Wars* he makes Mattathias kill the Syrian governor Bacchides; whereas, in the *Antiquities*, agreeing with the First Book of the Maccabees, he says that the Syrian officer who was slain at Modin was Appelles.

Josephus in the *Wars* follows his Hellenistic source for the history of the Hasmonean monarchy without introducing any Jewish knowledge and without criticism. His summary is of incidents, not of movements, and he has a liking for romantic color. The piercing of the king's elephant by the Maccabean Eleazar, the prediction by an Essene of the murder of Antigonus, the brother of King Aristobulus I, are detailed. The inner Jewish life is passed over in complete silence until he comes to the reign of Alexander. Then he describes the Pharisees as a sect of Jews that are held to be more religious than others and to interpret the laws more accurately.[1] The description is clearly derived from a Greek writer, who regards the Jewish people from the outside. It is quite out of harmony with the standpoint which Josephus himself later adopts. In this passage he presents the Pharisees as crafty politicians, insinuating themselves into the favor of the queen, and then ordering the country to suit their own ends. Without describing the other sects, he continues the narration of intrigues and wars till he reaches the intervention of Pompey in the affairs of Palestine.

[1: B.J. I. v. 2.]

From this point the treatment is fuller. No doubt the Hellenistic historians paid more attention to the Jews from the moment when they came within the orbit of the Roman Empire; but while in the ***Antiquities*** Josephus refers several times to the statements of two or three of the Greco-Roman writers, in the ***Wars*** he quotes no authority. From this it may be inferred that in the earlier work he is following but one guide.

He gives an elaborate account of the rise of the Idumean family of Antipater, and hence to the end of the book the history passes into a biography of Herod. The first part of Herod's career, when he was building up his power, is related in the most favorable light. His activity in Galilee against the Zealots, his trial by the Sanhedrin, his subsequent service to the Romans, his flight from Judea upon the invasion of the Parthians, his reception by Antony, his triumphal return to the kingdom that had been bestowed on him, his valiant exploits against the Arabians of Perea and Nabatea, his capture of Jerusalem, his splendid buildings, and his magnificence to foreigners--all these incidents are set forth so as to enhance his greatness. The description throughout has a Greek ring. There is scarcely a suggestion of a Jewish point of view towards the semi-savage godless tyrant. And when Josephus comes to the part of Herod's life which even an historian laureate could not misrepresent to his credit, his family relations, he adopts a fundamentally pagan outlook.

The foundation of the Greek drama was the idea that the fortunate incurred the envy of the gods, and brought on themselves the "nemesis," the revenge, of the divine powers, which plunged them into ruin. This conception, utterly opposed as it is to the Jewish doctrine of God's goodness, is applied to Herod, on whom, says Josephus, fortune was revenged for his external prosperity by raising him up domestic troubles.[1] He introduces another pagan idea, when he suggests that Antipater, the wicked son of the king, returned to Palestine, where he was to meet his doom, at the instigation of the ghosts of his murdered brothers, which stopped the mouths of those who would have warned him against returning. The notion of the avenging spirits of the dead was utterly opposed to Jewish teaching, but it was a commonplace of the Hellenistic thought of the time.

[1: B.J. I. xxii. 1.]

Of Hillel and Shammai, the great sages of the time, we have not a word; but when he recounts how, in the last days of Herod, the people under the lead of the Pharisees rose against the king in indignation at the setting up of a golden eagle over the Temple gate, he speaks of the sophists exhorting their followers, "that it was a glorious thing to die for the laws of their country, because the soul was immortal, and an eternal enjoyment of happiness did await such as died on that account; while the mean-spirited, and those that were not wise enough to show a right love of their souls, preferred death by disease to that which is a sign of virtue." The sentiments here are not so objectionable, but the description of the Pharisees as sophists, and the suggestion of a Valhalla for those who died for their country and for no others--for which there is no authority in Jewish tradition--betray again the uncritical copying of a Hellenistic source.

Finally, in summing up the character of Herod, all he finds to say is, "Above all other men he enjoyed the favor of fortune, since from a private station he obtained a kingdom, and held it many years, and left it to his sons; but yet in his domestic affairs he was a most unfortunate man." Not a word of his wickedness and cruelty, not a breath of the Hebrew spirit, but simply an estimate of his "fortune." This is the way in which the Romanized Jew continued the historical record of the Bible, substituting foreign superstitions about fate and fortune for the Jewish idea that all human history is a manifestation of God.

Josephus ends the first book of the **Wars** with an account of the gorgeous pomp of Herod's funeral, and starts the second book with a description of the costly funeral feast which his son Archelaus gave to the multitude, adding a note--presumably also derived from Nicholas-- that many of the Jews ruin themselves owing to the need of giving such a feast, because he who omits it is not esteemed pious. As his source fails him for the period following on the banishment of Archelaus, the treatment becomes fragmentary, but at the same time more original and independent. An account of the various Jewish sects interrupts the chronicle of the court intrigues and popular risings. Josephus distinguishes here four sects, the Essenes, the Pharisees, the Sadducees, and the Zealots, but his account is mainly confined to the first.[1] He describes in some detail their practices, beliefs, and organizations. Indeed, this passage and the account in Philo are our chief Jewish authorities for the tenets of the Essenes. He is anxious to establish their claim to be a philosophical community comparable with the Greek schools. In particular he represents that their notions of immortality correspond with the Greek ideas of the Isles of the Blessed and of Hades. "The divine doctrines of the Essenes, as he calls them, which consider the body as corruptible and the soul an immortal spirit, which, when released from the bonds of the flesh as from a long slavery, rejoices and mounts upwards, lay an irresistible bait for such as have once tasted of their philosophy." The ideas which the sect cherished were popular in a certain part of Greco-Roman society, which, sated with the luxury of the age, turned to the ascetic life and to the pursuit of mysticism. Pliny the Elder, who was on the staff of Titus at Jerusalem, appears to have been especially interested in the Jewish communists, and briefly described their doctrines in his books; and the circle for whom Josephus wrote would have been glad to have a fuller account.

[1: B. J. II. viii.]

Of the other two sects he says little here, and what he says is superficial. He places the differentiation in their contrasted doctrines of fate and immortality. The Pharisees ascribe all to fate, but yet allow freewill--a Hellenizing version of the saying ascribed to Rabbi Akiba, "All is foreseen, but freedom of will is given"[1]--and they say all souls are immortal, but those of the good only pass into other bodies, while those of the bad suffer eternal punishment. This attribution of the doctrine of metempsychosis and eternal punishment is another piece of Hellenization, or a reproduction of a Hellenistic misunderstanding; for the Rabbinic records nowhere suggest that such ideas were held by the Pharisees. "The Sadducees, on the other hand, deny fate entirely, and hold that God is not concerned in man's conduct, which is entirely in his own choice, and they likewise deny the immortality of the soul or retribution after death." Here the attempt to represent the Sadducees' position as parallel with Epicurean materialism has probably induced an overstatement of their distrust of Providence. Josephus adds that the Pharisees cultivate great friendships among themselves and promote peace among the people; while the Sadducees are somewhat gruff towards each other, and treat even members of their own party as if they were strangers.

[1: Comp. Abot, iii. 15.]

Of the fourth party, the Zealots, Josephus has only a few words, to the effect that when Coponius was sent as the first procurator of Judea, a Galilean named Judas prevailed on his countrymen to revolt, saying they would be cowards if they would endure to pay any tax to the Romans or submit to any mortal lord in place of God. This man, he says, was the teacher of a peculiar sect of his own. While the other three sects are treated as philosophical schools, Josephus does not attribute a philosophy to the Zealots, and out of regard to Roman feelings he says nothing of the Messianic hopes that dominated them.

After the digression about the sects, Josephus continues his narrative of the Jewish relations with the Romans. He turns aside now and then to detail the complicated family affairs of the Herodian family or to describe some remarkable geographical phenomenon, such as the glassy sands of the Ladder of Tyre.[1] The main theme is the growing irritation of the Jews, and the strengthening of the feeling that led to the outbreak of the great war. But Josephus, always under the spell of the Romans, or writing with a desire to appeal to them, can recognize only material, concrete causes. The deeper spiritual motives of the struggle escape him altogether, as they escaped the Roman procurators. He recounts the wanton insults of a Pontius Pilate, who brought into Jerusalem Roman ensigns with the image of Caesar, and spoiled the sacred treasures of the Korban for the purpose of building aqueducts; and he dwells on the attempt of Gaius to set up his statue in the Temple, which was frustrated only by the Emperor's murder. But about the attitude of the different sections of the Jewish people to the Romans, of which his record would have been so valuable, he is silent.

[1: B.J. II. x. 2. The same phenomenon is recorded in Pliny and Tacitus, and it was a commonplace of the geography of the age.]

After the brief interlude of Agrippa's happy reign, the irritation of Roman procurators is renewed, and under Comanus tumult follows tumult, as one outrage after another upon the Jewish feeling is countenanced or abetted. The courtier of the Flavian house takes occasion to recount the Emperor Nero's misdeeds and family murders; but he resists the desire to treat in detail of these things, because his subject is Jewish history.[1] He must have had before him a source which dealt with general Roman history more fully, and he shows his independence, such as it is, in confining his narrative to the Jewish story. But the reliance on his source for his point of view leads him to write as a good Roman; the national party are dubbed rebels and revolutionaries ([Greek: stasiastai]). The Zealots are regularly termed robbers, and the origin of war is attributed to the weakness of the governors in not putting down these turbulent elements. All this was natural enough in a Roman, but it comes strangely from the pen of a soi-disant Jewish apologist, who had himself taken a part in the rebellion. Characteristic is his account of the turbulent condition of Palestine in the time of Felix:

"Bands of Sicarii springing up in the chaos caused by the tyranny infested the country, and another body of abandoned men, less villainous in their actions, but more wicked in their designs, deluded the people under pretense of divine inspiration, and persuaded them to rise. Felix put down these bands, but, as with a diseased body, straightway the inflammation burst out in another part. And the flame of revolt was blown up every day more and more, till it came to a regular war."[2]

[1: B.J. II. xiii. 1.]

[2: B.J. II. xiii. 6.]

Josephus vents his full power of denunciation on the last procurator, Floras, who goaded the people into war, and by his repeated outrages compelled even the aristocratic party, to which the historian belonged, to break their loyalty to Rome: "As though he had been sent as executioner to punish condemned criminals, he omitted no sort of spoliation or extortion. In the most pitiful cases he was most inhuman; in the greatest turpitudes he was most impudent, nor could anyone outdo him in perversion of the truth, or combine more subtle ways of deceit." Josephus, not altogether consistently with what he has already said, seeks to exculpate his countrymen for their rising, up to the point in which he himself was involved in it; and though he admits that the high priests and leading men were still anxious for peace at any price, and he puts a long speech into Agrippa's mouth counseling submission, he is yet anxious to show that his people were driven into war by the wickedness of Nero's governors. His masters allowed him, and probably invited him, to denounce the oppression of the ministers of their predecessors, and the Roman historians Suetonius and Tacitus likewise state that the rapacity of the procurators drove the Jews into revolt. He had authority, therefore, for this view in his contemporary sources.

The die was cast. Menahem, the son of Judas the Galilean and the head of the Zealots, seized Jerusalem, drove the Romans and Romanizers into the fortress of Antonia, and having armed his bands with the contents of Herod's southern stronghold of Masada, overpowered the garrison and put it to the sword. Menahem himself, indeed, was so barbarous that the more moderate leader Eleazar turned against him and put him to death. But Josephus sees in the massacre of the Roman garrison the pollution of the city, which doomed it to destruction. In his belligerent ethics, massacre of the Romans by the Jews is always a crime against God, requiring His visitation; massacres of the Jews are a visitation of God, revealing that the Romans were His chosen instrument.

With the history of the war, so far as the historian was involved in it, we have already dealt. We are here concerned with the character and the reliability of his account. Josephus is somewhat vague and confused about the dispositions of the Jewish leaders, but when he is not justifying his own treachery, or venting his spite on his rivals, he shows many of the parts of a military historian. He surveys with clearness and conciseness the nature of the country that the Romans had to conquer, and he describes the Roman armies and Roman camp with greater detail than any Roman historian, his design being "not so much to praise the Romans as to comfort those who have been conquered and to deter others from rising."[1] It has, however, been pointed out with great force, in support of the theory that he is following closely and almost paraphrasing a Roman authority on the war, that his geographical and topographical lore is introduced not in its natural place, but on the occasions when Vespasian is the actor in a particular district.[2] Thus, he describes the Phoenician coast when Vespasian arrives at Ptolemais, Galilee when Vespasian

is besieging Tarichea, Jericho when Vespasian makes his sally to the Jordan cities.
[3]

[1: B.J. III. v. This remark must clearly have appeared in the original Aramaic.]

[2: Schlatter, Zur Topographie und Geschichte Palastinas, pp. 99 *ff.*]

[3: B.J. III. iii. 1 and x. 7.]

All this would be natural in a chronicler who was one of Vespasian's staff, but it is odd in the Jewish commander of Galilee. Again, he makes certain confusions about Hebrew names of places, which are easily explained in a Roman, but are inexplicable in the learned priest he represents himself to be. He says the town of Gamala was so called because of its supposed resemblance to a camel (in Greek, Kamelos), and the Jews corrupted the name.[1] A Roman writer no doubt would have regarded the Hebrew [Hebrew: Namal] as a corruption of the Greek word: a Jew should have known better.

[1: B.J. III. iv. 2.]

Again, he explains Bezetha, the name of the northeastern quarter of Jerusalem, as meaning the new house or city,[1] a mistake natural to a Roman who was aware that it was in fact the new part of the city, and alternatively called by the Greek name [Greek: kainopolis], but an extraordinary blunder for a Jew, who would surely know that it meant the House of Olives, while the Aramaic or popular name for "new city" would be Bet-Hadta. He does not once refer to Mount Zion, but knows the hill by its Greek name of Acra. Yet again it is significant that he inserts in his geography pagan touches that are part of the common stock of Greco-Roman notices of Palestine. At Joppa, he says, one may still see on the rock the trace of the chains of Andromeda,[2] who in Hellenistic legend was said to have been rescued there by the fictitious hero Perseus. Describing the Dead Sea,[3] he mentions the destruction of the cities of Sodom and Gomorrah as a myth, as a Greek or a Roman would have done.[4] His very accuracy about some topographical details is suspicious. Colonel Conder[5] points with surprise to the fact that his description of the fortress of Masada overlooking the Dead Sea, the siege of which he had not seen, is absolutely correct, while his account of Jotapata, which he defended, is full of exaggeration. The probable explanation is that in the one place he copied a skilled observer; in the other, he trusted to his own inaccurate memory. We may infer that as in the ***Antiquities*** he mainly compiled the work of predecessors that are known, so in the ***Wars*** he compiled the works of predecessors that are unknown, adding something from his personal experience and his national pride.

[1: B.J. V. v. 8.]

[2: B.J. IV. ix. 3. Pliny says the same thing in Latin.]

[3: B.J. IV. viii. 4.]

[4: Tac. Hist. v. 7.]

[5: Tent Work in Palestine, 1. 207.]

Apart from his dependence on others' work, his chronicle of the war is marred by the need of justifying his own submission, his Roman standpoint, and his ulterior purpose of pleasing and flattering his patrons. Vespasian and Titus are the righteous ministers of God's wrath against His people, His vicars on earth, and every action in their ruthless process of extermination has to be represented as a just retribution required to expiate the sin of Jewish resistance. Titus especially is singled out for his unfailing deeds of bravery; and when anything is amiss with the proceedings of the Romans, the Imperial family is always exculpated. Characteristic is the palliation of Vespasian's brutal treatment of the people of Tarichea. When they surrendered, they were promised their lives, but twelve hundred old men were butchered, and over three thousand men and women were sold as slaves. Josephus cannot find the execution of the divine will in this, and so he is driven to explain that Vespasian was overborne by his council, and gave them an ambiguous liberty to do as seemed good to them.

It is the pivot of the story of the wars, as has been stated, that the internal strife of the Jews brought about the ruin of the nation, and the testimony of Josephus has perpetuated that conception of the last days of Jerusalem. Our other records of the struggle go to suggest that civil strife did take place. Tacitus[1] states that there were three leaders, each with his own army in the city, and the Rabbinical authorities[2] speak of the three councils in Jerusalem. It is further said that the second Temple was destroyed because of the unprovoked hatred among the Jews, which was the equal of the sins of murder, unchastity, and idolatry that brought about the fall of the first Temple.[3] Yet the fact that the men who were the foremost agitators of the Rebellion were its leaders to the end suggests that the people had reliance on their leadership; and Josephus probably traded largely on his prejudices for the particulars of the civil conflicts, and he placed all the blame on the party that was least guilty. Adopting the Roman standpoint, he denounced the whole Zealot policy, and for John of Gischala, their leader, he entertained a special loathing. It is therefore his purpose to show that all the sedition was of John's making, while it would seem more probable that the disturbances arose because the Romanizing aristocrats were planning surrender.

[1: Hist. v. 12.]

[2: Midr. Kohelet, vii. 11.]

[3: Yoma, 9b.]

According to Josephus, the Zealots, who were masters of the greater part of Jerusalem during the struggle, established a reign of terror. They trampled upon the laws of man, and laughed at the laws of God. They ridiculed the oracles of the prophets as the tricks of jugglers. "Yet did they occasion the fulfilment of prophecies relating to their country. For there was an ancient oracle that the city should be taken and the sanctuary burnt when sedition should affect the Jews." Josephus shares the pagan outlook of the Roman historian Tacitus, who is horrified at the Jewish disregard of the omens and portents which betokened the fall of their city, and speaks of them as a people prone to superstition (what we would call faith) and deaf to divine warnings (what we would call superstition).[1] Josephus and his friends were looking for signs and prophecies of the ruin of the people as an excuse for surrender; the Zealots, men of sterner stuff and of fuller faith, were resolved to resist to the end, and would brook no parleying with the enemy. They were in fact political nationalists of a different school and leaning from the aristocrats and the priests. The latter regarded political life and the Temple service as vital parts of the national life, and believing that the legions were invincible were anxious to keep peace with Rome. The Zealots regarded personal liberty and national independence as vital, and, to vindicate them, fought to the end with Rome. Both the extreme political parties lacked the spiritual standpoint of the Pharisees, who believed that the Torah even without political independence would hold the people together till a better time was granted by Providence. The party conflicts induced violence and civil tumult, and Josephus would have us believe that "demoniac discord" was the main cause of the ruin of Jerusalem. During the respite which the Jews enjoyed before the final siege of Jerusalem, he alleges that a bitter feud was waged incessantly between Eleazar the son of Simon, who held the Inner Court of the Temple, Simon, the son of Gioras, who held the Upper and the greater part of the Lower city, and John of Gischala, who occupied the outer part of the Temple. He describes the situation rhetorically as "sedition begetting sedition, like a wild beast gone mad, which, for want of other food, falls to eating its own flesh." And he bursts into an apostrophe over the fighting that went on within the Temple precincts:

"Most wretched city! What misery so great as this didst thou suffer from the Romans, when they came to purify thee from thy internecine hatred! Thou couldst no longer be a fit habitation for God, nor couldst thou continue longer in being, after thou hadst been a sepulcher for the corpses of thine own people, and thy holy house itself had been a burial place in their civil strife."

[1: Hist. v. 13. Gens superstitioni prona, religioni obnoxia.]

It is curious that a little later, when he resumes the narrative of the Roman campaign, and returns presumably to a Roman source, he says that the Jews, elated by their unexpected success, made incursions on the Greek cities. The success referred to must be the defeat of Cestius Gallus, and it looks as if this lurid account of the horrors of the civil war in Jerusalem were not known to the Roman guide, and that at the least Josephus has embroidered the story of the feud to suit his thesis. The measure of the Jewish writer's dependence for the main part of his narrative of the siege is singularly illustrated by a small detail. Josephus throughout his account uses the Macedonian names of the months, and equates them loosely with those of the Jewish calendar; but it is notable that the three traditional Jewish dates in the siege which he inserts, the fourteenth of Xanthicus (Nisan), when it began, the seventeenth of Panemos (Tammuz), when the daily offering ceased, and the ninth and tenth of Loos (Ab), when the Temple was destroyed, conflict with the other dates he gives in his general account of the siege. So far from being a proof of his independence, as has been claimed, his Jewish dates show his want of skill in weaving his Jewish information into his scheme. When he is original, he is apt to be unhistorical. Josephus agrees with the Talmud that the fire lasted to the tenth of the month,[1] but while the Rabbis cursed Titus, who burnt the Holy of Holies and spread fire and slaughter, and Roman historians[2] declared that Titus had deliberately fired the center of the Jewish cult in order to destroy the national stronghold, Josephus is anxious to preserve his patron's reputation for gentleness and invest him with the appearance of piety and magnanimity. Voicing perhaps the conqueror's later regrets, he declares that he protested against the Romans' avenging themselves on inanimate things and against the destruction of so beautiful a work, but failed despite all his efforts to stay the conflagration. The historian writes a lurid description of the catastrophe, but he omits the simple details that make the account in the Talmud so pathetic. "The Temple," runs the Talmudic account[3] "was destroyed on the eve of the ninth day of Ab at the outgoing of Sabbath, at the end of the Sabbatic year; and the watch of Jehoiarib was on service, and the Levites were chanting the hymns and standing at their desks. And the hymn they chanted was, 'And He shall bring upon them their own iniquity, and shall cut them off with their own wickedness' (Ps. 94:23); and they could not finish to say, 'The Lord our God shall cut them off,' when the heathen came and silenced them." This account may not be historically true, but it represents the unquenchable spirit of Judaism in face of the disaster.

[1: Comp. Yer. Taanit, iv. 6.]

[2: Comp. Sulpicius Severus, who used Tacitus (Chron. I. xxx. 6.); and the poet Valerius Flaccus acclaims the victor of Solymae, who hurls fiery torches at the Temple. Dion Cassius (lxvi. 4.) declares that when the Roman soldiers refused to attack the Temple in awe of its holiness, Titus himself set fire to it; and this appears to be the true account.]

[3: Taanit, 29a.]

Josephus, on the other hand, regards the fall of the Temple as a favorable opportunity to give a list of the prodigies and omens that heralded it. For example, he finds a proof of Providence in the fulfilment of the oracle, that the city and the holy house should be taken when the Temple should become foursquare. By demolishing the tower of Antonia the Jews had made the Temple area foursquare, and so brought the doom upon themselves. He tells, too, the story of a prophet Jesus, who for years had cried, "Woe, woe to Jerusalem," and in the end, struck by a missile, fell, crying, "Woe, woe to me!" For any reflections, however, on the immortality of the religion or for any utterances of hope for the ultimate restoration of the Temple and the coming of the Messiah, we must not look to the **Wars**. Such ideas would not have pleased his patrons, had he entertained them himself. He pointed to the fulfilment of prophecy only so far as it predicted and justified the destruction and ruin of his people. The expression of the national agony at the destruction of the national center is to be found in the apocryphal book of Esdras II.

Over his account of the final acts of the tragedy we may pass quickly. Undismayed by the fall of the sanctuary and still hoping for divine intervention, John and Simon withdrew from the Temple to the upper city. Driven from this, they took refuge in the underground caverns and caves to be found everywhere beneath Jerusalem, and finally they stood their ground in the towers, until these too were captured, a month after the destruction of the Temple, on the eighth of Elul (Gorpiaeus, as the Greek month was called).

"It was the fifth time that the city was captured; and 2179 years passed between its first building and its last destruction. Yet neither its great antiquity, nor its vast riches, nor the diffusion of the nation over the whole earth, nor the greatness of the veneration paid to it on religious grounds, was sufficient to preserve it from destruction. And thus ended the siege of Jerusalem."

Though the war was not finished, the crisis of the drama was over, and Josephus, doubtless following his source, relaxes the narrative to digress about affairs in Rome and the East. The last book of the *Wars* is episodic and disconnected. It is a kind of aftermath, in which the historian gathers up scattered records, but does not preserve the dramatic character of the history. He had apparently here to fall back on his own feeble constructive power, and was hard put to it to eke out his material to the proportions of a book.

So careless, too, is he that he abstracts references from his source that are meaningless. In the excursion into general history, he refers to "the German king Alaric, whom we have mentioned before,"[1] though he is brought in for the first time; and in the account of the siege of the Zealots' fortress Machaerus he records the death of one "Judas whom we have mentioned before,"[2] though again there was no previous mention of the warrior. In the same chapter he describes some magical plant, "Baaras, possessing power to drive away demons, which are no other than the spirits of the wicked that enter into living men and kill them, unless they obtain some help against them." This apparently was a commonplace of Palestinian natural science, as known to the Greco-Roman world, and Josephus simply copied it.

[1: B.J. VII. iv. 4.]

[2: B.J. VII. vi. 4.]

The Zealots still maintained resistance in remote parts of the country, and the legate Bassus was sent to take their three fortresses. He died before the capture of Masada, the last stronghold, a natural fastness overlooking the Dead Sea, which had been fortified by Herod. In this region David and centuries later the Maccabean heroes had found a refuge at their time of distress, and here the Jewish people were to show that desperate heroism of their race which is evoked when all save honor is lost. Masada had been occupied by Eleazar, a grandson of Judas of Galilee, the leader of the most fanatical section of the Zealots; and it fell to the procurator Flavius Silva to reduce it.

Josephus utters a final outburst against the hated nationalist party and especially its two leaders, Simon of Gioras and John of Gischala, though both had become victims of Roman revenge. "That was a time," he exclaims, "most prolific in wicked practices, nor could anyone devise any new evil, so deeply were they infected, striving with each other individually and collectively who should run to the greatest lengths of impiety towards God and in unjust actions towards their neighbors." The more incongruous is it that after this invective he puts into Eleazar's mouth two long speeches, calling on his men to kill themselves rather than fall into the hands of the Romans, which sum up eloquently the Zealot attitude.[1] Josephus indeed introduces in the speech the Hellenized doctrine of immortality, which regards the soul as an invisible spirit imprisoned in the mortal body and seeking relief from its prison. He goes on, however, to make the Jewish commander point out how preferable is death to life servitude to the Romans, in a way in which Eleazar might himself have spoken.

[1: B.J. VII. viii.]

"'And as for those who have died in the war, we should deem them blessed, for they are dead in defending, and not in betraying, their liberty: but as to the multitude of those that have submitted to the Romans, who would not pity their condition? And who would not make haste to die before he would suffer the same miseries? Where is now that great city, the metropolis of the Jewish nation, which was fortified by so many walls round about, which had so many fortresses and large towers to defend it, which could hardly contain the instruments prepared for the war, and which had so many myriads of men to fight for it? Where is this city that God Himself inhabited? It is now demolished to the very foundations; and hath nothing but that monument of it preserved, I mean the camp of those that have destroyed it, which still dwells upon its ruins; some unfortunate old men also lie upon the ashes of the Temple, and a few women are there preserved alive by the enemy for our bitter shame and reproach. Now, who is there that revolves these things in his mind, and yet is able to bear the sight of the sun, though he might live out of danger? Who is there so much his country's enemy, or so unmanly and so desirous of living, as not to repent that he is still alive? And I cannot but wish that we had all died before we had seen that holy city demolished by the hands of our enemies, or the foundations of our holy Temple dug up after so profane a manner. But since we had a generous hope that deluded us, as if we might perhaps have been able to avenge ourselves on our enemies, on that account, though it be now become vanity, and hath left us alone in this distress, let us make haste to die bravely. Let us pity ourselves, our children, and our wives, while it is in our power to show pity to them; for we are born to die, as well as those whom we have begotten; nor is it in the power of the most happy of our race to avoid it. But for abuses and slavery and the sight of our wives led away after an ignominious manner with their children, these are not such evils as are natural and necessary among men; although such as do not prefer death before those miseries, when it is in their power to do so, must undergo even them on account of their own cowardice.'

"Responding to their leader's call, the defenders put their wives and children to the sword, and then turned their hands on themselves: and when the Romans entered the place, to their amazement and horror they found not a living soul."

Eleazar's speech is one of the few patriotic outbursts in the seven books of the Wars, and it reads like a cry of bitter regret wrung from the unhappy author at the end of his work. Like Balaam he set out to curse, and stayed to bless, his enemies, and cursed himself. Perhaps this apostrophe hides the tragedy of Josephus' life. Perhaps he inwardly repented of his cowardice, and rued the uneasy protection he had secured for himself. Perhaps he had denounced the Zealots throughout the history perforce, to please his taskmasters, and in his heart of hearts envied the party that had preferred death to surrender. We could wish he had ended with the story of Masada's noble fall, and left us at this pathetic doubt. But he had not the dramatic sense, and he rounds off the story of the wars with an account of the futile Jewish rising in Alexandria and Cyrene, fomented by the surviving remnants of the Zealots. The first led to the closing in Egypt of the Temple of Onias, the last sanctuary of the Jews; the second to slanderous attacks on the historian. Jonathan, who had stirred up the Cyrenaic rising and started the slanders, was tortured and burnt alive. As to Catullus, the Roman governor, who admitted the calumnies, though the Emperor spared him, he fell into a terrible distemper and died miserably. "Thus he became a signal instance of Divine Providence, and demonstrated that God punishes the wicked."

Instead of concluding upon some national reflection, Josephus, pathetically enough, disfigures the end of his work with a final revelation of personal vanity and materialistic views of a Providence intervening on his behalf. Egoism and incapacity to attain to the noble and sublime either in action or thought were the two defects that lowered Josephus as a man, and which mar him as an historian. In the last paragraph of the work he insists that he has aimed alone at agreement with the facts; but industrious as is the record of events, the claim is shallow. His history of the Jewish wars lacks authority because it is palpably designed to please the Roman taste, and because also it has to serve as a personal apology for one who, when heroism was called for, had failed to respond to the call, and who was thus rendered incapable in letters as in life of being a faithful champion of his people.

VI

JOSEPHUS AND THE BIBLE

In the preface to the *Antiquities* Josephus draws a distinction between his motives for the composition of that work and of the *Wars*. He wrote the latter because he himself had played a large part in the war, and he desired to correct the errors of other historians, who had perverted the truth. On the other hand, he undertook to write the earlier history of his people because of the great importance of the events themselves and of his desire to reveal for the common benefit things that were buried in ignorance. He was stimulated to the task by the fact that his forefathers had been willing to communicate their antiquity to the Greeks, and, moreover, several of the Greeks had been at pains to learn of the affairs of the Jewish nation.

It would appear that he is here referring to the Septuagint translation of the Bible, since he proceeds to summarize the well-known story of King Ptolemy recounted in the Letter of Aristeas, which he afterwards sets out more fully.[1] Josephus shares the aim of the Hellenistic-Jewish writers to make the Jewish Scriptures known to the Gentile world, and he inherits also, but in a much smaller degree, their method of presenting Judaism to suit Greek or Greco-Roman tastes, as a philosophical, i.e. an ethical- philosophical, religion. Perhaps he had become acquainted, either at Alexandria or at Rome, with Philo's *Life of Moses*, which was a popular text-book, so to speak, of universal Judaism. Certain it is that the prelude to the *Antiquities* is reminiscent of the earlier treatise. Josephus reproduces Philo's idea that Moses began his legislation not as other lawgivers, "with the detailed enactments, contracts, and other rites between one man and another, but by raising men's minds upwards to regard God and His creation." For Moses life was to be an imitation of the divine. Contemplation of God's work is the best of all patterns for man to follow. With Philo again, he points out the superiority of Moses over other legislators in his attack upon false ideas of the divine nature; "for there is nothing in the Scriptures inconsistent with the majesty of God or with His love of mankind: and all things in it have reference to the nature of the universe." He claims, too, that Moses explains some things clearly and directly, but that he hints at others philosophically under the form of allegory. And to these commonplaces of Alexandrian exegesis he adds as the lesson of the history of his people that "it goes well with those who follow God's will and observe His laws, and ill with those who rebel against Him and neglect His laws." To exhibit to the Greco-Roman world the power and majesty of the Jewish God and the excellence of the Jewish law--these are the two main purposes which he professes to set before himself in his rendering of the Bible story, which occupies the first half of the *Antiquities*. No Jewish writer before him had treated the Bible to suit Roman predilections, which attached supreme importance to material strength and the concrete manifestation of authority, and Josephus in order to carry out his aim had therefore to proceed on new lines.

[1: See below]

In effect, he rarely attempts to ethicize the Bible story. For the most part he paraphrases it, cuts out its poetry, and reduces it to a prosaic chronicle of facts. The exordium in fact has little relation to the book, and looks as if it were borrowed without discrimination. Josephus next, indeed, professes that he will accurately set out in chronological order the incidents in the Jewish annals, "without adding anything to what is therein contained or taking anything away from it." It may be that he regarded the oral tradition as an inherent part of the law, and therefore inserts selections of it in the narrative, but anyhow he does not observe strictly the command of Deuteronomy (4:2) that prompted his profession, "Ye shall not add unto the word I have spoken, neither shall ye diminish aught from it." Not only does he freely paraphrase the Septuagint version of the Bible, but, more especially in the earlier part of the work, he incorporates pieces of Palestinian Haggadah and to a smaller extent of Alexandrian interpretation, and he omits many episodes that did not seem to him to redound to the glory of his people. He seeks to improve the Bible, and though he did not invent new legends, he accepted uncritically those which he found in Hellenistic sources or in the oral tradition of his people. His work is, therefore, valuable as a storehouse of early Haggadah. It is unnecessary to accept his description of himself as one who had a profound knowledge of tradition, but he was acquainted with the popular exegesis of the Palestinian teachers; and twenty years of life at the Roman court had not entirely eliminated his knowledge.

In the very first section of the first book, he notes that Moses sums up the first day of Creation with the words, "and it was ***one*** day"; whereas afterwards it is said, "it was the second, the third day, etc." He does not indeed supply the interpretation, saying that he will give the reason in a separate treatise which he proposes to write; but the same point is discussed in the Rabbinic commentary. He gives the traditional interpretation of the four rivers of the Garden of Eden.[1] He derives the name Adam from the Hebrew word for red, because the first man was formed out of red earth.[2] He states that the animals in the Garden of Eden had one language, a piece of Midrash which occurs also in the Book of Jubilees. He relates that Cain, after the murder of his brother, was afraid of falling among wild beasts, agreeing with the Midrash that all the animals assembled to avenge the blood of Abel,[3] but God forbade them to destroy Cain on pain of their own destruction. Seth he describes as the model of the virtuous, and of him the Rabbis likewise say, "From Seth dates the stock of all generations of the virtuous." He pictures him also as a great inventor and the discoverer of astronomy, and tells how he set up pillars of brick and stone recording these inventions, so that they might not be forgotten if the world was destroyed either by fire or water: here again agreeing with the Book of Jubilees, which relates that Cainan found an inscription in which his forefathers had described their inventions. Examples might be multiplied from the first chapters of the ***Antiquities*** of the way in which Josephus weaves into the Bible account traditional Midrashim, but these instances will suffice.

[1: Gen. R. ii. and iii., quoted in Bloch, Die Quellen des Flavius Josephus, 1879. The rivers are the Ganges, Euphrates, Tigris, and Nile.]

[2: Yalkut Gen. 21, 22.]

[3: Gen. R. xxii.]

Besides embroidering the Bible text with Haggadic legends, Josephus is prone to place in the mouths of the characters rhetorical speeches in the Greek style, either expanding a verse or two in the Bible or composing them entirely. Thus God says to Adam and Eve in the Garden of Eden after the fall:

"I had before determined about you that you might lead a happy life without affliction and care and vexation of soul; and that all things which might contribute to your enjoyment and pleasure should grow up by My Providence of their own accord. And death would not overtake you at any period. But now you have abused My good-will and disobeyed My commands, for your silence is not the sign of your virtue but of your guilty conscience."

Anticipating, moreover, the methods of latter-day Biblical apologists, he loses no opportunity of adding any confirmation he can find for the Bible story in pagan historians. He cites for the truth of the story of the flood Berosus the Chaldean, Hieronymus the Egyptian, Menander the Phoenician, and a great many others[1]; and he finds confirmation of the early chapters of Genesis in general in Manetho, who wrote a famous Egyptian history, and Mochus, and Hestiaeus, and in some of the earliest Greek chroniclers, Hesiod and Hecataeus and Hellanicus and Acesilaus. In later years he was to deal more elaborately with the question of the authority of the Scriptural history,[2] and then he set out the pagan testimony more accurately. In the ***Antiquities*** he is usually content to refer to it. It is significant that in the passages in which he adduces pagan corroboration he refers to Nicholas of Damascus, and in the first of them repeats his words about the remains of the Ark lying on a mountain in Armenia. It is well-nigh certain that Josephus did not study the writings of any of these chroniclers and historians at first hand, for he shows no acquaintance with the substance of their works. They were quoted by Nicholas, and where his source had given excerpts from their writings that threw any light, or might be taken to throw light, on the Hebrew text, Josephus, following the literary ethics of his day, inserts them. His archeology extended only to the reading of one or more writers of universal ancient history and taking from them whatever bore upon his own subject. He finds authority for the story of the tower of Babel in the oracles of the Sibyl, which we now know to be Jewish forgeries, but which professed to be and were regarded by the less educated of his day as being the utterances of an ancient seeress. Josephus paraphrases the hexameters which described how, when all men were of one tongue, some of them built a high tower, as if they would thereby ascend to heaven; but the deity sent storms of wind and overthrew the tower, and gave everyone his peculiar language.

[1: Ant. I. iii. 3.]

[2: Comp. below,]

Josephus sets considerable store by the exact chronology of the Bible, stopping continually to enumerate the number of years that had passed from the Creation to some other point of reckoning. His habit in this respect is marred by a singular inaccuracy in dealing with dates and figures, varying as he often does from chapter to chapter, sometimes from paragraph to paragraph, according to the source he happens to be following. He gives the year of the flood as 2656, though the sum of the years of the Patriarchs who lived before it in his reckoning totals only 2256. It has been conjectured[1] that he followed the Septuagint chronology from the Creation to the flood and that of the Hebrew Bible from Abraham onwards, and for the intermediate period he has his own reckoning. The result is that his calculations are often inconsistent. In his desire to impress the Greco-Roman reader, he dates an event by the Macedonian as well as the Jewish month, whenever he knows it, i.e. when he found it in his source. Thus the flood is said to have taken place "in the month Dius, which is called by the Hebrews Marheshwan." From the same motive he dwells on the table of the descendants of Noah, identifying the various families mentioned in the Bible with peoples known to the Greek world. The sons of Noah inhabited first the mountains Taurus and Amanus, and proceeded along Asia to the river Tanais, and along Europe to Cadiz, giving their names to nations in the lands they inhabited.

[1: Comp. Destinon, Die Chronologie des Josephus, 1880.]

What Josephus then insists on in his paraphrase of Scripture is the fact and not the lesson, the letter and not the spirit; while Philo, who is the true type of Jewish Hellenist, was always looking for deeper meanings beneath the literal text. The Romans had no bent for such interpretations, and Josephus Romanizes. He treats, for example, the genealogies, the chronology, and the ethnology of Genesis as things of supreme value, and though he occasionally inserts Haggadic tradition, he misses the Haggadic spirit, which sought to draw new morals and new spiritual value from the narrative. In his account of Abram, indeed, he touches upon the patriarch's higher idea of God, which led him to leave Chaldea. But here, too, he distorts the genuine Hebraic conception, and presents Abram as a kind of Stoic philosopher.[1]

[1: Ant. I. vii. 1.]

He was the first that ventured to publish this notion, that there was but one God, the Creator of the Universe, and that, as to the other gods, if they contributed to the happiness of men, they afforded it according to their appointment and not according to their own power. His opinion was derived from the study of the heavenly bodies and the phenomena of the terrestrial world. If, said he, these bodies had power of their own, they would certainly have regular motions. But since they do not preserve such regularity, they show that in so far as they work for our good, they do it not of their own strength but as they are subservient to Him who commands them.

This is one of the few pieces of theology in the ***Antiquities***, and we are fain to believe that he borrowed it from Nicholas, who is quoted immediately afterwards, or from pseudo-Hecataeus, a Jewish pseudepigraphic historian, to whom a book on the patriarch was ascribed. So, later, following the Hellenistic tradition, he represents Abraham as the teacher of astronomy to the Egyptians.

Josephus was a wavering rationalist, as is shown by his acceptance of the story of Lot's wife being turned into a pillar of salt, "I have seen the pillar," he adds (though again he may be blindly copying), "and it remains to this day." It is not the place here to enter into the details of his version of the story of the patriarchs. He gives the facts, and loses much of the spirit, often spoiling the beauty of the Biblical narrative by a prosy paraphrase. Thus God assures Abraham after the offering of Isaac,[1] that it was not out of desire for human blood that he was commanded to slay his son; and Isaac says to Jacob, who comes to receive the blessing: "Thy voice is like the voice of Jacob, yet because of the thickness of thy hair thou seemest to be Esau." One is reminded of Bowdler's improvements of Shakespeare in the eighteenth century.

[1: Ant. I. xiii. 4.]

The first book of the ***Antiquities*** ends with the death of Isaac. The second deals with the story of Joseph and of the Exodus from Egypt. The method is the same: partly Midrashic and partly rhetorical embellishment of the Biblical text, conversion of the poetry into prose, and, where occasion offers, correlation of the Scripture with Hellenistic history. The chapters dealing with the life of Moses are particularly rich in legendary additions: Amram is told in a vision that his son shall be the savior of Israel;[1] the name of Pharaoh's daughter is given as Thermuthis, in accordance with Hellenistic, but not Talmudic, tradition. Moses in his childhood dons Pharaoh's crown, and is only saved from death by the king's daughter. [2] Finally a whole chapter is devoted to an account of the wars of Moses, as an Egyptian general fighting against the Ethiopians, which is taken from the histories of pseudo-Artapanus.[3] Josephus makes no attempt to rationalize the account of the plagues, but on the contrary dilates on them, "both because no such plagues did ever happen to any other nation, and because it is for the good of mankind, that they may learn by this warning not to do anything which may displease God, lest He be provoked to wrath and avenge their iniquity upon them." At the same time, following a tradition reflected in the Apocalyptic and Rabbinic literature, he modifies the Biblical statement, that the Jews spoiled the Egyptians before leaving the country, by explaining that they took their fair hire for their labor.[4] And after describing the drowning of the Egyptians in the Red Sea--which Moses celebrates with a thanksgiving song in hexameter verse[5]--he apologizes for the strangeness of the narrative and its miraculous incidents. He explains that he has recounted every part of the history as he found it in the sacred books, and people are not to wonder "if such things happened, ***whether by God's will or by chance***, to the men of old, who were free from the wickedness of modern times, seeing that even for those who accompanied Alexander the Greek, who lived recently, when it was God's will to destroy the Persian monarchy, the Pamphylian sea retired and afforded a passage." This homily smacks of some Hellenistic-Jewish rationalist, whom he copied. But he concludes the whole with a formula, which is regular when he has stated something which he fears will be difficult of belief for his audience, "As to these things, let everyone determine as he thinks best." He treats the account of the Decalogue in a similar way. "I am bound," he says, "to relate the history as it is described in the Holy Writ, but my readers may accept or reject the story as they please." Josephus therein applied the rule, "When at Rome, do as Rome does." For it is noteworthy that the Roman historian Tacitus, who wrote a little later than Josephus, manifests the same indecision about the interference of the divine agency in human affairs, the relation of chance to human freedom, and the necessity of fate; and in many cases he likewise places the rational and transcendental explanations of an event side by side, without any attempt to reconcile them.

[1: Comp. Mekilta, ed. Weiss, p. 52. This and the following Rabbinic parallels are collected by Bloch, *op. cit.*]

[2: Comp. Tanhuma, xii. 4.]

[3: Comp. Eusebius, Praep. vii. 2.]

[4: Comp. Book of Jubilees, xlviii. 18, and Sanhedrin, 91a.]

[5: He probably had in mind the Greek version of the Song of Moses made by the Jewish-Alexandrian dramatic poet Ezekiel, which was written in hexameter verse.]

Josephus deals summarily with the Mosaic Code in the *Antiquities*, but announces his intention to compose "another work concerning our laws." This work is, perhaps, represented by the second book *Against Apion*; or possibly the intention was never fulfilled. He does not set out the ten commandments at length, explaining that it was against tradition to translate them directly.[1] He refers probably to the rule that they were not to be recited in any language but Hebrew, though, of course, the Septuagint contained a full version. On the other hand, he describes the construction of the Tabernacle with some fulness, and dwells particularly on the robes of the priests and the pomp of the high priest. Ritual and ceremonial appealed to his public; and his account, which was based on the practice of his own day, supplements in some particulars the account in the Talmud. But unfortunately he does not describe the Temple service. He attaches marked importance to the Urim and Thummim, which formed a sort of oracle parallel with pagan institutions, and says that the breastplate and sardonyx, with which he identifies them, ceased to shine two hundred years before he wrote his book[2] (i.e. at the time of John Hyrcanus). The Talmud understands the mystic names of the Bible in a similar way,[3] but represents that the oracle ceased with the destruction of the first Temple, and was not known in the second Temple. Josephus enlarges, in a way common to the Hellenistic-Jewish apologists,[4] on the symbolism of the Temple service and furniture.

"One may wonder at the contempt men bear us, or which they profess to bear, on the ground that we despise the Deity, whom they pretend to honor: for if anyone do but consider the construction of the Temple, the Tabernacle, and the garments of the high priest, and the vessels we use in our service, he will find our lawgiver was inspired by God.... For if he regard these things without prejudice, he will find that everyone is made by way of imitation and representation of the Universe."[5]

[1: Ant. III. vi. 4.]

[2: Ant. III. vii. 7.]

[3: Yer. Sotah, ix. 13.]

[4: Comp. Philo, De V. Mos. iii. 6.]

[5: Ant. III. vii. 7.]

The ritual, in brief, typifies the universal character of Judaism, which Josephus was anxious to emphasize in reply to the charge of Jewish aloofness and particularism. The three divisions of the Tabernacle symbolize heaven, earth, and sea; the twelve loaves stand for the twelve months of the year; the seventy parts of the candlestick for the seventy planets; the veils, which were composed of four materials, for the four elements; the linen of the high priest's vestment signified the earth, the blue betokened the sky; the breastplate resembled the shape of the earth, and so forth. We find similar reflections in Philo, but in his work they are part of a continuous allegorical exegesis, and in the other they are a sudden incursion of the symbolical into the long narrative of facts.

Following the account of the Tabernacle and the priestly vestments, Josephus describes the manner of offering sacrifices, the observance of the festivals, and the Levitical laws of cleanliness. In his account of these laws Josephus makes no attempt either to derive a universal value from the Biblical commands or to read a philosophical meaning into them by allegorical interpretation. He normally states the law as it stands in the text, and in the selection he makes he gives the preference, not to general ethical precepts, but to regulations about the priests. He had a pride of caste and a love of the pomp and circumstance of the Temple service; and the national ceremony could be more easily conveyed to the Gentile than an understanding of the spiritual value of Judaism. The Hellenistic apologists enlarged on the humanitarian character of the Mosaic social legislation; Josephus mentions without comment the laws of the seventh year release and the Jubilee, though in his later apology, which was addressed to the Greeks, in the books ***Against Apion***,[1] he dwelt more carefully on them. His interpretation of the laws, so far as it goes, in places agrees with the Rabbinic Halakah, but he admits some modification of the accepted tradition. Thus he states that the high priest was forbidden to marry a slave, or a captive, or a woman who kept an inn. He translates the Hebrew [Hebrew: zonah], which probably here means a prostitute, by innkeeper, a meaning the word has in other passages;[2] but the Aramaic version of the Bible supports him. He gives, too, a rationalizing reason for the observance of Tabernacles, saying, "The Law enjoins us to pitch tabernacles so that we may preserve ourselves from the cold of the season of the year."[3] The Feast of Weeks he calls Asartha, perhaps a Grecized form of the Hebrew [Hebrew: Atzereth], which was its old name, and he does not regard it as the anniversary of the giving of the Law. He promises to explain afterwards why some animals are forbidden for food and some permitted, but he fails to fulfil his promise. Since, however, the interpretation of the dietary laws as a discipline of temperance was a commonplace of Hellenistic Judaism, which is very fully set forth in the so-called Fourth Book of the Maccabees,[4] the absence of his comments is not a great loss.

[1: See below.]

[2: Judges, 4:1; Josh. 2; and Ezek. 23:44.]

[3: Ant. IV. viii. 4.]

[4: See above]

In the next book of the ***Antiquities***, Josephus deals with other parts of the Mosaic Law, especially such as might appear striking to Roman readers. Thus he gives in detail the law as to the Nazarites, the Korban offering, and the red heifer, and he completes his account of the Mosaic Code by a summary description of the Jewish polity, in which he abstracts a large part of the laws of Deuteronomy together with some of the traditional amplifications.[1] Moses prefaces his farewell address with a number of moral platitudes. "Virtue is its own principal reward, and, besides, it bestows abundance of others."--"The practice of virtue towards other men will make your own lives happy," and so forth. Josephus again proclaims that he sets out the laws in the words of Moses, his only innovation being to arrange them in a regular system, "for they were left by him in writing as they were accidentally scattered." The influence of Roman law may have suggested the arranging and digesting of the Mosaic Code, as well as several of his variations from the letter of the Bible.

[1: Ant. IV. viii.]

A few of his interpretations are noteworthy as comprising either Palestinian or Hellenistic tradition. He understands the command not to curse those in authority ([Hebrew: Elohim], Exod. 22:28) as referring to the gods worshiped in other cities, following Philo and a Hellenistic tradition based on a mistranslation of the Septuagint. A late passage in the Talmud, on the other hand, says that all abuse is forbidden save of idolatry.[1] With Philo again, he inserts into the code a law prohibiting the possession of poison on pain of death,[2] which is based on an erroneous interpretation of the law against witchcraft. Josephus follows the Hellenistic school also when he deduces from the prohibition against removing boundary stones the lesson that no infraction of the law and tradition[3] is to be permitted. Nothing is to be allowed the imitation of which might lead to the subversion of the constitution. He introduces a law about evidence, to the effect that the testimony of women should not be admitted "on account of the levity and boldness of their sex."[4] The rule has no place in the Code of the Pentateuch, but is supported in the oral law. He adopts another traditional interpretation when he limits the commands against women wearing men's habits to the donning of armor in times of war.[5] He misrepresents, on the other hand, the law of [Hebrew: shemitah] (seventh year release), stating that if a servant have a child by a bondwoman in his master's house, and if, on account of his good-will to his master, he prefers to remain a slave, he shall be set free only in the year of jubilee. The Bible says he shall be branded if he refuse the proffered liberty in the seventh year, and Philo in his interpretation has drawn a fine homily about the regard set on liberty. But Josephus may have thought that the institution would appear ridiculous to the legal minds of Romans. To accommodate the Jewish law again to the Roman standard, he moderates the **lex talionis** (the rule of an eye for an eye), by adding that it is applied only if he that is maimed will not accept money in compensation for his injury, a half-way position between the Sadducean doctrine, which understood the Biblical law literally, and the Pharisaic rule, which abrogated it. But in several instances he makes offenses punishable with death, which were not so according to the tradition, **e.g.** the insulting of parents by their children and the taking of bribes by judges.[6] Summing up the version of Deuteronomy, it may be said that Josephus, by omitting a law here, adding one there, now softening, now modifying, in some places broadening, in others narrowing the scope of the command, presents a code which lacks both the ruggedness of the Torah and the maturer humaneness of the Rabbinical Halakah, but was designed to show the reasonableness of the Jewish system according to Roman notions.

[1: Sanhedrin, 63b.]

[2: Comp. Philo, De Spec. Leg. ii. 815.]

[3: Comp. Deut. 22:5, and Nazir, 59a, with Ant. IV. viii. 43.]

[4: Shebuot, 30a.]

[5: Comp. Philo, De Spec. Leg. ii.]

[6: Comp. C. Ap. ii. 27. It has been suggested by Judge Mayer Sulzberger that he falsely interpreted the Hebrew [Hebrew: 'Arur] (cursed be!) to mean death punishment. Comp. J.Q.R., n.s., iii. 315.]

Josephus, from a different motive, is silent about the golden calf and the breaking of the tablets of stone. Those incidents, to his mind, did not reflect credit on his people; therefore they were not to be disclosed to Greek and Roman readers. He omits, for other reasons, the Messianic prophecies of Balaam, which would not be pleasing to the Flavians. At the same time one of the blessings in the prophecies of Balaam gives him the opportunity of asserting some universal humanitarian doctrines, to which Philo affords a parallel. The Moabite seer talks like a Hellenistic apologist of the second century B.C.E. or a Sibylline oracle: "Every land and every sea will be full of the praise of your name. Your offspring will dwell in every clime, and the whole world will be your dwelling-place for eternity."[1] He is at pains to extol Moses as of superhuman excellence, as is proved by the enduring force of his laws, which is such that "there is no Jew who does not act as if Moses were present and ready to punish him if he should offend in any way."[2] He quotes examples of the Jewish steadfastness in the Law, which would have impressed a Roman: the regular pilgrimage from Babylon to the Temple, the abstention of the Jewish priests from touching a crumb of flour during the Feast of Passover, at a time when, during a severe famine, abundance of wheat was brought to the Temple. But he somewhat mars the effect of his praise by adding a not very exalted motive for the piety of his people--the dread of the Law and of the wrath which God manifests against transgressors, even when no man can accuse the actor. Josephus is in a way a loyal supporter of the Law, and he had a sincere admiration for its hold on the people, but he was led by the conditions of his appeal to materialize the idea of Jewish religious intensity and to present it as a fear of punishment. Nor is it the humanity, the inherent excellence of the Law which he emphasizes, but its endurance and the widespread allegiance it commands. Looking at Judaism through Roman spectacles, he treats it as a positive force comparable with the sway of the Roman Emperor.

[1: Comp. Orac. Sib. 111. 271: [Greek: pasa de gaia sethen plaeres kai pasa thalassa] and Philo, De V. Mos. ii. 126.]

[2: Ant. IV. vi 4.]

In the description of the death of Moses the same habit of enfeebling the majesty of the Biblical text to suit the current taste is manifested. Moses weeps before he ascends the mountain to die. He exhorts the people not to lament over his departure. As he is about to embrace Joshua and Eleazar, he is covered with a cloud and disappears in a valley, although he piously wrote in the holy books that he died lest the people should say that, because of his marvelous virtue, he was taken up to God. For the last statement Josephus has the authority of some sages, who discussed whether the last verses of Deuteronomy were written by Moses himself.[1]

[1: Baba Batra, 15a.]

Josephus continues the Biblical narrative in less detail in the fifth book, which covers the period of Joshua and the Judges and the first part of Samuel. The Book of Joshua is compressed into the limits of one chapter, but the exploits of each of the judges of Israel, with one or two omissions, are recounted in order, and the episode of Ruth is inserted after the story of Samson. He substitutes for the famous declaration of Ruth to Naomi the prosy statement: "Naomi took Ruth along with her, as she was not to be persuaded to stay behind, but was resolved to share her fortune with her mother-in-law, whatsoever it should prove." And he justifies his insertion of the episode by the reflection that he desires to demonstrate the power of God, who can raise those that are of common parentage to dignity and splendor, even as He advanced David, though he was born of mean parents.

With his fondness for royal history, and no doubt with an eye to his noble audience, he devotes a whole book to the account of Saul's reign, adhering closely to the narrative in Samuel, but occasionally adding a passage from the Book of Chronicles, or softening what seemed an asperity in Scripture. Samuel, for example, orders Agag to be killed, whereas in the Bible he puts him to death with his own hand.[1] The incident of Saul and the Witch of Endor is expanded and invested with further pathos.[2] The Witch devotes her only possession, a calf, for the king's meal, and the historian expatiates first on her kindness and then on Saul's courage in fighting, though he knew his approaching doom. We may suspect that this digression was induced by a supposed analogy in the king of Israel's lot to the author's conduct in Galilee, when, as he claimed, he fought on though knowing the hopelessness of resistance.

[1: Ant. VI. viii. 5.]

[2: Ant. VI. viii. 14.]

The next book is taken up entirely with the reign of David, and contains little that is noteworthy. On one point Josephus cites the authority of Nicholas of Damascus to support the Bible, and here and there he adopts a traditional interpretation. David's son by Abigail is said to be Daniel,[1] whereas the Book of Samuel gives the name as Kitab. Absalom's hair was so thick that it could be cut with difficulty every eight days.[2] David chose a pestilence as the punishment for his sin in numbering his people, because it was an affliction common to kings and their subjects.[3] The historian ascribes the Psalms to David, and says they were in several (Greek) meters, some in hexameters and others in pentameters. Lastly he enlarges on the wonderful wealth of David, which was greater than that of any other king either of the Hebrews or of other nations. Benjamin of Tudela relates, and the Mohammedans believe to this day, that vast treasure is buried with the king, and lies in his reputed sepulcher. The story must have been accepted in the days of Josephus, for he records how Hyrcanus, the son of Simon the Maccabee, being in straits for money to buy off the Seleucid invader, opened a room of David's sepulcher and took out three thousand talents, and how, many years later, King Herod opened another room, and took out great store of money; yet neither lighted on the body of the king. Such romantic tales pleased the readers of the Jewish historian, who lived amid the wonderful material splendor of Rome, and prized, above all things, material wealth.

[1: Comp. Ant. VII. i. 4; Berakot, 4a.]

[2: Ant. VII. viii.; comp. Nazir, 4b.]

[3: Ant. VII. xiii.; comp. Yalkut, ii. 165.]

When he comes to the history of Solomon, he speaks of his proverbial writings, and inserts a long account of his miraculous magical powers, based no doubt on popular legend.[1]

"He composed books of odes and songs one thousand and five [here he follows Chronicles] and of parables and similitudes three thousand. For he spoke a parable on every sort of tree, from the hyssop to the cedar, and in like manner about every sort of living creature, whether on the earth or in the air or in the seas. He was not unacquainted with any of their natures, nor did he omit to study them, but he described them all in the manner of a philosopher. God also endowed him with skill in expelling demons, which is a science useful and health-giving to men."[2]

[1: Comp. Yalkut, ii. 177. The apocryphal Wisdom of Solomon similarly credits the king with power over spirits (vii. 20).]

[2: Ant. VIII. ii. 5.]

Josephus goes on to describe how, in the presence of Vespasian, a compatriot cured soldiers who were demoniacal. We know from the New Testament that the belief in possession by demons was widespread among the vulgar in the first century of the common era, and the Essenes specialized in the science of exorcism. As the belief was invested with respectability by the patronage which the Flavian court extended to all sorts of magic and witchcraft, Josephus enlarges on it. Solomon is therefore represented as a thaumaturgist, and while not a single example is given of the proverbs ascribed to him, his exploits as a miracle-monger are extolled. Josephus sets out at length the story of the building of the Temple, and dwells on Solomon's missions to King Hiram, of which, he says, copies remained in his day, and may be seen in the public records of Tyre. This he claims to be a signal testimony to the truthfulness of his history.[1] He modernizes elaborately Solomon's speech at the dedication of the sanctuary, and converts it into an apology for the Jews of his own day. Again he follows an Alexandrian model, and describes God in Platonic fashion: "Thou possessest an eternal house, and we know how, from what Thou hast created for Thyself, Heaven and Air and Earth and Sea have sprung, and how Thou fillest all things and yet canst not be contained by any of them."[2] Solomon is here a preacher of universalism; he prays that God shall help not the Hebrews alone when they are in distress, "but when any shall come hither from the ends of the earth and repent of their sins and implore Thy forgiveness, do Thou pardon them and hear their prayer. For thereby all shall know that Thou wast pleased with the building of this house, and that we are not of an unsociable nature, nor do we behave with enmity to such as are not of our people, but are willing that Thou shouldst bestow Thy help on all men in common, and that all alike may enjoy Thy benefits." Solomon's dream after the dedication service provides another occasion for pointing to the Jewish disaster of the historian's day. For he foresees that if Israel will transgress the Law, his miseries shall become a proverb, and his neighbors, when they hear of them, shall be amazed at their magnitude.

[1: Comp. below, p. 223.]

[2: Ant. VIII. iv. 2. Comp. Philo, De Confus. Ling. i. 425.]

The description of the Temple is followed by a glowing account of the king's palace, of which the roof was "according to the Corinthian order, and the decorations so vivid that the leaves seemed to be in motion." We are told, too, of the great cities which the king built, Tadmor in the wilderness of Syria, and Gezer, the Bible narrative being supplemented here with passages from Nicholas. The Queen of Sheba is represented as the Queen of Egypt and Ethiopia, and it is to her gift that Josephus attributes "the root of balsam which our country still bears." Reveling in the material greatness of the Jewish court during the golden age of the old kingdom, Josephus catalogues the wealth of Solomon, the number of his horses and chariots.

He reproaches him not only for marrying foreign wives, but for making images of brazen oxen, which supported the brazen sea, and the images of lions about his throne. For these sins against the second commandment he died ingloriously.

With the death of Solomon the legendary and romancing character of this part of the ***Antiquities*** comes to an end. In the summary of the fortunes of the kingdoms of Israel and Judah, Josephus adheres almost exclusively to the Biblical text, and allows himself few digressions. He moralizes a little about the decay of the people under Rehoboam, reflecting that the aggrandizement of a kingdom and its sudden attainment of prosperity often are the occasion of mischief; and he controverts Herodotus, who confused Sesostris with Shishak when relating the Egyptian king's conquests. It is, he claims, really Shishak's invasion of Jerusalem which the Greek historian narrates, as is proved by the fact that he speaks of circumcised Syrians, who can be no other than Jews. The fate of Omri and Zimri[1] moves him to moralize again about God's Providence in rewarding the good and punishing the wicked; and Ahab's death evokes some platitudes concerning fate, "which creeps on human souls and flatters them with pleasing hopes, till it brings them to the place where it will be too hard for them."[2] Artapanus, or one of the Jewish Hellenists masking as a pagan historian, may have provided him with this reflection.

[1: Ant. IX. xii. 6.]

[2: Ant. IX. xv. 6.]

He spoils the grandeur of the scene on Mount Carmel, when Elijah turned the people from Baal-worship back to the service of God. In place of the dramatic description in the Book of Kings he states that the Israelites worshiped one God, and called Him the great and the only true God, while the other deities were names. He omits altogether the account of Elijah's ascent to Heaven, probably from a desire not to appear to entertain any Messianic ideas with which the prophet was associated. He says simply that Elijah disappeared from among men. But he gives in detail the miraculous stories of Elisha, which were not subject to the same objection. Occasionally his statements seem in direct conflict with the Hebrew Bible, as when he says that Jehu drove slowly and in good order, whereas the Hebrew is that "he driveth furiously."[1] Or that Joash, king of Israel, was a good man, whereas in the Book of Kings it is written, "he did evil in the sight of the Lord."[2] But these discrepancies may be due, not to a different Bible text, but to aberrations of the copyists.

[1: Ant. IX. vi. 3; II Kings, 9:20.]

[2: II Kings, 13:11.]

The story of dynastic struggles and foreign wars is varied with a short summary of the life of Jonah, introduced at what, according to the Bible, is its proper chronological place,[1] in the reign of Jeroboam II, king of Israel. The picturesque and miraculous character of the prophet's adventures secured him this distinction, for in general Josephus does not pay much regard to the lives or writings of the prophets. It is only where they foretold concrete events that their testimony is deemed worthy of mention. Of the other minor prophets he mentions Nahum, and paraphrases part of his prophecy of the fall of Nineveh, cutting it short with the remark that he does not think it necessary to repeat the rest,[2] so that he may not appear troublesome to his readers. In the account of Hezekiah he mentions that the king depended on Isaiah the prophet, by whom he inquired and knew of all future events,[3] and he recounts also the miracle of putting back the sun-dial. For the rest, he says that, by common consent, Isaiah was a divine and wonderful man in foretelling the truth, "and in the assurance that he had never written what was false, he wrote down his prophecies and left them in books, that their accomplishment might be judged of by posterity from the events.[4] Nor was he alone, but the other prophets [i.e. the minor prophets presumably], who were twelve in number, did the same." It is notable that this phrase of the *Antiquities* about the prophets bears a resemblance to the "praise of famous men" contained in the apocryphal book of Ben Sira, which Josephus probably used in the Greek translation.

[1: Ant. IX. x. 1.]

[2: Ant. IX. xi. 3.]

[3: Ant. IX. xiii.]

[4: Ant. X. ii. 2. Comp. Is. 30:8*f*.]

While he thus cursorily disposes of the prophetical writers, he seizes on any scrap of Hellenistic authors which he could find to confirm the Bible story, or rather to confirm the existence of the personages mentioned in the Bible. Thus he quotes the Phoenician historian Menander, who confirms the existence and exploits of the Assyrian king Shalmaneser. So, too, he brings forward Herodotus and Berosus to confirm the existence and doings of Sennacherib.[1] He refutes Herodotus again, doubtless on the authority of a predecessor, for saying that Sennacherib was king of the Arabs instead of king of the Assyrians.

[1: Ant. X. ii. 4.]

As with Ahab, so with Josiah, Josephus sees the power of fate impelling him to his death, and substitutes the Hellenistic conception of a blind and jealous power for the Hebrew idea of a just Providence. He ascribes to Jeremiah "an elegy on the death of the king, which is still extant,"[1] apparently following a statement in the Book of Chronicles, which does not refer to our Book of Lamentations. Jeremiah is treated rather more fully than Isaiah. Besides a notice of his writings we have an account of his imprisonment. He ascribes to Ezekiel two books foretelling the Babylonian captivity. Possibly the difference between the last nine and the first forty chapters of the exile prophet suggested the idea of the two books, unless these words apply rather to Jeremiah,

"The two prophets agreed [he remarks] on all other things as to the capture of the city and King Zedekiah, but Ezekiel declared that Zedekiah should not see Babylon, while Jeremiah said the king of Babylon should carry him thither in bonds. Because of this discrepancy, the Jewish prince disbelieved them both, and condemned them for false tidings.[2] Both prophets, however, were justified, because Zedekiah came to Babylon, but he came blind, so that, as Ezekiel had predicted, he did not see the city."

[1: Ant. X. v. 2. Comp. II Chron. 35:25.]

[2: Ant. X. vii. 2.]

The episode is possibly based on some apocryphal book that has disappeared, and the historian extracts from it the lesson, which he is never weary of repeating, that God's nature is various and acts in diverse ways, and men are blind and cannot see the future, so that they are exposed to calamities and cannot avoid their incidence.[1]

[1: Ant. X. viii. 3.]

Following on the account of the fall of the last of the Davidic line and the destruction of the Temple, Josephus gives a chronological summary of the history of Israel from the Creation, together with an incomplete list of all the high priests who held office. The latter may be compared with the list of high priests with which he closes the *Antiquities*.[1] These chronological calculations were dear to him, but perhaps he borrowed them from one of the earlier Hellenistic Jewish chroniclers. He takes an especial pride throughout the *Antiquities* as well as in the *Wars* in recording the priestly succession, which served to emphasize the antiquity not only of his people, but of his own personal lineage, and was moreover congenial to the ideas of the Romans, who paid great heed to the records of their priests.

[1: See below,]

As might be expected, he dwells at some length on Daniel,[1] whose book was full of the miraculous legends and exact prophecies loved by his audience, and he recommends his book to those who are anxious about the future. He elaborates the interpretation of the vision of the image (ch. 3:7), but finds himself in a difficulty when he comes to the explanation of the stone broken off from the mountain that fell on the image and shattered it. According to the traditional interpretation, it portended the downfall of Rome, or maybe the coming of the Messiah, an idea equally hateful to the Roman conquerors. He excuses himself by saying that he has only undertaken to describe things past and present, and not things that are future. Later he disclaims responsibility for the story of Nebuchadnezzar's madness, on the plea that he has translated what was in the Hebrew book, and has neither added nor taken away. The story probably looked too much like an implied reproach on a mad Caesar. He adds a new chapter to the Biblical account of the prophet: Daniel is carried by Darius to Persia, and is there signally honored by the king. He builds a tower at Ecbatana,[2] which is still extant, says the historian, "and seems to be but lately built. Here the kings of Persia and Media are buried, and a Jewish priest is the custodian." Josephus borrowed this addition from some apocalyptic book recounting Daniel's deeds, and he speaks of "several books the prophet wrote and left behind him, which are still read by us." The short story in the Apocrypha of ***Bel and the Dragon***, with its apologue about Susannah, affords an example of the post-Biblical additions to Daniel, and in the first century, when Messianic hopes were rife among the people, such apocryphal books had a great vogue. Daniel is in fact elevated to the rank of one of the greatest of the prophets, because he not only prophesied generally of future events like the others, but fixed the actual time of their accomplishment. It is claimed for him that he foretold explicitly the persecution of Antiochus Epiphanes and the Roman conquest of Judea. Anticipating the theological controversialists of later times, Josephus sets special store on the Bible book that is most miraculous, because miracle and exact prognostication of the future are for his audience the clearest testimony of God. Hence the predictions of Daniel are the best refutation of the Epicureans, who cast Providence out of life, and do not believe that God has care of human affairs, but say that things move of their own accord, without a ruler and guide.

[1: Ant. X. x.]

[2: Ant. X. xi. 7.]

When he comes to the history of the Restoration from Babylon, Josephus follows what is now known as the apocryphal Book of Esdras, in preference to the Biblical Ezra and Nehemiah, probably because a Hellenistic guide whom he had before him did likewise. It is clear that he based his paraphrase on the Greek text. His chronicle therefore differs considerably from that given in our Scripture, and on one point he differs from his guide. For while Esdras represents Artaxerxes as the king under whom the Temple was rebuilt, Josephus, relying on a fuller knowledge of Persian history, derived probably from Nicholas of Damascus, substitutes

Cambyses.[1] Our Greek version of Esdras I is unfortunately not complete, but the book, differing from that included in the Bible, must have originally comprised an account of Nehemiah. According to Josephus, Ezra dies before Nehemiah[2] arrives in Judea, whereas in the canonical books they appear for a time together. He states also that Nehemiah built houses for the poor in Jerusalem out of his own means, an incident which has not the authority of the Bible, but which may well have reposed on an ancient tradition. The account of the marriage of Sanballat with the daughter of Manasseh the high Priest, which is touched on in our Book of Nehemiah, is described more fully by Josephus,[3] who based this account on some uncanonical source. And following the Rabbis, who shortened the Persian epoch in order to eke out the Jewish history over the whole period of the Persian kingdom till the conquest of Alexander, he makes the marriage synchronize with the reign of Philip of Macedon. Josephus was anxious to avoid a vacuum, and by a little vague chronology and the aid of the fragmentary records of Ezra and Nehemiah and a priestly chronicle, the few Jewish incidents known in that tranquil, unruffled epoch are spread over three centuries.

[1: Ant. XI. ii.]

[2: Ant. XI. v.]

[3: Ant. XI. vii. 2.]

The episode of Esther is treated elaborately, and, following the apocryphal version, is placed in the reign of Artaxerxes. The Greek Book of Esther, which embroidered the Hebrew story, and is generally attributed to the second century B.C.E., is laid under contribution as well as the Canonical book; from it Josephus extracted long decrees of the king and elaborate anti-Semitic denunciations of a Hellenized Haman. He omits the incident of casting lots, and contrives to explain Purim, by means of a Greek etymology, as derived from [Greek: phroureai], which denotes protection. Here and there the Biblical simplicity is elaborated: Mordecai moves from Babylon to Shushan in order to be near Esther, and soldiers with bared axes stand round the king to secure the observance of the law that he shall not be approached. We have some moralizing on Haman's fall and the working of Providence ([Greek: to theion]), which teaches that "what mischief anyone prepares against another, he unconsciously contrives against himself." Less edifying is the addition that "God laughed to scorn the wicked expectations of Haman, and as He knew what the event would be, He was pleased at it, and that night He took away the king's sleep." The Book of Esther does not mention God: Josephus calls in directly the operation of the Divine Power, but represents it unworthily.

With the completion of the eleventh book of the ***Antiquities***, we definitely pass away from the region of sacred history and miracles, and find ourselves in the more spacious but more misty area of the Hellenistic kingdom, in which Jewish affairs are only a detail set in a larger background. Though Josephus himself does not explicitly mark the break, the character of his work materially changes. He has come to the end of the period when the Bible was his chief guide; he has now to depend for the main thread on Hellenistic sources, filling in the details when he can from some Jewish record. His function becomes henceforth more completely that of compiler, less of translator, and his work becomes much more valuable for us, because in great part he has the field to himself. Although, however, the Bible paraphrase, with the embroidery of a little tradition and comparative history and its Romanizing reflections, which constitutes the first part of the ***Antiquities***, had not a great permanent value, for a very long period it was accepted as the standard history of the Jewish people; and in the pagan Greco-Roman world it appealed to a public to which both the Hebrew Bible and the Septuagint translation were sealed books. It was written for a special purpose and served it, doing for the Jewish early history what Livy did for the hoary past of the Romans. If it was not a worthy record in many parts, it was yet of great value as an antidote to the crude fictions of the anti-Semites about the origin and the institutions of the people of Israel, which had for some two centuries been allowed to poison the minds of the Greek-speaking world, and had fanned the prejudices of the Roman people against a nationality of whose history they were ignorant and of whose laws they were contemptuous.

VII
JOSEPHUS AND POST-BIBLICAL JEWISH HISTORY

(THE ANTIQUITIES, BOOKS XII-XX)

Josephus is the sole writer of the ancient world who has left a connected account of the Jewish people during the post-Biblical period, and the meagerness of his historical information is not due so much to his own deficiencies as to the difficulty of the material. From the period when the Scriptures closed, the affairs of the Jews had to be extracted, for the most part, out of works dealing with the annals of the whole of civilized humanity. With the conquest of Alexander the Great, the Jewish people enter into the Hellenistic world, and begin to command the attention of Hellenistic historians. They are an element in the cosmopolis which was the ideal of the world-conqueror. At the same time the nature of the history of their affairs vitally changes. The continuous chronicle of their doings, which had been kept from the Exodus out of Egypt to the Restoration from Babylon, and which was designed to impress a religious lesson and illustrate God's working, comes to an end; and their scribes are concerned to draw fresh lessons from that chronicle. The religious philosophy of history is not extended to the present. The Jews, on the other hand, chiefly engage the interest of the Gentiles when they come into violent collision with the governing power, or when they are involved in some war between rival Hellenistic sovereigns. Hence their history during the two centuries following Alexander's conquests, i.e. until the time when we again have adequate Jewish sources, is singularly shadowy and incoherent.

Josephus was not the man to pierce the obscurity by his intuition or by his research. Yet we must not be too critical of the want of proportion in his writing when we remember that he was a pioneer; for it was an original idea to piece together the stray fragments of history that referred to his people. It has been shown that in his attempt to stretch out the Biblical history till it can join on to the Hellenistic sources, Josephus interposes between the account of Esther and the fall of the Persian Empire a story of intrigue among the high priests. He there describes the crime of the high priest John in killing his brother in the Temple as more cruel and impious than anything done by the Greeks or Barbarians--an expression which must have originated in a Jewish, probably a Palestinian, authority, to whom Greek connoted cruelty. And in the next chapter Josephus inserts the story of the Samaritan Sanballat and the building of the Samaritan Temple on Mount Gerizim,[1] as though these events happened at the time of Alexander's invasion of Persia. Rabbinical chronology interposes only one generation between Cyrus and Alexander. The Sanballat who appears in the Book of Nehemiah is represented as anticipating the part played by the Hellenists of a later century, and calling in the foreign invader against Judea and Jerusalem in order to set up his own son-in-law Manasseh as high priest. Probably, in the fashion of Jewish history, the events of a later time were placed in the popular Midrash a few generations back and repeated. Jewish legendary tradition is more certainly the basis of the account of Alexander's treatment of the Jews. The Talmud has preserved similar stories.[2] According to both records, the Macedonian conqueror did obeisance before the high priest, who came out to ask for mercy, because he recognized in the Jewish dignitary a figure that had appeared to him in a dream. And when Alexander is made to revere the prophecies of Daniel and to prefer the Jews to the Samaritans and bestow on them equal rights with the Macedonians, the historian is simply crystallizing the floating stories of his nation, which are parallel with those invented by every other nation of antiquity about the Greek hero.

[1: Comp. Neh. 13: 23.]

[2: Comp. Megillat Taanit, 3, and Yoma, 69a.]

Passing on to Alexander's successors, he has scarcely fuller or more reliable sources. For Ptolemy's capture of Jerusalem on the Sabbath day, when the Jews would not resist, he calls in the confirmation of a Greek authority, Agatharchides of Cnidus. But he has to gloss over a period of nearly a hundred years, till he can introduce the story of the translation of the Scriptures into Greek,[1] for which he found a copious source in the romantic history, or rather the historical romance, now known as the Letter of Aristeas. This Hellenistic production has come down to us intact, and therefore we can gather how closely Josephus paraphrases his authorities. Not that he refrained altogether from embellishment and improvement. The Aristeas of his version, as of the original, professes that he is not a Jew, but he adds that nevertheless he desires favor to be done to the Jews, because all men are the work of God, and "I am sensible that He is well pleased with all those that do good." Josephus states a large part of the story as if it were his own narrative, but in fact it is a paraphrase throughout. He reproduces less than half of the Letter, omitting the account of the visit of the royal envoy to Jerusalem and the discourse of Eleazar the high priest. For the seventy-two questions and answers, which form the last part, he refers curious readers to his source. But he sets out at length the description of the presents which Ptolemy sent to Jerusalem, rejoicing in the opportunity of showing at once the splendor of the Temple vessels and the honor paid by a Hellenistic monarch to his people.

[1: Ant. XII. ii.]

From his own knowledge also, he adds a glowing eulogy, which Menedemus, the Greek philosopher, passed on the Jewish faith. The Letter of Aristeas says that the authors of the Septuagint translation uttered an imprecation on any one who should alter a word of their work; Josephus makes them invite correction,[1] adding inconsequently--if our text is correct--that this was a wise action, "so that, when the thing was judged to have been well done, it might continue forever."

[1: Josephus may have used a different text of Aristeas from that which has come down to us. Or the passage in our Aristeas may be a later insertion introduced as a protest against Christian interpolations in the LXX.]

Having disposed of the Aristeas incident, Josephus has to fill in the blank between the time of Ptolemy Philadelphus (250 B.C.E.) and the Maccabean revolt against Antiochus Epiphanes, nearly one hundred years later, which was the next period for which he had Jewish authority. He returns then to his Hellenistic guides and extracts the few scattered incidents which he could find there referring to the

Jewish people. But until he comes to the reign of Antiochus, he can only snatch up some "unconsidered trifles" of doubtful validity. Seleucus Nicator, he says, made the Jews citizens of the cities which he built in Asia, and gave them equal rights with the Macedonians and Greeks in Antioch. This information he would seem to have derived from the petition which the Jews of Antioch presented to Titus when, after the fall of Jerusalem, the victor made his progress through Syria. The people of Antioch then sought to obtain the curtailment of Jewish rights in the town, but Titus refused their suit.[1] Josephus takes this opportunity of extolling the magnanimity of the Roman conqueror, and likewise of inserting a reference to the friendliness of Marcus Agrippa, who, on his progress through Asia a hundred years before, had upheld the Jewish privileges.[2] He derived this incident from Nicholas' history, and thus contrived to eke out the obscurity of the third century B.C.E. with a few irrelevancies.

[1: Comp. B.J. VII. v. 3.]

[2: Ant. XIII. iii. 2.]

His material becomes a little ampler from the reign of Antiochus the Great, because from this point the Greek historians serve him better. Several of the modern commentators of Josephus have thought that his authorities were Polybius and Posidonius, who wrote in Greek on the events of the period. He cites Polybius explicitly as the author of the statement about Ptolemy's conquest of Judea, and then reproduces two letters of Antiochus to his generals, directing them to grant certain privileges to his Jewish subjects as a reward for their loyal service. We know that Polybius gave in his history an account of Jerusalem and its Temple, and his character-sketch of Antiochus Epiphanes has been preserved in an epitome. Josephus, however, be it noted, has only these scanty extracts from his work. The letters are clearly derived, not from him, but from some Hellenistic-Jewish apologist, and the passages from Polybius, it is very probable, are extracted from some larger work.[1] Here, as elsewhere, both facts and authorities were found in Nicholas of Damascus.

[1: Dr. Buechler (J.Q.R. iv. and R.E.J. xxxii. 179) has argued convincingly that Josephus had not gone far afield. For the genuineness of the Letter, comp. Willrich, Judaica, p. 51, and Buechler, Oniaden und Tobiaden, p. 143.]

We know from Josephus himself that Nicholas had included a history of the Seleucid Empire in his **magnum opus**. He is quoted in reference to the sacking of the Temple by Antiochus Epiphanes and the victory of Ptolemy Lathyrus over Alexander Jannaeus.[1] Josephus, indeed, several times appends to his paragraphs about the general history a note, "as we have elsewhere described." Some have inferred from this that he had himself written a general history of the Seleucid epoch, but a more critical study has shown that the tag belongs to the note of his authority, which he embodied carelessly in his paraphrase.[2]

[1: Ant. XIII. xii. 6.]

[2: Comp. Ant. XIV. I. 2-3; xi. I.]

Josephus supplements the Jewish references in the Seleucid history of Nicholas by an account of the intrigues of the Tobiades and Oniades, which reveals a Hellenistic-Jewish origin.[1] Possibly he found it in a special chronicle of the high-priestly family, which was written by one friendly to it, for Joseph ben Tobias is praised as "a good man and of great magnanimity, who brought the Jews out of poverty and low condition to one that was more splendid." The chronology here is at fault, since at the time at which the incidents are placed both Syria and Palestine were included in the dominion of the Seleucids; yet Tobias is represented at the court of the Ptolemies. Josephus follows the story of these exploits with the letters which passed between Areas, king of the Lacedemonians, and the high priest Onias, as recorded in the First Book of the Maccabees (ch. 12). The letters are taken out of their true place, in order to bridge the gap between the fall of the Tobiad house and the Maccabean rising. Areas reigned from 307-265, so that he must have corresponded to Onias I, but Josephus places him in the time of Onias III.

[1: Ant. XII. iv.]

For his account of the Maccabean struggle he depends here primarily upon the First Book of the Maccabees, which in many parts he does little more than paraphrase. Neither the Second Book of the Maccabees nor the larger work of Jason of Cyrene, of which it is an epitome, appears to have been known to him. It is well-nigh certain that in writing the *Wars* he had no acquaintance with the Jewish historical book, but was dependent on the less accurate and complete statement of a Hellenistic chronicle; and in the later work, though he bases his narrative on the Greek version of the Maccabees, and says he will give a fresh account with great accuracy, he yet incorporates pieces of non-Jewish history from the Greek guide without much art or skill or consistency. Thus, in the *Wars* he says that Antiochus Epiphanes captured Jerusalem by assault, while in the *Antiquities* he speaks of two captures: the first time the city fell without fighting, the second by treachery. And while in the Book of the Maccabees the year given for the fall of the city is 143 of the Seleucid era, in the *Antiquities* the final capture is dated 145[1] of the era. He no doubt found this date in the Greek authority he was following for the general history of Antiochus--he gives the corresponding Greek Olympiad--and applied it to the pillage of Jerusalem. For the story of Mattathias at Modin, which is much more detailed than in the *Wars*, he closely follows the Book of the Maccabees, though in the speeches he takes certain liberties, inserting, for example, an appeal to the hope of immortality in Mattathias' address to his sons.[2] He turns to his Greek authority for the death of Antiochus, and controverts Polybius, who ascribes the king's distemper to his sacrilegious desire to plunder a temple of Diana in Persia. Josephus, with a touch of patriotism and an unusual disregard of the feelings of his patrons, who can hardly have liked the implied parallel, says it is surely more probable that he lost his life because of his pillage of the Jewish Temple. In confirmation of his theory he appeals to the materialistic morality of his audience, arguing that the king surely would not be punished for a wicked intention that was not successful. He states also that Judas was high priest for three years, which is not supported by the Jewish record;[3] and he passes over the miracle of the oil at the dedication of the Temple, and ascribes the name of the feast to the fact that light appeared to the Jews. The celebration of Hanukkah as the feast of lights is of Babylonian-Jewish origin, and was only instituted shortly before the destruction of the Temple.[4]

[1: Ant. XII. v. 3.]

[2: Ant. XIII. vi. 3.]

[3: In his own list of high priests at the end of the work, the name of Judas does not appear.]

[4: Comp. Krauss, R.E.J. xxx. 32.]

His use of the Book of the Maccabees stops short at the end of chapter xii. He presumably did not know of the last two chapters of our text, which contain the history of Simon, and probably were translated later. Otherwise we cannot explain his dismissal, in one line, of the league that Simon made with the Romans.[1] The incident is dwelt on in the extant version of the First Book of the Maccabees, and Josephus would surely not have omitted a syllable of so propitious an event, had he possessed knowledge of it. On the other hand, he inserts into the history of the Maccabean brothers an account of the foundation of a Temple by Onias V in Leontopolis,[2] in the Delta of Egypt, and describes at length the negotiations that led up to it;[3] and in the same connection he narrates a feud between the Jewish and Samaritan communities at Alexandria in the days of Ptolemy Philometor. From these indications it has been inferred that he had before him the work of a Helle-nistic-Jewish historian interested in Egypt--the collection of Alexander Polyhistor suggests that there were several such at the time--while for the exploits of the later Maccabees he relied on the chronicle of John Hyrcanus the son of Simon, which is referred to in the Book of the Maccabees,[4] but has not come down to us,

[1: Ant. XIII. vii. 3.]

[2: Ant. XII. ix. 7. The ruins of the Temple were unearthed a few years ago by Professor Flinders Petrie.]

[3: Ant. XIII. iii.]

[4: I Macc, xvi, 23.]

From this period onwards till the end of the ***Antiquities***, Josephus had no longer any considerable Jewish document to guide him, nor have we any Jewish history by which to check him. For an era of two hundred years he was more completely dependent on Greek sources, and it is just in this part of the work where he is most valuable or, we should rather say, indispensable. Save for a few scattered references in pagan historians, orators, and poets, he is our only authority for Jewish history at the time. It is, therefore, the more unfortunate that he makes no independent research, and takes up no independent attitude. For the most part he transcribes the pagan writer before him, unable or unwilling to look any deeper. And he tells us only of the outward events of Jewish history, of the court intrigues and murders, of the wars against the tottering empires of Egypt and Syria, of the ignoble feuds within the palace. Of the more vital and, did we but know it, the profoundly interesting social and religious history of the time, of the development of the Pharisee and Sadducee sects, we hear little, and that little is unreliable and superficial. Josephus reproduces the deficiencies of his sources in their dealings with Jewish events. He brings no original virtue compensating for the careful study which they made of the larger history in which the affairs of Judea were a small incident.

The foundation of his work in the latter half of book xiii and throughout books xiv-xvii is Nicholas, who had devoted two special books to the life of Herod, and by way of introduction to this had dealt more fully with the preceding Jewish princes. [1] We must therefore be wary of imputing to Josephus the opinions he expresses upon the different Jewish sects in this part of the ***Antiquities***. He introduces them first during the reign of Jonathan, with the classification which had already been made in the ***Wars***:[2] the Pharisees as the upholders of Providence or fate and freewill, the Essenes as absolute determinists, the Sadducees as absolute deniers of the influence of fate on human affairs.[3] The next mention of the Pharisees occurs in the reign of Hyrcanus,[4] when he states that they were the king's worst enemies.

"They are one of the sects of the Jews, and they have so great a power over the multitude that, when they say anything against the king or against the high priest, they are presently believed.... Hyrcanus had been a disciple of their teaching; but he was angered when one of them, Eleazar, a man of ill temper and prone to seditious practices, reproached him for holding the priesthood, because, it was alleged, his mother had been a captive in the reign of Antiochus Epiphanes, and he, therefore, was disqualified."

[1: Buechler, Sources of Josephus for the History of Syria, J.Q.R. ix. 311.]

[2: B.J. II. viii.]

[3: Ant. XIII. v. 9.]

[4: Ant. XIII. x. 5.]

This account is taken from a source unfriendly to the Pharisees. Though the story is based apparently on an old Jewish tradition, since we find it told of Alexander Jannaeus in the Talmud,[1] it looks as if Josephus obtained his version from some author that shared the aristocratic prejudices against the democratic leaders. The reign of Hyrcanus had been described by a Hellenistic-Jewish chronicler or a non-Jewish Hellenist, from whom Josephus borrowed a glowing eulogy,[2] with which he sums it up: "He lived happily, administered the government in an excellent way for thirty-one years, and was esteemed by God worthy of the three greatest privileges, the principate, the high priesthood, and prophecy." To the account of the Pharisees is appended a paragraph, seemingly the historian's own work, where he explains that "the Pharisees have delivered to the people the tradition of the fathers, while the Sadducees have rejected it and claim that only the written word is binding. And concerning these things great disputes have arisen among them; the Sadducees are able to persuade none but the rich, while the Pharisees have the multitude on their side." Again, in the account of the reign of Queen Alexandra, he represents the Pharisees as powerful but seditious, and causing constant friction, and ascribes the fall of the royal house to the queen's compliance with those who bore ill-will to the family.

[1: Comp. I. Levi, Talmudic Sources of Jewish History, R.E.J. xxxv. 219; I. Friedlaender, J.Q.R., n.s. iv. 443*ff.*]

[2: Ant. XIII. x. 7.]

Whenever the opportunity offers, Josephus brings in references to Jewish history from pagan sources. He quotes Timagenes' estimate of Aristobulus as a good man who was of great service to the Jews and gained them the country of Iturea; and he notes Strabo's agreement with Nicholas upon the invasion of Judea by Ptolemy Lathyrus.[1] General history takes an increasingly larger part in the account of the warlike Alexander Jannaeus and the queen Alexandra, and reference is made to the consuls of Rome contemporary with the reigns of Aristobulus and Hyrcanus, in order to bring Jewish affairs into relation with those of the Power which henceforth played a critical part in them.

[1: Ant. XIII. xii. 6.]

Josephus marks the new era on which he was entering by a fresh preface to book xiv. His aim, he says, is "to omit no facts either through ignorance or laziness, because we are dealing with a history of events with which most people are unacquainted on account of their distance from our times; and we purpose to do it with appropriate beauty of style, so that our readers may entertain the knowledge of what we write with some agreeable satisfaction and pleasure. But the principal thing to aim at is to speak truly."[1] It is not impossible that the prelude is based on something in Nicholas; but it is turned against him; for in the same chapter Josephus controverts his predecessor for the statement that "the Idumean Antipater [the father of Herod] was sprung from the principal Jews who returned to Judea from Babylon." The assertion, he says, was made to gratify Herod, who by the revolution of fortune came to be king of the Jews. He shows here some national feeling, but in general he accepts Nicholas, and borrows doubtless from him the details of Pompey's invasion of Judea and of the siege of Jerusalem. He appeals as well to Strabo and the Latin historian Titus Livius.[2] But though it is likely that he had made an independent study of parts of Strabo, since he drags in several extracts from his history that are not quite in place,[3] there is no reason to think he read Livy or any other Latin author. He would have found reference to the work in the diligent Nicholas. We may discern the hand of Nicholas, too, in the praise of Pompey for his piety in not spoiling the Temple of the holy vessels.[4] Josephus writes altogether in the tone of an admirer of Rome's occupation, attributing the misery which came upon Jerusalem to Hyrcanus and Aristobulus.

[1: Ant. XIV. i. 1.]

[2: Ant. XIV. iv. 3; vi. 4.]

[3: Comp. Ant. XIV. vii. 2; viii. 3.]

[4: Ant. XIV. iv. 5.]

Thanks to his copious sources, he is able to give a detailed account of the relation of the Jews to Julius Caesar and of the decrees which were made in their favor at his instance. It has been conjectured with much probability that Josephus obtained his series of documents from Nicholas, who had collected them for the purpose of defending the Jews of Asia Minor in the inquiry which Marcus Agrippa conducted during the reign of Herod.[1] He says that he will set down the decrees that are treasured in the public places of the cities, and those which are still extant in the Capitol of Rome, "so that all the rest of mankind may know what regard the kings of Asia and Europe have had for the Jewish people." In a subsequent book, when he is recounting the events of Herod's reign,[2] Josephus sets forth a further series of decrees in favor of the Jews, issued by Caesar Augustus and his lieutenant Marcus Agrippa. These likewise he probably derived from Nicholas, who was the court advocate and court chronicler at the time they were promulgated. But he enlarges on his motive for giving them at length, pointing to them with pride as a proof of the high respect in which the Jews were held by the heads of the Roman Empire before the disaster of the war. Though in his own day they were fallen to a low estate, at one time they had enjoyed special favor:

"And I frequently mention these decrees in order to reconcile other peoples to us and to take away the causes of that hatred which unreasonable men bear us. As for our customs, he continues, each nation has its own, and in almost every city we meet with differences; but natural justice is most agreeable to the advantage of all men equally, and to this our laws have the greatest regard, and thereby render us benevolent and friendly to all men, so that we may expect the like return from others, and we may remind them that they should not esteem difference of institutions a sufficient cause of alienation, but join with us in the pursuit of virtue and righteousness, for this belongs to all men in common."[3]

[1: Comp. Bloch, Die Quellen des Flavius Josephus.]

[2: Ant. XVI. ii.]

[3: Comp. below,]

The Jewish rising and defeat had increased the odium of the Greco-Roman world towards the peculiar people, and the captive in the gilded prison was fain to dwell on their past glory in order to cover the wretchedness of their present.

Josephus claims to have copied some of the decrees from the archives in the Roman Capitol.[1] The library was destroyed with the Capitol itself during the civil war in 69.[2] It was restored, it is true, during the reign of Vespasian, and it is not impossible that the old decrees were saved. But Josephus might have collected from the Jewish communities those documents which he did not find ready to hand in Nicholas, if they formed part of an apology for the Jews of Antioch in 70 C.E. At least there is no good reason to doubt their authenticity, and they are in quite a different class from the letters and decrees attributed to the Hellenistic sovereigns, which lack all authority.

[1: Ant. XIV. x. 20.]

[2: Comp. Tac. Hist. iii. 71.]

The story of Herod's life, which is set out in great detail in these books, has more dramatic unity than any other part of the *Antiquities*. It bears to the whole work the relation which the story of the siege of Jerusalem bears to the rest of the *Wars*. Josephus seems to manifest suddenly a power of vivid narrative and psychological analysis, to which he is elsewhere a stranger. But at the same time, where the story is most vivid and dramatic, its framework is most pagan. The Greco-Roman ideas of fate and nemesis, which dominate the shorter account of the king's life in the *Wars*, are still the underlying motives. The reason for the dramatic power and the pagan frame are one and the same: Josephus uses here a full source, and that source is a pagan writer.

It is apparent at the same time that Josephus had a better acquaintance with the historical literature about Herod than when he wrote the *Wars*, and that he compared his various authorities and exercised some judgment in composing his picture. For example, in relating the murder of the Hasmonean Hyrcanus, he first gives the account which he found in Herod's memoirs, designed of course to exculpate the king, and then sets out the version of other historians, who allege that Herod laid a snare for the last of the Maccabean princes. Josephus proudly contrasts his own critical attitude towards Herod with the studied partisanship of Nicholas,[1] who wrote in Herod's lifetime, and in order to please him and his courtiers,

"touching on nothing but what tended to his glory, and openly excusing many of his notorious crimes and diligently concealing them. We may, indeed, say much by way of excuse for Nicholas, because he was not so much writing a history for others as doing a service for the king. But we, who come of a family closely connected with the Hasmonean kings, and have an honorable rank, think it unbecoming to say anything that is false about them, and have described their actions in an upright and unvarnished manner. And though we reverence many of Herod's descendants, who still bear rule, yet we pay greater regard to truth, though we may incur their displeasure by so doing."

[1: Ant. XIV. xvi. 7.]

It was not so difficult for the historian to write impartially of Herod as to write impartially of Vespasian and Titus. At the same time Josephus, though in these books more critical, seldom escapes the yoke of facts, and says little of the inner conditions of the people. Of Hillel we do not hear the name, and Shammai is only mentioned, if indeed he, and not Shemaya, is disguised under the name of Sameas, as the member of the Sanhedrin who denounced Herod.[1]

[1: Ant. XV. i. 1. Schlatter ingeniously conjectures that Pollio, who is men-

tioned as predicting to the Sanhedrin, that this Herod would be their enemy if they acquitted him, is identical with Abtalion, of whom the Talmud
tells a similar story. [Greek: pollion] may be an error for [Greek: Eudalion]
as the Hebrew name would be transcribed in Greek.]

The speeches, which are put into the mouth of the king on various occasions,
are rhetorical declamations in the Greek style, which must be derived either from
Nicholas or from Herod's Memoirs, to which the historian had access through his
intimacy with the royal family. Yet, prosaic as the treatment is, it has provided
the picture of the "magnificent barbarian" which has inspired many writers and
artists of later ages. It is from the Jewish point of view that it is most wanting. He
does indeed say that Herod transgressed the laws of his country, and violated the
ancient tradition by the introduction of foreign practices, which fostered great sins,
through the neglect of the observances that used to lead the multitude to piety. By
the games, the theater, and the amphitheater, which he instituted at Jerusalem,
he offended Jewish sentiment; "for while foreigners were amazed and delighted at
the vastness of his displays, to the native Jews all this amounted to a dissolution of
the traditions for which they had so great a veneration."[1] And he points out that
the Jewish conspiracy against him in the middle of his reign arose because "in the
eyes of the Jewish leaders, he merely pretended to be their king, but was in fact
the manifest enemy of their nation." It has been suggested that Justus of Tiberias
supplied him with this Jewish view of Herod, which is unparalleled in the **Wars**.
But in another passage, where he must be following an Herodian and anti-Pharisaic
source, he makes some remarks in quite an opposite spirit, as if the Pharisees were
in the wrong, and provoked the king. He says of them: "They were prone to offend
princes;[2] they claimed to foresee things, and were suddenly elated to break out
into open war." He calls them also Sophists,[3] the scornful name which the Greeks
gave to their popular lecturers of morality.

[1: Ant. XV. viii. 1.]

[2: Ant. XVII. ii. 8.]

[3: Ant. XVII. vi. 2.]

In dealing with Herod's character, Josephus is more discriminating than in the **Wars**. He sums him up as "cruel towards all men equally, a slave to his passions, and claiming to be above the righteous law: yet was he favored by fortune more than any man, for from a private station he was raised to be a king."[1] One piece of characterization may he quoted,[2] which is not the less interesting because we may suspect that it is stolen:

"But this magnificent temper and that submissive behavior and liberality which he exercised towards Caesar and the most powerful men at Rome, obliged him to transgress the customs of his nation and to set aside many of their laws, by building cities after an extravagant manner, and erecting Temples, not in Judea indeed, for that would not have been borne, since it is forbidden to pay any honors to images or representations of animals after the manner of the Greeks, but in the country beyond our boundaries and in the cities thereof. The apology which he made to the Jews was this, that all was done not of his own inclination, but at the bidding of others, in order to please Caesar and the Romans, as though he set more store on the honor of the Romans than the Jewish customs; while in fact he was considering his own glory, and was very ambitious to leave great monuments of his government to posterity: whence he was so zealous in building such splendid cities, and spent vast sums of money in them."

[1: Ant. XVII. viii. 1.]

[2: Ant. XV. ix. 5.]

He bursts out, too, with unusual passion against Herod for his law condemning thieves to exile, because it was a violation of the Biblical law, "and involved the dissolution of our ancestral traditions."

If the account of the Jewish spiritual movement at a time of great spiritual awakening is meager, the picture of Herod's great buildings, despite occasional confusion and vagueness, is full and valuable. He gives us an excellent description of Caesarea and Sebaste, the two cities which the king established as a compliment to the Roman Emperor, and an account of the Temple and the fortress of Antonia, which he himself knew so well. Of the Temple we have another description, in the Mishnah, which in the main agrees with Josephus. Where the two differ, however, the preference cannot be given to the writer who had grown up in the shadow of the building, and might have been expected to know its every corner.[1] As we have seen in the *Wars*, he was in topography as in other things under the influence of Greco-Roman models.

[1: Comp. George A. Smith, Jerusalem, ii. 495 *ff.*]

Josephus did not enjoy the advantage of a full chronicle to guide him much beyond the death of Herod. Nicholas died, or ceased to write, in the reign of Antipater, who succeeded his father. Apparently he had no successor who devoted himself to recording the affairs of the Jewish court. Hence, though the events of the troubled beginning of Antipater's reign are dealt with at the same length as those of Herod, and we have a vivid story of the Jewish embassy that went to Rome to petition for the deposition of the king, the history afterwards becomes fragmentary. Such as it is, it manifests a Roman flavor. The nationalists are termed robbers, and the pseudo-Messiahs are branded as self-seeking impostors.[1] After an enumeration of various pretenders that sought to make themselves independent rulers, there is a sudden jump from the first to the tenth year of Archelaus, who was accused of barbarous and tyrannical practices and banished by the Roman Emperor to Gaul. His kingdom was then added to the province of Syria. Josephus dwells on the story of two dreams which occurred to the king and his wife Glaphyra, and justifies himself because his discourse is concerning kings, and also because of the advantage to be drawn from it for the assurance both of the immortality of the soul and the Providence of God in human affairs. "And if anybody does not believe such stories, let him keep his own opinion, but let him not stand in the way of another who finds in them an encouragement to virtue."

[1: Ant. XVII. xiii. 2.]

The last three books of the *Antiquities* reveal the weaknesses of Josephus as an historian: his disregard of accuracy, his tendency to exaggeration, his lack of proportion, and his mental subservience. He had no longer either the Scriptures or a Greek chronicler to guide him. He depended in large part for his material on oral sources and scattered memoirs, and he is not very successful in eking it out so as to produce the semblance of a connected narrative. His chapters are in part a miscellany of notes, and the construction is clumsy. The writer confesses that he was weary of his task, but felt impelled to wind it up. Yet, just because we are so ignorant of the events of Jewish history at the period, and because the period itself is so critical and momentous, these books (xviii-xx) are among the most important which he has left, and on the whole they deal rather more closely than their predecessors with the affairs of the Jewish people. The palace intrigues do not fill the stage so exclusively, and some of the digressions carry us into byways of Jewish history.

At the very outset[1] Josephus devotes a chapter to a fuller delineation than he has given in any other place of the various sects that flourished at the time. The account, ampler though it is than the others, does not reveal the true inwardness of the different religious positions. He repeats here what he says elsewhere about the Pharisaic doctrine of predestination tempered by freewill, but he enlarges especially on the difference between the parties in their ideas about the future life. [2] The Pharisees believe that souls have an immortal vigor, and that they will be rewarded or punished in the next world accordingly as they have lived virtuously or wickedly in this life; the wicked being bound in everlasting prisons, while the good have power to live again. The Sadducees, on the other hand, assert that the souls die with the bodies, and the Essenes teach the immortality of souls and set great store on the rewards of righteousness. Their various ideas are wrapped up in Greco-Roman dress, to suit his readers, and the doctrine of resurrection ascribed to the Pharisees is almost identical with that held by the neo-Pythagoreans of Rome. [3] But Josephus' account is more reliable when he refers to the divergent attitudes of the sects to the tradition.

"The Pharisees strive to observe reason's dictates in their conduct, and at the same time they pay great respect to their ancestors; and they have such influence over the people because of their virtuous lives and their discourses that they are their friends in divine worship, prayers, and sacrifice. The Sadducees do not regard the observance of anything beyond what the law enjoins them, but since their doctrine is held by the few, when they hold the judicial office, they are compelled to addict themselves to the notions of the Pharisees, because the mass would not otherwise tolerate them. The Essenes live apart from the people in communistic groups, and exceed all other men in virtue and righteousness. They send gifts to the Temple, but do not sacrifice, on which account they are excluded from the common court of the Temple."

[1: Ant. XVIII. i. 1.]

[2: Comp. B.J. II. viii.]

[3: Comp. Vergil, Aeneid, vi.]

Lastly, Josephus turns to the fourth sect, the Zealots, whose founder was Judas the Galilean:

"These men agree in all other things with the Pharisees, but they have an inviolable attachment to liberty, and they say that God is to be their only Ruler and Lord. Moreover they do not fear any kind of death, nor do they heed the death of their kinsmen and friends, nor can any fear of the kind make them acknowledge anybody as sovereign."

Josephus, however, cannot refrain from imputing low motives to those who belonged to the party opposed to himself and hated of the Romans. "They planned robberies and murders of our principal men," he says, "in pretense for the public welfare, but in reality in hopes of gain for themselves." And he saddles them with the responsibility for all the calamities that were to come. About the Messianic hope, which appears to have inspired them, he is compulsorily silent.

The historical record that follows is very sketchy. We have a bare list of procurators and high priests down to the time of Pontius Pilate, a notice of the foundation of Tiberias by the tetrarch Herod, and an irrelevant account of the death of Phraates, the king of the Parthians, and of Antiochus of Commagene, who was connected by marriage with the Herodian house. Still there is rather more detail than in the corresponding summary in the second book of the *Wars*, and Josephus must in the interval have lighted on a fuller source than he had possessed in his first historical essay. It is not impossible that the new authority was again Justus of Tiberias. Of the unrest in the governorship of Pontius Pilate he has more to say, but the genuineness of the passage referring to the trial and death of Jesus, which is dealt with elsewhere,[1] has been doubted by modern critics. It is followed in the text by a long account of a scandal connected with the Isis worship at Rome, which led to the expulsion of Jews from the capital. In this way the chronicler wanders on between bare chronology and digression, until he reaches the reign of Agrippa, when he again finds written sources to help him. The romance of Agrippa's rise from a bankrupt courtier to the ruler of a kingdom is treated with something of the same full detail as the events of Herod's career, and probably the historian enjoyed here the use of royal memoirs. He may have obtained material also from the historical works of Philo of Alexandria, which were partly concerned with the same epoch. He refers explicitly to the embassy which the Alexandrian Jews sent to the Roman Emperor to appeal for the rescission of the order to set up in the synagogue the Imperial image, at the head of which went Philo, "a man eminent on all accounts, brother to Alexander the Alabarch, and not unskilled in philosophy." Bloch[2] indeed is of the opinion that the later historian did not use his Alexandrian predecessor, either in this or any other part of his writings, and points out certain differences of fact between the two accounts; but in view of the references to Philo and the fact that Josephus subsequently wrote two books of apology, one of which was expressly directed in answer to Philo's bitter opponent Apion, it is at least probable that he was acquainted with Philo's narrative. He may, however, have used it only to supplement the memoirs of the Herodian house, which served him as a chief source. Josephus devotes less attention to the Alexandrian embassy than to the efforts of the Palestinian Jews to obtain a rescission of the similar decree which Petronius, the governor of Syria, was sent to enforce in Jerusalem. His account is devised to glorify the part which Agrippa played. The prince appears as a kind of male Esther, endangering his own life to save his people; and indeed higher critics have been found to suggest that the Biblical book of Esther was written around the events of the reign of Gaius.

[1: Ant. XVIII. iii. Comp. below, p. 241.]

[2: Die Quellen des Flavius Josephus.]

The story of Agrippa is interrupted by a chapter about the Jews of Babylon, which has the air of a moral tale on the evils of intermarriage, and may have formed part of the popular Jewish literature of the day. Another long digression marks the beginning of the nineteenth book of the ***Antiquities***, where Josephus leaves Jewish scenes and inserts an account of Caligula's murder and the election of Claudius as Emperor. This narrative, while of great interest for students of the Roman constitution, is out of all proportion to its place in the Jewish chronicle. Josephus, it has been surmised, based it on the work of one Cluvius (referred to in the book as an intimate friend of Claudius), who wrote a history about 70 C.E.; he may besides have received hitherto unpublished information from Agrippa II, whose father had been an important actor in the drama, or from his friend Aliturius, the actor at Rome, who had mixed in affairs of state. Anyhow, he took advantage of this chance of making a literary sensation. Doubtless also, the recital, which threw not a little discredit on the house of the earlier Caesars, was for that reason not unwelcome to the upstart Flavians, and may have been inserted at the Imperial wish.

Agrippa I is the most attractive figure in the second part of the ***Antiquities***. He is contrasted with Herod,

"who was cruel and severe in his punishments, and had no mercy on those he hated, and everyone perceived that he had more love for the Greeks than for the Jews.... But Agrippa's temper was mild and equally liberal to all men. He was kind to foreigners and was of agreeable and compassionate feeling. He loved to reside at Jerusalem, and was scrupulously careful in his observance of the Law of his people. On his death he expressed his submission to Providence; for that he had by no means lived ill, but in a splendid and happy manner."

His peaceful reign, however, was only the lull before the storm, and the last book of the ***Antiquities*** is mainly taken up with the succession of wicked procurators, who, by their extortions and cruelties and flagrant disregard of the Jewish Law and Jewish feeling, goaded the Jews into the final rebellion. It contains, however, a digression on the conversion of the royal house of Adiabene to Judaism, which is tricked out with examples of God's Providence. Yet another digression records the villainies of Nero (which no doubt was pleasing to his patrons) and the amours of Drusilia, the daughter of Agrippa I. But of the rising discontent of the Jewish people in Palestine we have no clear picture. Josephus fails as in the ***Wars*** to bring out the inner incompatibility of the Roman and the Jewish outlook, and represents, in an unimaginative, matter-of-fact, Romanizing way, that it was simply particular excesses--the rapacity of a Felix, the knavery of a Florus--which were the cause of the Rebellion. This is just what a Roman would have said, and when the Jewish writer deals at all with the Jewish position, it is usually to drag in his political feud. He especially singles out the sacrilege of the Zealots in assassinating their opponents within the Temple precincts as the reason of God's rejecting the city; "and as for the Temple, He no longer deemed it sufficiently pure to be His habitation, but brought the Romans upon us and threw a fire on the city to purge it, and brought slavery on us, our wives, and our children, to make us wiser by our calamities." Thus the priestly apologist, accepting Roman canons, finds in the ritual offense of a section of the people the ground for the destruction of the national center. He is torn, indeed, between two conflicting views about the origin of the rebellion: whether he shall lay the whole blame on the Jewish irreconcilables, or whether he shall divide it between them and the wicked Roman governors; and in the end he exaggerates both these motives, and leaves out the deeper causes.

The penultimate chapter contains a list of the high priests, about whom the historian had throughout made great pretensions of accuracy. He enumerates but eighty-three from the time of Aaron to the end of the line, of whom no less than twenty-eight were appointed after Herod's accession to his kingdom; whereas the Talmud records that three hundred held office during the existence of the second Temple alone.[1] That number is probably hyperbolical, but the statement in other parts of the Rabbinical literature, that there were eighty high priests in that period,[2] throws doubt on this list, which besides is manifestly patched in several places.

[1: Yoma, 9a.]

[2: Yer. Yoma, ix., and Lev. R. xx.]

With the procuratorship of Florus, Josephus brings his chronicle to an end, the later events having been treated in detail in the *Wars;* and in conclusion he commends himself for his accuracy in giving the succession of priests and kings and political administrators:

"And I make bold to say, now I have so completely perfected the work which I set out to do, that no other person, be he Jew or foreigner, and had he ever so great an inclination to it, could so accurately deliver these accounts to the Greeks as is done in these books. For members of my own people acknowledge that I far exceed them in Jewish learning, and I have taken great pains to obtain the learning of the Greeks and understand stand the elements of the Greek language, though I have so long accustomed myself to speak our own tongue that I cannot speak Greek with exactness."

He makes explicit his standpoint with this *envoi*, which shows that he was writing for a Greek-speaking public and in competition with Greeks, and this helps to explain why he sets special store on the record of priests and kings and political changes, and why he so often disguises the genuine Jewish outlook. As an account of the Jewish people for the prejudiced society of Rome, the *Antiquities* undoubtedly possessed merit. History, indeed, at the time, was far from being an exact science, nor was accuracy esteemed necessary to it. Cicero had said a hundred years earlier, that it was legitimate to lie in narratives; and this was the characteristic outlook of the Greco-Roman writers. The most brilliant literary documents of the age, the *Annals* and *Histories* of Tacitus, are rather pieces of sparkling journalism than sober and philosophical records of facts; and therefore we must not judge Josephus by too high a standard. Weighed in his own balance, he had done a great service to his people by setting out the main heads of their history over three thousand years, so that it should be intelligible to the cultured Roman society; and had he been reproached with misrepresenting and distorting many of their religious ideas, he would have replied, with some justice, that it was necessary to do so in, order to make the Romans understand. On the same ground he would have justified the omission of much that was characteristic and the exaggeration of much that was normal. He shows throughout some measure of national pride. To-day, however, we cannot but regret that he weakly adopted much of the spiritual outlook of his Gentile contemporaries, and that he did not seek to convey to his readers the fundamental spiritual conceptions of the Jews, which might have endowed his history with an unique distinction. His record of two thousand years of Israel's history gives but the shadow of the glory of his people.

VIII
THE APOLOGY FOR JUDAISM

In every age since the dispersion began, the Jews have appeared to their neighbors as a curious anomaly. Their abstract idea of God, their peculiar religious observances, their refusal to intermarry with their neighbors, their serious habits of life--all have served to mark them out and attract the wonder of the philosophical, the vituperation of the vulgar, and the dislike of the ignorant. Their enemies in every epoch have repeated with slight variation the charge which Haman brought in his petition to King Ahasuerus, "There is a people scattered abroad and dispersed among the peoples in all the provinces of thy kingdom; and their laws are diverse from those of every people, neither keep they the king's laws" (Esther 3:8). In the cosmopolitan society that arose in the Hellenistic kingdoms, it was their especial offense that they retained a national cohesion, and refused to indulge in the free trade in religious ideas and social habits adopted by civilized peoples. The popular feeling was fanned by a party that had a more particular grievance against them. Though certain philosophical sects, notably the schools of Pythagoras and Aristotle, were struck with admiration for the lofty spiritual ideas and the strict discipline of Judaism, another school, and that the most powerful of the time, was smitten with envy and hatred.

The Stoics, who aspired to establish a religious philosophy for all mankind, and pursued a vigorous missionary propaganda, particularly in the East, saw in the Jews not only obstinate opponents but dangerous rivals, who carried on a competing mission with provoking success. The children of Israel were spread over the whole of the civilized world, and everywhere they vigorously propagated their teaching. Of all enmities, the enmity of contending creeds is the bitterest. The Stoics became the first professional Jew-haters, and set themselves at the head of those who resented

Jewish particularism, either from jealousy or from that unreasoning dislike which is universally felt against minorities that live differently from the mass about them.

The ill-will and sectarian hatred were most prevalent at Alexandria, where the powerful Jewish community excited the attacks of the half-Hellenized natives. The campaign was fought mainly as a battle of books. The Hebrew Scriptures represented the early Egyptians in no favorable light. The Greco-Egyptian historians retaliated by a malevolent account of the origin and history of the Hebrew people, of which Manetho's story is the prototype. In this work of the third century B.C.E. the children of Israel were represented as sprung from a pack of lepers, who were expelled from Egypt because of their foul disease. A still more virulent attack on the Jewish teaching is found in two Stoic writers of the first century B.C.E., Posidonius of Apamea, a town of Phrygia, and Molon,[1] who taught at Rhodes. The former raised the charge that the Jews alone of all peoples refused to have any communication with other nations, but regarded them as their enemies. Molon, besides a general travesty of their early history, wrote a special diatribe against them--the first document of the kind which history records--accusing them of atheism and misanthropy, cowardice and stupidity. These remained the stock charges for centuries, and they assumed an added bitterness after the Roman conquest, when to the peculiarity of Jewish customs was added the stigma of being a subject people. The hatred of Greek and Jew, despite all the ostentatious friendliness of a Herod for Greek things, became deeper, and it showed itself as well without as within Palestine. At Alexandria, in the beginning of the first century, the antagonism developed into open riots, and the leaders of the anti-Jewish party were again two Stoics, Apion and Chaeremon, the one orator and grammarian, the other priest and astrologer. There is nothing very original in their libels, which are modeled upon those of Posidonius and Molon; but some fresh detail is added. It was said that the deity worshiped at Jerusalem was the head of an ass, to which human sacrifices were offered, and that the Jews took an oath to do no service for any Gentile. Apion, a man of some repute, was the head of the Alexandrian Stoic school, and called "the toiler," because of his industry. He was, however, also known as "the quarrelsome"[2] ([Greek: ho pleistonikeas]). Another critic of ancient times says he was notorious for advertising his ideas (***in doctrinis suis praedicandis venditator***)[3], and the Emperor Augustus declares that he was the drum of his own fame (i.e. the blower of his own trumpet).

He was in fact a mixture of scholar and charlatan, as many of his successors have been, the Houston Chamberlain of the first century.

[1: Schuerer (iii. 503*ff*) has brought cogent reasons to show that Molon is not the same as Apollonius, another Jew-baiter, with whom he has often been identified.]

[2: Clemens, Strom. i. 21, 101.]

[3: Gallus, Noctes Atticae, v. 2.]

Apion wrote a history of Egypt in which his attack upon the Jews appears to have been an episode,[1] but his prominence as an anti-Semite is shown by the fact that he went as the spokesman of the Greek embassy to Caligula on the memorable occasion when Philo was the champion of the Jewish cause. In that capacity Philo prepared an elaborate apology for his people, which he had not the opportunity to deliver; but it contained in part an account of the religious sects, designed to show their philosophical excellence, and it was known to the Church fathers of the early centuries of the Christian era. Only small fragments of it are preserved by Eusebius, and the rest of the apologetic writing of Alexandria, which was in all probability very extensive, has disappeared. Yet the Hellenistic-Jewish literature is colored throughout by an apologetic purpose. Whether the work is a professedly historical or ethical or philosophical treatise, the idea is always present of representing Judaism as a sublime and a humanitarian doctrine, and of refuting the calumnies of the Greek scribes. Thus, besides his elaborate apology prepared for the Roman Emperor, Philo had written a popular presentation of Judaism in the form of a Life of Moses, with appended treatises on Humanity and Nobility, which was but a thinly-veiled work of apologetics. Another part of the defensive literature took the form of missionary propaganda under a heathen mask. The oracles of the Sibyl and Orpheus, a forged history of Hecataeus, and monotheistic verses foisted on the Greek poets, were but attempts to carry the war into the enemy's territory. Further, there must have been a more direct presentation of the Jewish cause by way of public lectures and popular addresses in the synagogues. Nevertheless, the specific answers to the charges advanced by the anti-Jewish scribblers are now to be found most fully stated in Josephus. In his day the literary campaign against the Jewish name was as remorseless as the military campaign that had destroyed their political independence. The Romans, tolerant themselves in religion, had long been intolerant of Jewish separatism and national exclusiveness, and Cicero,[2] shortly after the capture of Jerusalem by Pompey, had denounced their "barbarian superstition" in language that is typical of the outlook of the Roman aristocracy. "Even when Jerusalem was untouched, and the Jews were at peace with us, their religious ceremonies ill accorded with the splendor of our Empire; still less tolerable are they to-day, when the nation has shown, by taking up arms, its attitude towards us, while the fact that it has been conquered and reduced to servitude proves how much the gods care for it."

[1: The idea, which is derived from the Church fathers, that he wrote a separate [Greek: logos] against the Jews, appears to be based by them on a misunderstanding of Ant. XVIII. viii. 1. Comp. Schuerer, *op. cit.* iii. 541.]

[2: Pro Flacco, 68.]

The later poets of the Augustan age, Horace, Tibullus, and Ovid, expressed a supercilious disdain for the Jewish customs of Sabbath-keeping, etc., which were spreading even in the politest circles. As the political conflict between the Romans and their stubborn subjects became more pronounced, the Roman impatience of their obstinacy increased. Seneca, writing after Palestine had been placed under a Roman governor, speaks bitterly of "the accursed race whose practices have so far prevailed that they have been received all over the world." Hating the Jews as he did with the double hatred of a Roman aristocrat and a Stoic philosopher, he is yet fain to admit that their religion is diffused over the Empire, and anxious as he is to decry their superstition, he reveals part of the reason of their success. "They at least can give an explanation of their religious ceremonies, whereas the pagan masses cannot say why they carry out their practices." The pagan cults were languishing because of the frigidity of their forms and their incapacity for providing men with an ideal or a discipline or a solace; and the people turned to a living religion. The day had come that was foretold by the prophet, when men shall catch hold of the skirts of a Jew, saying, "We will go with you, because we have heard that God is with you" (Zech. 8:23).

The bitterest and the most envenomed attacks on the Jews were written after the destruction of Jerusalem, when the failure of Rome to break the stubborn spirit of her conquered foe became apparent. The legions could destroy Jerusalem; they could not uproot Judaism or even stay its progress. The presence of thousands of Jewish captive slaves at Rome accelerated indeed the march of conversion. Vespasian and Titus forebore to take the title "Judaicus" after their triumph, lest it should be taken to mean that they had Judaized. The speedy defection of Roman citizens to the superstition of a conquered people was an insult, which, added to the injury of their obstinate resistance, roused to fury the remnants of the Roman conservatives. The entanglement of Titus with the Jewish princess Berenice was the final outrage. The satiric poets Martial and Juvenal inserted frequent ribald references to Jewish customs; but the nature of their works precluded a serious criticism. Martial was a master of flouts, jeers, and gibes, and Juvenal was a soured and disappointed provincial, who delighted to hurl wild reproaches. He declaimed against the passing away of the old manners of Republican Rome, and for him the spread of Jewish habits was among the surest signs of degeneracy. The poets, however, did not so much endeavor to misrepresent as to ridicule the Jews and their converts. But the classical exponent of Roman anti-Semitism is Tacitus, the historian who wrote in the time of Nerva and Trajan, i.e. just after Josephus, and who treated of the Jews both in his ***Annals***, which were a history of the last century, and in his ***Histories***, which dealt with his own times. He surpassed all his predecessors, Greek or Roman, in distortion and abuse, and he combined the charges invented by the jealousy and rancor of Greek sophists with the abuse of Jewish character induced by Imperial Roman passion. His account cannot be mistaken for a sober judgment. By the transparent combination of earlier, discredited sources, by blatant inconsistencies, and by neglect of the authorities that would have provided him with reliable information, he shows himself the partisan pamphleteer. But the indictment is none the less illuminating. Mommsen speaks of the solemn enmity which Tacitus cherishes to the section of the human race "to whom everything pure is impure, and everything impure is pure." Doubtless his hatred was founded on intense national pride, but it was fed by his tendency to blacken and exaggerate. His audience was composed, as Renan says, of "aristocrats of the race of English Tories, who derived their strength from their very prejudices." Their ideas about the Jewish people were as vague as those of the ordinary man of to-day about the people of Thibet, and they were willing to believe anything of them.

Tacitus gives several alternative accounts of the origin of the Jews.[1] According to some they were fugitives from the Isle of Crete (deriving their name from Mount Ida), who settled on the coast of Libya. According to others they sprang from Egypt, and were driven out under their captains Hierosolymus and Judas; while others stated that they were Ethiopians whom fear and hatred obliged to change their habitation. He supplies himself a fanciful account of the Exodus, tricked out with a variety of misrepresentations of their observances, which are ludicrously inconsistent with each other:

"They bless the image of that animal [the ass], by whose indication they had escaped from their vagrant condition in the wilderness and quenched their thirst. They abstain from swine's flesh as a memorial of the miserable destruction which the mange brought on them. That they stole the fruits of the earth, we have a proof in their unleavened bread. They rest on the seventh day, because that day gave them rest from their labors, and, affecting a lazy life, they are idle during every seventh year. These rites, whatever their origin, are at least supported by their antiquity.[2] Their other institutions are depraved and impure, and prevailed by reason of their viciousness; for every vile fellow despising the rites of his ancestors brought to them his contribution, so that the Jewish commonwealth was augmented. The first lesson taught to converts is to despise their gods, to renounce their country, and to hold their parents, children, and brethren in utmost contempt: but still they are at pains to increase and multiply, and esteem it unlawful to kill any of their children. They regard as immortal the souls of those who die in battle, or are put to death for their crimes.[3] Hence their love of posterity and their contempt of death. They have no notion of more than one Divine Being, who is only grasped by the mind. They deem it profane to fashion images of gods out of perishable matter, and teach that their Being is supreme and eternal, immutable and imperishable. Accordingly, they erect no images in their cities, much less in their temples, and they refuse to grant this kind of honor to kings or emperors."

[1: Hist. v. 2*ff.*]

[2: Ch. lvii.]

[3: This statement agrees remarkably with what Josephus puts into the mouth of several of his speakers. See above, p. 114.]

The sage Pliny, who himself laughed at the crude paganism of his time, could also point the finger of scorn at the Jews as "a people notorious by their contempt of divine images." To the genuine Roman, the state religion might not be true, but it was part of the civic life, and therefore its rejection was unsocial and disloyal. Yet the account of Tacitus contains several remarks which, in their author's despite, reveal the moral superiority of the conquered over the conquerors. He notes their national tenacity, their ready charity, their freedom from infanticide, their conviction of the immortality of the soul, their purely spiritual and monotheistic cult. Tacitus certainly wrote after the works of Josephus had been published, so that the apology is not an answer to him; but his methods of misstatement were anticipated at Rome by a host of anti-Semitic writers. Though Josephus never mentions a single Roman detractor of his people, and confines his reply to Greeks who were long buried, it was doubtless against this class that he was anxious to defend himself and his faith.

He declared at the end of the *Antiquities* his intention to write three books about "God and His essence, and about our laws," proposing, perhaps, to imitate Philo's apology for Judaism, which was in three parts. But the virulence of the calumny against Judaism induced him to modify his plan and write a specific reply to the charges made against the Jews. It was necessary to refute more concisely and more definitely than he had done in his long historical works the false tales about the Jewish past and the Jewish law that were circulated and believed in the hostile Greco-Roman world. He directed himself more particularly to uphold the antiquity of the Jews against those who denied their historical claims and to disprove the charges leveled against the Jewish religious ideas and legislation. These two subjects form the content of the two books commonly known to us as *Against Apion*. Only the second, however, deals with Apion's diatribe, and the current title is certainly unauthentic. Origen,[1] Eusebius, and Hieronymus[2] refer to the first book as ***About the Antiquity of the Jews***, and Hieronymus adds the description [Greek: antirraetikos logos], ***A Refutation***. Eusebius similarly[3] speaks of the second book as the Refutation of Apion the grammarian. Porphyry calls it simply [Greek: pros tous Hellaenas], ***The Address to the Greeks***, and it is possible that Josephus so entitled his work. It is noteworthy that he directed his pleading to the Greek-speaking and not to the Latin public; the Greeks, he recognized, were the source of the misrepresentations of his people, and, as Greek was read by all cultured people in his day, in refuting them he would incur less obloquy and attain his end equally well.

[1: Orig. C. Cels. i. 14.]

[2: De Viris Illustr. 13.]

[3: H.E. III. viii. 2.]

The first point that Josephus seeks to make good in his apology is the antiquity of the Hebrew people and the historical character of their Scriptures. In the Greco-Roman world, which had lost confidence in itself, and looked for inspiration to the past, age was a title to respectability, and it was the aim of the Jewish apologist to explain away the silence of the Greeks. For the certificate of the Hellenic historians was in the Hellenistic world the most convincing mark of genuineness.

"By my works on the Antiquity of the Jews--thus Josephus begins--I have proved that our Jewish nation is of very great antiquity and had a distinct existence. Those Antiquities contain the history of five thousand years, and are derived from our sacred books, but are translated by me into the Greek tongue."

Josephus loosely represents that the whole of the ***Antiquities*** is based on the Bible, and reckons the period of history at nearly a thousand years more than it covered.

"But since I observe that many people give ear to the reproaches that are laid against us by those who bear us ill-will, and will not believe what I have written concerning the antiquity of our nation, while they take it for a plain sign that our nation is of late date because it is not so much as vouchsafed a bare mention by the most famous historians among the Greeks, I therefore have thought myself under an obligation to write somewhat briefly about these subjects, in order to convict those who reproach us of spite and deliberate falsehood and to correct the ignorance of others, and withal to instruct all those who are desirous of knowing the truth of what great antiquity we really are. As for the witnesses whom I shall produce for the proof of what I say, they shall be such as are esteemed by the Greeks themselves to be of the greatest reputation for truth and the most skilful in the knowledge of all antiquity. I will also show that those who have written so reproachfully and falsely about us are to be convicted by what they have themselves written to the contrary, and I shall endeavor to give an account of the reasons why it has happened that a great number of Greeks have not made mention of our nation in their histories."

Acting on the principle that the best defense is attack, Josephus starts by turning on the Greeks themselves and discrediting their antiquity. They were a mushroom people, or at least their records were modern, and not to be compared in age with the records of the Phoenicians, the Hebrews, or the Babylonians. Comparative sciences had flourished in the cosmopolitan city of Alexandria, and in the light of them the Greek claim to exclusive wisdom had been shattered. Josephus had made himself master of the current knowledge of the subject. The Greeks learnt their letters from the Phoenicians, they have no record more ancient than the Homeric poems, and even Homer did not leave his poems in writing,[1] while their earliest historians lived but shortly before the Persian expedition into Greece, and their earliest philosophers, Pythagoras and Thales, learnt what they knew from Egyptians and Chaldeans. Having shown the lateness and Oriental origin of Greek culture, Josephus accuses Greek writers of unreliability, as is manifest by their mutual disagreement. He makes a great show of learning on the subject and uses his material effectively. Doubtless he found the topic ready to hand in some predecessor, and it is somewhat ironical that a Josephus should throw stones at a Thucydides on the score of inaccuracy.

> [1: It is interesting that this casual statement of Josephus was one of the starting points of modern Homeric criticism.]

The reason for the want of authority in the Greek historians--continues Josephus--is to be found in the fact that the Greeks in early times took no care to preserve public records of their transactions, which afforded those who afterwards would write about them scope for making mistakes and displaying invention: conditions which favored literary art, but marred historical accuracy. Those who were the most zealous to write history were more anxious to demonstrate that they could write well than to discover the truth.

The contrast between the individual creative impulse of the Hellene and the respect for tradition of the Hebrew, which anticipates in a way Matthew Arnold's contrast between Hellenic "spontaneity of consciousness" and Hebraic "strictness of conscience," is pointedly made by the apologist:[1]

"We Jews must yield to the Greek writers as to style and eloquence of composition, but we concede them no such superiority in regard to the verity of ancient history, and least of all as to that part which concerns the affairs of our country. The reliability of the Hebrew records is vouched for by the unbroken succession of official annals handed down by priests and prophets. The purity of the priestly caste was strictly maintained by the law of marriage, which impelled every priest to make a scrutiny into the genealogy of his wife and forward a register of it to Jerusalem, where it was duly recorded in the archives. And we possess the names of our high priests from father to son for a period of two thousand years. Nor is there individual liberty of writing among us: only the prophets (i.e. inspired persons) have written the earliest accounts of things as they learned them of God Himself by inspiration, and others have written about what happened in their own times, and that too in a very distinct manner. We have no mass of books disagreeing with each other, but only twenty-two books containing the records of all our past, which are rightly believed to be inspired."

[1: C. Ap. 6*ff.*]

The reckoning of the Canon is interesting:[1] there are five books of Moses, thirteen books of the prophets, recording the history from the death of Moses to the reign of Artaxerxes, and the remaining four books, the Ketubim, contain hymns to God and precepts for the conduct of human life. The books written since the time of Artaxerxes have not the same trustworthiness, because the exact succession of prophets has not been maintained. The intense sentiment which the Jews feel for their Scriptures is proved by their willingness to die for them.

[1: The accepted number of books in the Jewish Canon is twenty-four, and
this number is found in the Book of II Esdras, xiv. 41, which is probably
contemporaneous with Josephus. The number 22 is to be explained by the
fact that Josephus must have linked Ruth with Judges and Lamentations
with Jeremiah. See J.E., s.v. Canon.]

Again a contrast is pointed between the seriousness of the Hebraic and the levity of the Greek attitude towards literature. Josephus egotistically draws an example
from the record of the recent war. The Greeklings who wrote about it

"put a few things together by hearsay, and, abusing the word, call their writings by the name of histories. But I have composed a true history of the whole war
and of all the events that occurred, having been concerned in all its transactions;
for I acted as general of those among us that are named Galileans, as long as it was
possible for us to make any resistance. I was then seized by the Romans, and became
a captive. Vespasian and Titus kept me under guard, and forced me to attend on
them continually. At the first I was put into bonds, but later was set at liberty and
sent to accompany Titus when he came from Alexandria to the siege of Jerusalem,
during which time nothing was done that escaped my knowledge. For what happened in the Roman camp I saw, and wrote down carefully; and what information
the deserters brought out of the city, I was the only man to understand. Afterwards,
when I had gotten leisure at Rome, and when all my material was prepared for the
work, I obtained some persons to assist me in learning the Greek tongue, and by
these means I composed the history of the events, and I was so well assured of the
truth of what I related, that I first of all appealed to those that had the supreme
command in that war, Vespasian and Titus, as witnesses for me. For to them first
of all I presented my books, and after them to many of the Romans that had been
engaged in the war. I also recited them to many of my own race that understood
Greek philosophy, among whom were Julius Archelaus, Herod, king of Chalcis, a
person of great authority, and King Agrippa himself, a person that deserved the
greatest respect. Now all these bore their testimony to me that I had the strictest
regard to truth; who yet would not have dissembled the matter, nor been silent, if
I, out of ignorance, or out of favor to any side, either had given a false color to the
events, or omitted any of them."

Josephus here indignantly replies to his Roman detractors, who accused him of having composed a mere partisan thesis. As a priest he had a special knowledge of the Scriptures, which were the basis of his ***Antiquities***, and as an important actor in the drama of the Roman war, he wrote of its events with the knowledge of an eye-witness. He excuses his digression as being made in self-defense, and claims to have proved that historical writing is indigenous rather to those called Barbarians than to the Greeks. He then returns to the task of refuting those who say that the Jewish polity is of late origin because the Greek authors are silent about it. One main cause of the silence was the isolation of Judea and the character of the Jewish people, who did not delight in merchandise and commerce, but devoted themselves to the cultivation of the soil. This, of course, is a picture of the Bible times, because in the writer's days they were beginning their mercantile development. Hence the Jews were in quite a different condition from the Phoenicians, the Thracians, the Persians, and the Medes, with all of whom the Hellenes came into contact. They are rather to be compared with the Romans, who only entered into the Greek sphere of interest later in their history.

Josephus makes the point that it would be as reasonable for the Jews to deny the antiquity of the Greeks because there is no mention of them in Hebrew records, as for the Greeks to deny the antiquity of the Jews for the converse reason. And if the Greeks are ignorant of the Hebrews, he argues that there is abundant testimony in the histories of other peoples. He starts with the Egyptian evidence, and quotes from Manetho, the anti-Jewish historian, giving extracts about the Hyksos tribes and Hyksos kings, whom he identifies with Joseph and his brethren. The identification was popular till recent times, but modern historical criticism has rejected it. Josephus dates the invasion of the Hyksos at three hundred and ninety-three years before Danaus came to Argos, which in turn was five hundred and twenty years before the Trojan war. Thus he puts the Bible story far ahead in age of Greek myth. Passing on to the testimony in the Phoenician records, he derives from the public archives of Tyre, to which reference was made also in the ***Antiquities***,[1] evidence of the relations between Solomon and Hiram, and further quotes the account given by the Hellenistic historian Alexander of Ephesus, who mentions the same incident. This Alexander had written a world-history, and had collected the chronicles of the various peoples that formed part of Alexander's empire. Josephus, who probably knew of his work through Nicholas or some other chronicler, cites him to confirm the Bible. Collections of extracts about the Jewish people and references to the Bible in Greek literature were already in vogue, for it was an age similar to our own in its love of encyclopedias. Josephus uses with not a little skill these foreign sources, and supplements the comparative material which he had introduced in the ***Antiquities***. Confirmation of the account of the flood, as also of the rebuilding of the Temple after the return of the Jews from Babylon, is found in the Chaldean history of Berosus; and other long extracts from Babylonian history are inserted that furnish a casual mention of Judea or Jerusalem. Josephus attempts, too, with doubtful success, to combine the Phoenician and Babylonian records in order to prove that they agree about the date of the rebuilding of the Temple. The only justifiable inference from the passages, however, appears to be that both sources agreed on the existence of Cyrus, king of Persia.

[1: Comp. above,]

Finally he adduces passages from various Greek writers, to show that the Jews were not entirely unknown to the Hellenes before Alexander's conquests. Josephus had no doubt predecessors among the Hellenistic Jewish litterateurs in the search for testimony, as well as successors among the Christian apologists; but his collection has alone survived, and has become invaluable to modern scholars, who have ploughed the same field for a different purpose. Authority is brought forward to show that Pythagoras had connection with the Hebrews, and Herodotus, it is argued, referred to the Jews as circumcised Syrians.[1] More apposite is a passage quoted from Clearchus, a pupil of Aristotle, about a discussion which his master had with a Jew of Soli, "who was Greek not only in language but in thought." The genuineness of this excerpt has been questioned, but without good reason. Aristotle's school had a scientific interest in the Jews as in other peoples that had come under Greek sway through Alexander's conquests.

[1: Comp. Ant. VIII. x. 3.]

Josephus then sets out some very eulogistic passages about his people, purporting to be from Hecataeus of Abdera, which are very much to his taste and his purpose. Unfortunately, however, they are too good to be true, and modern criticism has established that, while the genuine Hecataeus, an historian who wrote at the end of the fourth century B.C.E., did insert in his work an account of Jerusalem and the Jews, the glowing testimonials which Josephus adduces are from forged books devised by Jews to their own glory. A passage of a less favorable tone, and of which the genuineness is therefore not open to suspicion, is quoted from Agatharchides, a Seleucid historian. Finally, with an incidental mention of a half-dozen Hellenistic writers that have made distinct reference to the Jewish people, and of three Jewish writers, Demetrius, the elder Philo, and Eupolemus, "who have not greatly missed the truth about our affairs," Josephus closes his evidence as to the antiquity of his nation.[1] Possibly he did not realize that his last three witnesses were of his own race, and it is not improbable that this string of names was to him also a string of names culled from Alexander Polyhistor or a similar authority.

[1: C. Ap. 23.]

The latter part of the first book is devoted to the refutation of the anti-Jewish diatribes of several Greeks, and starts off with a few commonplaces upon the topic, to the effect that every great nation incurs the jealousy and ill-will of others. "The Egyptians," says Josephus, "were the first to cast reproaches upon us, and in order to please them, some others undertook to pervert the truth. The causes of their enmity are their chagrin at the events of the Exodus and the difference of their religious ideas."[1] Josephus deals with Manetho's description of the going-out from Egypt, and undertakes to demonstrate that "he trifles and tells arrant lies." He dissects the charge that the Hebrews were a pack of lepers exiled from the country, and insists upon its absurdity and the lack of consistency in the details. He offers ingenuously as a proof of the falsity of the allegation that Moses was a leper the Mosaic legislation about lepers. "How could it be supposed," he asks, "that Moses should ordain such laws against himself, to his own reproach and damage?" Chaeremon is unworthy of reply, because his account, though equally scurrilous, is inconsistent with that of Manetho. But the story of Lysimachus, a writer of the same genus, is more critically examined and found wanting, because it gives no explanation of the origin of the Hebrews. Lysimachus derived the name Jerusalem from the Greek Hierosylen--to commit sacrilege--the Hebrews, according to his story, owing their settlement to the plunder of temples; and Josephus points out triumphantly that that idea is not expressed by the same word and name among the Jews and Greeks. But, to vary a saying of Doctor Johnson, this section of Josephus must be read for the quotations, for if one reads it for the argument of either assailant or apologist, one would shoot oneself.

[1: C. Ap. 24.]

The second book of the apology, which is a continuation of the first, opens with an elaborate refutation of Apion. Josephus questions whether he should take the trouble to confute the scurrilous stories of the Alexandrian grammarian, "which are all abuse and vulgarity"; but because many are pleased to pick up mendacious fictions, he thinks it better not to leave the charges without an answer. He disposes first of Apion's tales about Moses and the Exodus, which are of the same character as those of Manetho and Chaeremon. Loaded abuse and unmeasured invective color the refutation, but Apion apparently deserved it. We may take, as a fair specimen of his veracity, the statement that the Hebrews reached Palestine six days after they left Egypt and rested on the seventh day, which they called Sabbath, because of some disease from which they suffered, and of which the Egyptian name was Sabbaton. Apion had in particular attacked the Alexandrian Jews, and Josephus takes the opportunity of enlarging on the privileged position of his people, not only in the Egyptian capital, but in the other Hellenistic cities where they had been settled.[1] He elaborates and amplifies what he had stated on this subject in the ***Antiquities***, and adds a short account of the miraculous delivery of the Egyptian Jews during the short-lived persecution of Ptolemy Physcon, which is recorded more fully and with some variation of detail in the so-called Third Book of the Maccabees. In reply to Apion's charge, that the Jews show a lack of civic spirit because they do not worship the same gods as the Alexandrians, Josephus launches out into an explanation of their conception of God, describes their abhorrence of idolatry, and deals also with their refusal to set up in their temples the image of the Emperor. "But at the same time they are willing," he says, "to pay honors to great men and to offer sacrifices in their name." He deals also, in a digression, with calumnies derived from Posidonius and Melon about the worship of an ass in the sanctuary at Jerusalem.

[1: This part of the book, it may be noted, has only been preserved in the

Latin version; the Greek original has been lost.]

Apion had invented a detailed story of ritual murder to justify Antiochus Epiphanes for his spoliation of the Temple. The origin of this charge is instructive of the methods of a classical anti-Semite. There was, in the innermost sanctuary, a stone[1] on which the blood of the burnt offering was sprinkled by the high priest on the Day of Atonement. It was known as the [Hebrew: Even Shtiah] and tradition said that the ark of the covenant had rested on it. Mystery centered around it, and the Greek scribes imagined that it was the object of worship. Now, the Greek word for a stone was Onos, which likewise meant an ass, and it was probably on the strength of this blunder that prejudice for centuries accused Jews and Christians of worshiping an ass' head. Josephus brings proof of the emptiness of the charge, and retorts that Apion had himself the heart of an ass; and then, describing the ritual of the Temple, insists that there was no secret mystery about it. It gives a touch of pathos that he speaks as if the Temple services were still being carried out, whether because he was copying a source written before the destruction, or because he deliberately disregarded that event. Apion, like Cicero, had taunted the Jews on account of their political subjection, which proved, he argued, that their laws were not just nor their religion true. Josephus meets the charge--which in the materialistic thinking of the Roman world was hard to answer--by the not very happy plea that the Egyptians and Greeks had suffered a like fortune. So, too, he meets the gibe that the Jews do not eat pork, by saying that the Egyptian priests abstain likewise. He omits in both cases the true religious answer, which would probably not have appealed to his public.

[1: Yer. Yoma, v. 2.]

At this point the reply to the Alexandrian anti-Semite comes to an end, and the rest of the book comprises a defense of the Jewish legislation, "which is intended not as an eulogy but as an apology." The broad aim is to show that the Law inculcates humanity and piety; but Josephus, before setting himself to this, again labors to point out that it is pre-eminent in antiquity over any of the Greek codes. This done, he gives a summary of the principles of Judaism, which is unlike anything else he wrote in its masterly grasp of the spirit of the religion and in its philosophical attitude. So great indeed is the contrast between this epilogue and the bald summary of the Mosaic laws in the ***Antiquities*** that it is safe to say that Josephus had for his later work lighted on a fresh and more inspired source. His presentation has the regular characteristic of the Alexandrian school, an insistence on the universal and philanthropic elements of the Mosaic law; and it is likely that he had before him either Philo's work on the Life of Moses, or another work, which his predecessor had used. It matters little that there are differences of detail between his and Philo's interpretations: the manner and the general purport are the same, and the manner is not the usual manner of Josephus, and altogether different from the treatment in the ***Antiquities***.

He lays down with great clearness the dominant features of the Mosaic constitution. It is a theocracy, i.e. the state depends on God. The passage in which he makes good this principle is a striking piece of reasoning in comparative religion, worthy to be quoted in full:

"Now there are innumerable differences in the particular customs and laws that hold among all mankind, which a man may briefly reduce under the following heads: Some legislators have permitted their governments to be under monarchies, others put them under oligarchies, and others under a republican form; but our legislator had no regard to any of these forms, but he ordained our government to be what, by a strained expression, may be termed a Theocracy, by ascribing the authority and the power to God, and by persuading all the people to have a regard to Him as the Author of all the good things enjoyed either in common by all mankind or by each one in particular, and of all that they themselves obtain by praying to Him in their greatest difficulties. He informed them that it was impossible to escape God's observation, either in any of our outward actions or in any of our inward thoughts. Moreover he represented God as un-begotten and immutable through all eternity, superior to all mortal conceptions in form, and though known to us by His power, yet unknown to us as to His essence. I do not now explain how these notions of God are in harmony with the sentiments of the wisest among the Greeks. However, their sages testify with great assurance that these notions are just and agreeable to the divine nature; for Pythagoras and Anaxagoras and Plato and the Stoic philosophers that succeeded them, and almost all the rest profess the same sentiments, and had the same notions of the nature of God; yet durst not these men disclose those true notions to more than a few, because the body of the people were prejudiced beforehand with other opinions. But our legislator, whose actions harmonized with his laws, did not only prevail with those who were his contemporaries to accept these notions, but so firmly imprinted this faith in God upon all their posterity that it could never be removed. The reason why the constitution of our legislation was ever better directed than other legislations to the utility of all is this: that Moses did not make religion a part of virtue, but he ordained other virtues to be a part of religion--I mean justice, and fortitude, and temperance, and a universal agreement of the members of the community with one another. All our actions and studies have a reference to piety towards God, for he hath left none of these in suspense or undetermined. There are two ways of coming at any sort of learning and a moral conduct of life: the one is by instruction in words, the other by practical exercises. Now, other lawgivers have separated these two ways in their opinions, and, choosing the one which best pleased each of them, neglected the other. Thus did the Lacedemonians and the Cretans teach by practical exercises, but not by words; while the Athenians and almost all the other Greeks made laws about what was to be done, or left undone, but had no regard to exercising them thereto in practice.

"But our legislator very carefully joined these two methods of instruction together; for he neither left these practical exercises to be performed without verbal instruction, nor did he permit the learning of the law to proceed without the exercises for practice; but beginning immediately from the earliest infancy and the regulation of our diet, he left nothing of the very smallest consequence to be done at the pleasure and disposal of the individual. Accordingly, he made a fixed rule of law, what sorts of food they should abstain from, and what sorts they should use; as also what communion they should have with others, what great diligence they should use in their occupations, and what times of rest should be interposed, in order that, by living under that law as under a father and a master, we might be guilty of no sin, neither voluntary nor out of ignorance. For he did not suffer the guilt of ignorance to go without punishment, but demonstrated the law to be the best and the most necessary instruction of all, directing the people to cease from their other employments and to assemble together for the hearing and the exact learning of the law,--and this not once or twice or oftener, but every week; which all the other legislators seem to have neglected."

This passage contains, in many ways, an admirable explanation of Judaism as a law of conduct, inculcating morality by good habit; it lacks, indeed, any deep spiritual note or mystical exaltation, but it was likely for that reason to appeal to the practical, material-minded Roman. Josephus corroborates what Seneca had grudgingly remarked, that the Jews understood their laws; and it is this, he says, which made such a wonderful accord among us, to which no other nation can show a parallel. The eloquent insistence on the harmony uniting the Jewish people is another proof that Josephus is here reproducing the ideas of others, for it is in complete and glaring contrast with what he had repeatedly written in his *Antiquities* and his *Wars* about the strife of different sects. His books would have supplied the best argument to any pagan criticising his apology. Josephus further ascribes to the singleness of the tradition the absence of original genius among the people. The excellence of the Law produces a conservative outlook, whereas the Greeks, lacking a fixed law, love a new thing. S.D. Luzzatto, the Hebraist of the middle of the nineteenth century, emphasized the same contrast between Hellenism and Hebraism.

Turning in detail to the precepts of the Law, Josephus gives eloquent expression in the Hellenistic fashion to the idea of the divine unity. "God," he says, "contains all: He is a being altogether perfect, happy, and self-sufficient, the beginning, the middle, and the end of all things; God's aim is reflected in human institutions. Rightly He has but one Temple, which should be common to all men, even as He is the common God of all men." He develops, too, the humanitarian aspect of Judaism in the manner of the Hellenistic school. "And for our duty at the sacrifices, we ought in the first place to pray for the common welfare of all and after that for ourselves, for we were made for fellowship, one with another, and he who prefers the common good before his own is above all dear to God." He points to the excellence of the Jewish conception of marriage, another commonplace of the Hellenistic apologist, as we know from the Sibylline oracles; to the respect for parents and to the friendliness for the stranger. He insists with Philo[1] that kinship is to be measured not by blood, but by the conduct of life. He dwells, likewise in company with the Hellenists, on a law that lacks Bible authority: that the Israelites should give, to all who needed it, fire and water, food and guidance.[2] The impulse to this interpretation of the Torah is found in the charge made by the Jews' enemies, that they were to assist only members of their own race.[3] Josephus appears to be original, and, as is quite pardonable, he may be writing with a view to Roman proclivities, when he praises the law for the number of offenses to which it attaches the capital penalty. Like many a later Jewish apologist living amid an alien and dominant culture, Josephus accepts foreign standards, and he is silent about the Pharisaic teaching which softened the literal prescripts of the Bible.[4]

[1: Comp. De Nobilitate.]

[2: Comp. Philo, II. 639.]

[3: Comp. Juvenal, Sat. xiv. 102.]

[4: It has been noticed above that Josephus appears to misunderstand or deliberately misinterpret the Hebrew [Hebrew: aror] (cursed be!), which precedes many prohibitions of the Mosaic law, to mean "he shall be put to death."]

In a peroration Josephus returns to a general eulogy of the Jewish Law, on account of the faithful allegiance which it commands, and denounces the pagan idolatry in the manner of the Greek rationalists, who had made play with the Olympian hierarchy. While the inherent excellence of the Jewish Law is dependent on the sublime conception of God, the inherent defect of the Greek religion is that the Greek legislators entertained a low conception of God, and did not make the religious creed a part of the state law, but left it to the poets to invent what they chose. The greatest of the Greek philosophers, indeed, agreed with the Jews as to the true notions about God: "Plato especially imitated our legislation in enjoining on all citizens that they should know the laws accurately." A later generation made bold to declare that Plato had listened to Jeremiah in Egypt and learnt his wisdom from the Jewish prophet. Josephus compares with the Jewish separateness the national exclusiveness of the Lacedemonians, and claims that the Jews show a greater humanity in that they admit converts from other peoples. They have, moreover, shown their bravery not in wars for the purpose of amassing wealth, but in observing their laws in spite of every attempt to wean them away. The Mosaic law is being spread over the civilized world:

"For there is not any city of the Greeks, nor any of the barbarians, nor any nation whatsoever whither our custom of resting on the seventh day has not come, and by which our fasts and lighting up of lamps and divers regulations as to food are not observed. They also endeavor to imitate our mutual accord with one another, and the charitable distribution of our goods, and our diligence in our trades, and our fortitude in bearing the distresses that befall us; and what is here matter of the greatest admiration, our Law hath no bait of pleasure to allure men to it, but it prevails by its own force; and as God Himself pervades all the world, so hath our Law passed through all the world also."

The task of the apologist is completed; "for whereas our accusers have pretended that our nation are a people of late origin, I have demonstrated that they are exceedingly ancient, and whereas they have reproached our lawgiver as a vile man, God of old bare witness to his virtues, and time itself hath been proved to bear witness to the same thing."[1] In a final appreciation he concludes:

"As to the laws themselves, more words are unnecessary, for they are visible in their own nature, and are seen to teach not impiety, but the truest piety in the world. They do not make men hate one another, but encourage people to communicate what they have to one another freely. They are enemies to injustice, they foster righteousness, they banish idleness and expensive living, and instruct men to be content with what they have and to be diligent in their callings. They forbid men to make war from a desire of gain, but make them courageous in defending the laws. They are inexorable in punishing malefactors. They admit no sophistry of words, but are always established by actions, which we ever propose as surer demonstrations than what is contained in writing only; on which account I am so bold as to say that we are become the teachers of other men in the greatest number of things, and those of the most excellent nature only. For what is more excellent than inviolable piety? What is more just than submission to laws? And what is more advantageous than mutual love and concord? And this prevails so far that we are to be neither divided by calamities nor to become oppressive and factious in prosperity, but to contemn death when we are in war, and in peace to apply ourselves to our handicrafts or to the tilling of the ground; while in all things and in all ways we are satisfied that God is the Judge and Governor of our actions."

[1: C. Ap. ii. 41.]

As we read this final outburst of the Jewish apologist and think of what he had himself written to gainsay it, and what he was yet to write in his autobiography, we are fain to exclaim, *o si sic omnia*! One would like to believe that in the defense of the Jewish Law we have the true Josephus, driven in his old age by the goading of enemies to throw off the mask of Greco-Roman culture, and standing out boldly as a lover of his people and his people's law. Such latter-day repentance has been known among the Flavii of other generations. And the two books ***Against Apion*** show that when Josephus had not to qualify his own weakness nor to flatter his patrons, he could rise to an appreciation and even to an eloquent exposition of Jewish ideals. Yet it was not the Greek-writing historian, but the Palestinian Rabbis, that were to prove to the world the undying vigor, the unquenchable power of resistance of the Jewish Law. The Vineyard of Jabneh founded by Johanan ben Zakkai was the sufficient refutation of Roman scoffers, while the apology of Josephus became the guide of the early Church fathers in their replies to heathen calumniators who repeated against them the charges that had been invented against the Jews. It is significant that Tacitus, who wrote his history some few years after the defense of Josephus was published, repeated with added virulence the fables which the Jewish writer had refuted. The charges of anti-Semites have in every age borne a charmed life: they are hydra-headed, and can be refuted, not by literature, but by life.

Nevertheless literary libels, if unanswered in literature, tend to become fixed popular beliefs, and in the Dark and Middle Ages the Jewish people were to suffer bitterly from the lack of apologists who could obtain a hearing before the peoples of Europe. In the early centuries of the Christian era, before the Christian Church was allied with the Roman Empire, tolerance ruled in the Greco-Roman world, and the narrow Roman hatred of Judaism was in large part broken down. Celsus, Numenius, and Dion Cassius, three of the most notable authors of the second century, speak of the Jewish people and Jewish Scriptures in a very different tone from that of a Tacitus and an Apion. And as it has been said, "Who shall know how many cultured pagans were led by the books of Josephus to read the Bible and to look on Judaism with other eyes?"[1] If the apologies of Philo and Josephus could not pierce

the armor of prejudice and hatred which enwrapped a Tacitus or a Christian eccle-
siastic, they at least found their way through the lighter coating of ignorance and
misunderstanding which had been fabricated by Hellenistic Egyptians, but which
had not fatally warped the minds of the general Greco-Roman society.

[1: Comp. Joel, Blicke in die Religionsgeschichte, ii. 118.]

IX
CONCLUSION

The works of Josephus early passed into the category of standard literature. It is recorded that they were placed by order of the Flavian Emperors in the public library of Rome; and though Suetonius, the biographer of the Caesars, who wrote in the second century, and Diogenes, the biographer of the philosophers, who wrote a century later, do not apparently hold them of any account, it is certain that they were carefully preserved till the triumph of the Christian Church gave them a new importance. For centuries henceforth they were the prime authority for Jewish history of post-Biblical times, and were treasured as a kind of introduction to the Gospels, illuminating the period in which Christianity had its birth. The traitor-historian was soon forgotten by his own people, if they ever had regard for him, and with the rest of the Hellenistic writers he dropped out of the Rabbinical tradition. Possibly the Aramaic version of the *Wars* survived for a time in the Eastern schools, but while the Jews were struggling to preserve their religious existence, they had little thought for such a history of their past.

The Christians, on the other hand, had a special interest in the works of Josephus, since they found in them not only the model of their defense against pagan calumnies, but the earliest external testimony to support the Gospels. Josephus was venerated as the Jew who had recorded the fate of Jesus of Nazareth. The *Antiquities* contain two references to John the Baptist and an account of the execution of James, the brother of Jesus; but the most celebrated of the "evidential" passages occurs in book xviii of the *Antiquities*, where in our text, following on the account of Pilate's persecution, occurs this paragraph:

"Now, there lived about this time Jesus, a wise man, if it be lawful to call him a man, for he was a doer of wonderful works, a teacher of such men as receive the truth with pleasure. He drew over to him both many of the Jews and many of the Gentiles. He was the Christ; and when Pilate, at the suggestion of the principal men amongst us, had condemned him to the cross, those that loved him at the first did not forsake him, for he appeared alive to them again the third day, as the divine prophets had foretold these and ten thousand other wonderful things concerning him. And the tribe of Christians, so named from him, are not extinct at this day (ch. 3)."

An enormous literature has been provoked by these lines, and the weight of modern opinion is that they are altogether spurious. The passage is first quoted by Eusebius,[1] the historian of Caesarea, who wrote about the beginning of the fourth century C.E.;[2] but Origen, his predecessor by a hundred years, significantly enough does not know of it. Josephus, he says simply, did not acknowledge the Christ.[3] At the same time Origen quotes a passage from the same book of the *Antiquities*,[4] to show that the Jews ascribed the defeat of the Tetrarch Herod to his murder of John the Baptist. The earliest of the Patristic writers, Clement of Alexandria, quotes Josephus as to chronology, but it is fairly certain that he did not know the works at first hand, since the era he refers to runs from Moses to the tenth year of Antoninus,[5] i.e. till the better part of a century after the death of Josephus. Origen likewise probably knew Josephus only at second hand, and the inference is that both the Alexandrian ecclesiastics derived their citations and their interpolation in the text of Josephus from a pious Christian abstract and improvement. The uncompromisingly Christian character of the text, the discrepancy between Origen and Eusebius, and the notorious aptitude of early Christian scribes for interpolating manuscripts, and especially the manuscripts of Hellenistic Jewish writers, with Christological passages make it well nigh certain that the paragraph was foisted in between the second and third century. That was a period when, as has been said, "faith was more vivid than good-faith." The will to believe its genuineness, however, persisted to our own day, and some have made a compromise between their sentiment and their critical faculty, by arguing that the passage, though partly corrupt, is founded on something Josephus wrote.[6]

[1: Comp. Schlatter, *op. cit.* 403.]

[2: H.E. i. 41; Comp. Freimann, Wie verhielt sich das Judenthum zu Jesus? (Monatsschrift fur die Geschichte und Wissenschaft des Judenthums, 1911, p. 296).]

[3: Comm. in Matth. ch. xvii.]

[4: Ant. XVIII. v. 5.]

[5: Strom. I. xxi. 409.]

[6: Among those who uphold this view is the Franco-Jewish savant Theodore Reinach, whose opinion is that the Christian scribe changed a ***testimonium de Christo*** into a ***testimonium pro Christo*** (R.E.J. xxxv. 6). Both Renan and Ewald hold that our passage is a corrupted fragment of a much fuller account of Jesus in the ***Antiquities***. See Joel. ***op. cit***. p. 52.]

It is alleged that many of the words are such as Josephus might have used, but, apart from the fact that this is contested by other authorities, it is unreasonable to suppose that the interpolator would go out of his way to stamp the insertion as a forgery by using extraordinary words. It is urged again that the passages about John and James in the ***Antiquities*** support the likelihood of Josephus' having mentioned Jesus. But these passages are themselves open to very grave suspicions. There is no reference to them in the epitome of the chapters furnished at the head of each book, which according to Niese dates from the age of the Antonines, or the end of the second century. Nor does the Slavonic version of Josephus contain the passage about James, and while Origen refers to that passage, he had a different version of it from that which appears in our manuscripts. It seems that he has incorporated the gloss of a Christian believer. And again, while our text imputes the blame of the stoning of James to the Sadducees, and gives credit to the Pharisees for endeavoring to prevent it, Hegesippus, the Christian writer of the second century, uses the alleged account of the incident by Josephus to gird at the Pharisees. The probability is then that different Christological insertions were made in the manuscripts of Josephus according to the leaning of the scribe, but that none of the supposed evidences are genuine, or based on a genuine narrative. The absence of any reference to Jesus and the apostles in Josephus would have seemed damaging to the truth of the Christian testament, and therefore the passages were supplied.

Nevertheless we may be grateful to the interpolators, because, on the strength of these passages, Josephus was especially treasured through the Dark and Middle Ages, and he alone survived of the Hellenistic apologists. When Christianity established its center at Rome, Josephus was soon translated into Latin, and in the Vulgate version (if we may so call it) he was best known for centuries. The seven books of the *Wars* were rendered into Latin by one Tyrannus Rufinus of Aquilea, who was a contemporary of Jerome (Hieronymus, 345-410 C.E.), and a very industrious translator of the works of the Greek Patristic writers. The translation of the *Antiquities*, though ascribed to the same author, was made later. Jerome apparently was invited to undertake the task, for in one of his letters he writes:[1] "The rumor that the works of Josephus and Papian and Polycarp have been translated by me is false. I have neither the leisure nor the strength to render his writings into another tongue with the same elegance" [as those already done]. It is uncertain who the translator was, but the work was carried out at the instigation of Cassiodorus (480-575), who lived in the time of Justinian, and was a versatile historian. He wrote himself a chronicle of events from Adam to his own day as well as a history of the Goths. In his book on the Institutions of Holy Literature he says:

"As to Josephus, who is almost a second Livy, and is widely known by his books on the *Antiquities of the Jews*, Jerome declared that he was unable to translate his works because of their great volume. But one of my friends has translated the twenty-two books [i.e. the *Antiquities* and the two books of the *Apology*], in spite of their difficulty and complexity, into the Latin tongue. He also wrote seven books of extreme brilliancy on the Conquest of the Jews, the translation of which some ascribe to Jerome, others to Ambrose, and others to Rufinus."

[1: Epist. ad Lucrinum, 5.]

The autobiography of Josephus, alone of his writings, does not appear to have been done into the language of the Western Church. Perhaps its worthlessness was apparent even in the dark days. More ancient, however, and even more popular than the complete Latin version of Josephus, was an abridgment of his works which passed under the name of Hegesippus. The name is not found till the ninth century, but it is likely that the work was written in the time of Ambrosius, the famous bishop of Milan (C.E. 350). In this form the seven books of the *Wars* are compressed into five, and the words and phrases of the original are modified throughout. The writer in his preface explicitly declares that it is a kind of revised version, and he improves the original by Christological insertions, explaining, for example, the destruction of Jerusalem as a judgment upon the Jews for the murder of Christ. Josephus, he says, aims at the careful unraveling of events and at sobriety of speech, but he lacks faith (*religio*) and truth; "and so we have been at pains, relying not on intellectual force but on the promptings of faith, to probe for the inner meaning of Jewish history and to extract from it more of value to our posterity." Josephus is often mentioned by name as authority for the statements, but at the same time considerable additions are made from other Roman sources. Some have thought that there was a compiler named Hegesippus, others that the word is but a corruption of the Latinized form of the Jewish historian's name: Josippus, formed from [Greek: Io saepos], would become Egesippus, and finally Hegesippus.

A Greek epitome of Josephus also existed. We find it used by a Byzantine historian, John Zonaras, during the tenth and the eleventh century, in the composition of his chronicles. It omitted the speeches and historical evidences of the fuller work and pruned its excessive garrulousness. By the uncritical scholiasts and the prolix chroniclers of the Byzantine and Papal courts, Josephus was esteemed as a distinguished and godlike historian, and as a truthloving man ([Greek: philalaethaes anaer]). He was dubbed by Jerome "the Greek Livy," and to Tertullian and his followers he was an unfailing guide. Choice passages in his writings are frequently extracted, often with a little purposive modification, to emphasize some Christological design. Eustathius of Antioch in the sixth century, Syncellus in the eighth, and Cedrenus and Glycas some three or four hundred years later, are among those whose extant fragments prove a frequent use of Josephus. And the neo-Platonist philosopher Porphyry (ab. 300 C.E.), who was well acquainted with Jewish literature, reproduces in his treatise on Abstinence the various passages about the Essenes from the *Wars* and the *Antiquities*. The Emperor Constantine later ordered extracts from the *Wars* to be put together for his edification in a selection bearing the title *About Virtue and Vice*.

Owing to this popularity, we have abundant manuscripts of Josephus. The oldest of the Latin is as early as the sixth century; the Greek date from the tenth century and later. Niese, the most authoritative editor of Josephus in modern times, thinks that our manuscript families go back to one archetype of the second century in the epoch of the Antonines. The earliest printed copy like the earliest manuscript of his work contains the Latin version, being a part of the *Antiquities*, which was issued in 1470 at Augsburg. The whole corpus was printed in 1499, and, after a number of Latin editions, the first Greek edition was published at Basel by Arten, in 1544, together with the Fourth Book of the Maccabees, which was ascribed to the historian.

In the days of vast but undiscriminating scholarship that followed the Renaissance, Josephus still enjoyed a great repute, and Scaliger, prince of polymaths, regarded him as superior to any pagan historian. The great Dutch scholar Havercamp made a special study of the manuscripts, and produced, in 1726, a repertory of everything discovered about his author. A little later Whiston, professor of mathematics at Cambridge, published an English translation of all the works, which is still serviceable, but not critical, together with some dissertations, which are neither serviceable nor critical. Later translations into English and almost every other language were made, but the greatest work of modern times on Josephus is the edition of Niese. Lastly, it may be mentioned that we have a Slavonic version, which goes back to the eighth or the ninth century, and a Syriac version of the sixth book of the *Wars*, which is included, immediately after the Fourth Book of the Maccabees, in a manuscript of the Syriac version of the Bible dating from the sixth century, and is entitled the Fifth Book of the Maccabees. It has been suggested that the Syriac was based on the work which Josephus published in Aramaic before he wrote the Greek; but Professor Noeldeke has shown that the theory is not probable, since the translator clearly used the Greek text.[1] Somewhat late in the day a Hebrew translation of the books *Against Apion*, which were regarded as the most Jewish part of his work, was made in the Middle Ages, and printed, together with Abraham Zacuto's Yuhasin, at Constantinople, in 1506, by Samuel Shullam. The Hebrew translation is very free, and is marred by several large omissions. It was very probably made with the help of the Latin version.

[1: Literarisches Centralblatt, 1880, no. 20, p. 881.]

While Josephus enjoyed great honor among Christian scholars, for centuries he passed out of the knowledge of his own people. The Talmud has no reference to him, for the surmise that he is the "philosopher" visited by the four sages who journeyed from Palestine to Rome[1] is no more than a vague possibility. Nor has the supposed identification with the Joseph Hakohen that is mentioned in the Midrash anything more solid to uphold it.[2] In the Middle Ages, however, when Spain, Italy, and North Africa witnessed a remarkable revival of Jewish literature, both secular and religious, and when scientific studies again interested the people, the historical literature of other peoples became known to their scholars, and several Jewish writers mention the chronicles of one Yosippon, or "little Joseph." The text of the chronicle itself is widely known from the eleventh century onwards. The first author to mention it is David ben Tammum (ab. 950), and an extract from the book is found about a century later. Four manuscripts of it have come down to us: two in the Vatican, one in Paris, and one in Turin, and it was among the earliest Hebrew books printed. Professing to be the work of Joseph ben Gorion, one of the Jewish commanders in the war with Rome and a prefect of Jerusalem, it is written in a Rabbinical Hebrew that is nearer the classical language than most medieval compositions. It was indeed argued on the ground of its pure classical idiom that it dated from the fourth century, but Zunz[3] showed that this was impossible. It bears all the traces of the pseudepigraphic tendency of a period that produced the first works of the Cabala, the Seder Olam Zutta of Rabbi Joshua, and the neo-Hebraic apocalypses. The attempt to write an archaic Hebrew is marred by the presence of Rabbinical and novel terms. Reference to events or things only known to later times is combined with the pretension of an ancient chronicle. The country and the date of the author are uncertain, but probabilities point to Italy, where in the ninth and tenth centuries Jewish culture flourished, and where both Arabic and Latin works were well known in the Ghettos. The transcription of foreign names, the frequent introduction of the names of places in Italy, the acquaintance with Roman history, and the fact that Italian Jews are among the first to recognize Yosippon favor this theory. It is fitting that the country where Josephus wrote his history should also have produced a Jewish imitation of his work. Yosippon indeed was soon translated into Arabic, and its narratives and legends passed into the current stock of Ghetto history. The book was swollen by later additions, which Zunz has proved to belong to the twelfth century. One Yerahmeel ben Shelomoh who flourished in that epoch is mentioned in an early manuscript as a compiler of Yosippon and other histories; and it is possible that he was himself responsible for parts of the work in its present form.

[1: Derek Erez, ed. Goldberg, iii. 10.]

[2: Moed Katon, 23a. See above, p. 177.]

[3: Comp. Zunz, Gottesdienstliche Vortraege, pp. 154*ff*.]

The chronicle of Yosippon is a summary of Jewish history, with considerable digressions--many of them later interpolations--about the history of the nations with whom the Hebrew people came into contact, Babylon, Greece, and Rome. Like the Book of Chronicles, it begins with Adam and genealogies, explains the roll of the nations in Genesis, and then springs suddenly from the legendary origin of Babel and Rome to the relation of the Jews with Babylon. The history proper contains the record of the Jews from the first to the second captivity, but is broken by a mass of legendary material about Alexander the Great--reproducing much of what is found in pseudo-Callisthenes--and by a short account of the Carthaginian general Hannibal and several incidents of Roman history. These include a description of a coronation of the Emperor, which, it is suggested, applies to the medieval and not the classical period of the Empire.

The book was known throughout the later part of the Middle Ages and down to the eighteenth century as the Hebrew Josephus, and contrasted with the [Hebrew: Yosifon la-Romim], or "Latin Josephus." When the genuine works of our worthy became known to the Jews, Yosippon was regarded as the true representative of the Jewish point of view against the paganizing traitor. Its author had not a first-hand acquaintance with our Josephus. He knew him only through the Latin versions, which were mixed with much later material. Possibly he meant to pass off his work as the Hebrew original of the Jewish history, and confused Joseph ben Gorion with Joseph ben Mattathias; for in the introduction to one manuscript we read, "I am Joseph, called Josephus the Jew, of whom it is written that he wrote the book of the wars of the Lord, and this is the sixth part." This, however, may be the gloss of a later scribe, who found an anonymous book, and thought fit to supply the omission. In places the Hebrew translator reproduces, though with some blunders, the Latin Hegesippus, but he sought to give charm to his work by legendary additions, which more often show Arabic and other foreign influences than traces of the Jewish Haggadah. Interpolations have served to increase the legendary element, and take away from the historical value. But it is this element, reflecting the ideas of the age, that gives the composition a peculiar literary interest.

Though only to a small extent representing Jewish tradition, the book remained very popular among the Jews both of the West and the East, and was long regarded as authoritative. The first printed edition was issued at Mantua, in 1476, and was followed by the edition of Constantinople, in 1520, arranged in chapters and enlarged, and an edition of Basel, in 1541, containing a Latin preface and a Latin translation of the greater part. In 1546 a printed Yiddish edition appeared in Zurich, and in the Ghetto it retains its popularity to the present day. Other editions and translations have followed. Steinschneider has noted that as late as 1873 an abstract of the Arabic translation together with the Arabic version of the Book of the Maccabees was published at Beirut.[1] The spuriousness of the work has now been established, and of modern scholars Wellhausen[2] is almost alone in ascribing to it any independent historical worth. In the Spanish period of Jewish culture the real as well as the spurious Josephus was read by many of his race, and some hard things were said of him. Thus Rabbi Isaac Abrabanel, the statesman and apologist (1457-1508), regarded him as a common sycophant and wrote, "In many things he perverted the truth, even where we have the Scriptures before us, in order to court favor with the Romans, as a slave submits himself to the will of his master." Azariah de Rossi (ab. 1850), anticipating the ideas of a later age, alone balanced his merits against his demerits. Among the great Christian scholars of the Renaissance, however, he enjoyed great fame. Joseph Scaliger, the most eminent of the seventeenth century critics, could write of him, "Josephus was the most diligent and the most truthloving of all writers, and one can better believe him, not only as to the affairs of the Jews, but also as to the Gentiles, than all the Greek and Latin writers, because his fidelity and his learning are everywhere conspicuous."[3] It is illustrative of his popularity that Rembrandt named one of his great Jewish pictures after him. Whiston's English translation of his works became a household book, found side by side with the Bible and *The Pilgrim's Progress*.[4]

[1: J.Q.R. xvi. 393.]

[2: Der arabische Josippus; see J.E., s.v. Joseph ben Gorion.]

[3: De Emend. Temp. Proleg. 17.]

[4: Readers of Rudyard Kipling may recall that in ***Captains Courageous*** one of the seamen on board the "We're Here" Schooner reads aloud on Sunday from a book called Josephus: "It was an old leather-bound volume very solid and very like a Bible, but enlivened with accounts of battles and sieges."]

In modern times his reputation as a trustworthy authority has depreciated considerably, and it is still depreciating. More accurate study and wider knowledge have exposed his grave defects as an historian, and the critical standpoint has dissipated the halo with which his supposed Christian sympathies had invested him, and laid bare his weakness and his essential unreliability. Yet with all his glaring faults and unlovable qualities he has certain solid merits. The greatest certainly is that his works so appealed to later generations as to have been preserved, and thereby posterity has been enabled to get some knowledge, however inadequate, of the history of the Jewish polity during its last two hundred years--between the time of the Maccabees and the fall of the nation--which would otherwise have been buried in almost unrelieved darkness. And at the same time he has preserved a record of some interesting pieces of Egyptian, Syrian, and Roman history. Just because he was so little original, he has a special usefulness; for he reproduces the statements of more capable writers than himself, who have disappeared, and he has embodied an aspect of the Hellenistic-Jewish literature which had otherwise been lost. We can estimate his value to us as an historian from our ignorance of what was happening in Judea during the fifty years after his account comes to an end.

It is true that he brings before us, for the most part, but the external facts and the court scandals in place of the vital movements and the underlying principles; and in dealing with contemporary events he has a perverted view, borrowed largely from Roman foes and feebly corrected. But it is something to have preserved even these facts, and in the account of the *Wars* he often draws a vivid picture. The siege of Jerusalem has passed into the roll of the world's heroic events, and it owes its place there largely to the narrative of Josephus. Moreover, in spite of his pusillanimity and his subservience to his Roman patrons, Josephus did possess a distinct pride of race and a love of his people. It led him at times to glorify them in a gross way, but notably in the books *Against Apion* it could inspire a certain eloquence; and many hostile outsiders must have learnt from his pages to appreciate some of the great qualities of the Jewish people.

To appraise him fairly is difficult. He has few of the qualities, either personal or literary, that attract sympathy and many of the defects that repel. He is at once vain and obsequious, servile and spiteful, professing candor and practising adulation, prolix and prosaic. As a general he proved himself a traitor; as apologist of the Jews, a function which he asserted for himself, he marred by a lack of independence the service which he sought to render his people. In his account of their past he was often false to their fundamental ideas of God and history. Whether he was really under the influence of the debased Greco-Roman culture of the day, which consigned mankind to the dominion of fatality, or whether he deliberately masked his own standpoint to please his audience, he presented the history of the Hebrew nationality in the light of ideas of fate strange to it. He has perpetuated a false picture of the Zealots, whose avowed enemy he was, and he reveals an inadequate understanding of the deeper ideas and deeper principles of the Pharisees, whose champion he professed to be. Generally, in dealing with the struggle against Rome, his dominating desire to justify his own submission and please the Romans led him to distort the facts, and rendered him blind to the real heroism of his countrymen. The client in him prevails over the historian: we can never be sure whether he is expressing his own opinion or only what he conceives will be pleasing to his patrons and masters. This dependence affects his presentation of Judaism as well as of the Jewish people. He dissembled his theological opinions in his larger historical works, and it is only in his last apologetic composition that he asserts confidently a Jewish point of view.

Yet it is but fair to Josephus to consider the times and circumstances in which he wrote. It was an age when the love of truth was almost dead, extinguished partly by the crushing tyranny of omnipotent Emperors, partly by the intellectual and moral degeneration of pagan society. The Flavian house soon showed the same characteristics of a vainglorious despotism as the line of Caesars which it had supplanted. Under Domitian "the only course possible for a writer without the risk of outlawry or the sacrifice of personal honor was that followed by Juvenal and Tacitus during his reign, viz., silence." It was an age when, in the words of Mazzini, "a hollow sound as of dissolution was heard in the world. Man seemed in a hideous case: placed between two infinities, he knew neither. He knew not past nor future. All belief was dead; dead the belief in the gods, dead the belief in the Republic." The material power of Rome, while it dazzled by its splendor, seemed invincible, and it crushed, in all save the strongest, independence of thought and independence of national life. Unfortunately it fell to Josephus to write amid these surroundings his account of the Jewish wars and the history of the Jews, and he may have been driven to distortion to keep his perilous position at court. The moral environment, too, was such as to contaminate those who had not a deep faith and a strong Hebrew consciousness. At Alexandria it was possible to achieve a harmony between Judaism and the spiritual teaching of Greek philosophy; but the basic conceptions of Roman Imperialism were not to be brought into accord with Jewish ideas.

Josephus had no conception of the moral weakness, he felt only the invincible power, of the conqueror. He was a Jew, isolated in Rome, estranged from his own people, and not at home in his environment, a favored captive in a splendid court, a member of a subject people living in the halls of the mighty. Did ever situation more strongly conduce to moral servility and mental dependence! It was well nigh impossible for him, even had he possessed the ability, to write an honest and independent history of the Jews. It required some courage and steadfastness to write of the Jews at all. In such circumstances he might well have become an apostate, as his contemporary Tiberius Alexander had done, and it is a tribute to his Jewish feeling that he remained in profession and in heart true to his people, that he was not among those who with the fall of the second Temple exclaimed, "Our hope is perished: we are cut off." He had indeed chosen the easier and less noble way on the destruction of the national life of his people; he preferred the palace of the Palatine with its pomp to the Vineyard at Jabneh with its wise men. While Johanan ben Zakkai was saving Judaism, Josephus was apologizing for it. Yet he too has done some service: he preserved some knowledge of his people and their religion for the Gentiles, and became one of the permanent authorities for that heretical body of Jewish proselytes who in his own day were beginning to mark themselves off as a separate sect, and who carried on to some extent the work of Hellenistic Judaism. Perhaps the true judgment about him is that he was neither noble nor villainous, neither champion nor coward, but one of those mediocre men of talent but of weak character and conflicting impulses struggling against adversity who succumb to the difficulties of the time in which their life is passed, and sacrifice their individuality to comfort. But he wrote something that has lived; and for what he wrote, if not for what he was, he has a niche in the literary treasure house of the Jewish people as well as in the annals of general history. As a man, if he cannot inspire, he may at least stand as a warning against that facile subservience to external powers and that fatal assimilation of foreign thought which at once destroy the individuality of the Jew and deprive him of his full humanity.

The Codes Of Hammurabi And Moses
W. W. Davies

QTY

The discovery of the Hammurabi Code is one of the greatest achievements of archaeology, and is of paramount interest, not only to the student of the Bible, but also to all those interested in ancient history...

Religion   **ISBN:** *1-59462-338-4*   Pages:132

MSRP $12.95

The Theory of Moral Sentiments
Adam Smith

QTY

This work from 1749. contains original theories of conscience amd moral judgment and it is the foundation for systemof morals.

Philosophy **ISBN:** *1-59462-777-0*   Pages:536

MSRP $19.95

Jessica's First Prayer
Hesba Stretton

QTY

In a screened and secluded corner of one of the many railway-bridges which span the streets of London there could be seen a few years ago, from five o'clock every morning until half past eight, a tidily set-out coffee-stall, consisting of a trestle and board, upon which stood two large tin cans, with a small fire of charcoal burning under each so as to keep the coffee boiling during the early hours of the morning when the work-people were thronging into the city on their way to their daily toil...

Pages:84

Childrens **ISBN:** *1-59462-373-2*   *MSRP $9.95*

My Life and Work
Henry Ford

QTY

Henry Ford revolutionized the world with his implementation of mass production for the Model T automobile. Gain valuable business insight into his life and work with his own auto-biography... "We have only started on our development of our country we have not as yet, with all our talk of wonderful progress, done more than scratch the surface. The progress has been wonderful enough but..."

Pages:300

Biographies/ **ISBN:** *1-59462-198-5*   *MSRP $21.95*

The Art of Cross-Examination
Francis Wellman

QTY

I presume it is the experience of every author, after his first book is published upon an important subject, to be almost overwhelmed with a wealth of ideas and illustrations which could readily have been included in his book, and which to his own mind, at least, seem to make a second edition inevitable. Such certainly was the case with me; and when the first edition had reached its sixth impression in five months, I rejoiced to learn that it seemed to my publishers that the book had met with a sufficiently favorable reception to justify a second and considerably enlarged edition. ...

Pages:412

Reference   ISBN: *1-59462-647-2*   *MSRP $19.95*

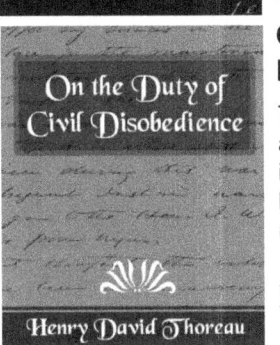

On the Duty of Civil Disobedience
Henry David Thoreau

QTY

Thoreau wrote his famous essay, On the Duty of Civil Disobedience, as a protest against an unjust but popular war and the immoral but popular institution of slave-owning. He did more than write—he declined to pay his taxes, and was hauled off to gaol in consequence. Who can say how much this refusal of his hastened the end of the war and of slavery?

Law   ISBN: *1-59462-747-9*   Pages:48
MSRP $7.45

Dream Psychology
Psychoanalysis for Beginners

Sigmund Freud

Dream Psychology Psychoanalysis for Beginners
Sigmund Freud

QTY

Sigmund Freud, born Sigismund Schlomo Freud (May 6, 1856 - September 23, 1939), was a Jewish-Austrian neurologist and psychiatrist who co-founded the psychoanalytic school of psychology. Freud is best known for his theories of the unconscious mind, especially involving the mechanism of repression; his redefinition of sexual desire as mobile and directed towards a wide variety of objects; and his therapeutic techniques, especially his understanding of transference in the therapeutic relationship and the presumed value of dreams as sources of insight into unconscious desires.

Psychology   ISBN: *1-59462-905-6*   Pages:196

MSRP $15.45

The Miracle of Right Thought
Orison Swett Marden

QTY

Believe with all of your heart that you will do what you were made to do. When the mind has once formed the habit of holding cheerful, happy, prosperous pictures, it will not be easy to form the opposite habit. It does not matter how improbable or how far away this realization may see, or how dark the prospects may be, if we visualize them as best we can, as vividly as possible, hold tenaciously to them and vigorously struggle to attain them, they will gradually become actualized, realized in the life. But a desire, a longing without endeavor, a yearning abandoned or held indifferently will vanish without realization.

Self Help   ISBN: *1-59462-644-8*   Pages:360
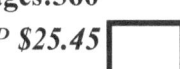
MSRP $25.45

www.bookjungle.com *email: sales@bookjungle.com fax: 630-214-0564 mail: Book Jungle PO Box 2226 Champaign, IL 61825*

QTY

☐ **The Rosicrucian Cosmo-Conception Mystic Christianity** *by Max Heindel*   ISBN: *1-59462-188-8*   **$38.95**
The Rosicrucian Cosmo-conception is not dogmatic, neither does it appeal to any other authority than the reason of the student. It is: not controversial, but is: sent forth in the, hope that it may help to clear...   New Age/Religion Pages 646

☐ **Abandonment To Divine Providence** *by Jean-Pierre de Caussade*   ISBN: *1-59462-228-0*   **$25.95**
"The Rev. Jean Pierre de Caussade was one of the most remarkable spiritual writers of the Society of Jesus in France in the 18th Century. His death took place at Toulouse in 1751. His works have gone through many editions and have been republished...   Inspirational/Religion Pages 400

☐ **Mental Chemistry** *by Charles Haanel*   ISBN: *1-59462-192-6*   **$23.95**
Mental Chemistry allows the change of material conditions by combining and appropriately utilizing the power of the mind. Much like applied chemistry creates something new and unique out of careful combinations of chemicals the mastery of mental chemistry...   New Age Pages 354

☐ **The Letters of Robert Browning and Elizabeth Barret Barrett 1845-1846 vol II**   ISBN: *1-59462-193-4*   **$35.95**
by Robert Browning and Elizabeth Barrett   Biographies Pages 596

☐ **Gleanings In Genesis (volume I)** *by Arthur W. Pink*   ISBN: *1-59462-130-6*   **$27.45**
Appropriately has Genesis been termed "the seed plot of the Bible" for in it we have, in germ form, almost all of the great doctrines which are afterwards fully developed in the books of Scripture which follow...   Religion/Inspirational Pages 420

☐ **The Master Key** *by L. W. de Laurence*   ISBN: *1-59462-001-6*   **$30.95**
In no branch of human knowledge has there been a more lively increase of the spirit of research during the past few years than in the study of Psychology, Concentration and Mental Discipline. The requests for authentic lessons in Thought Control, Mental Discipline and...   New Age/Business Pages 422

☐ **The Lesser Key Of Solomon Goetia** *by L. W. de Laurence*   ISBN: *1-59462-092-X*   **$9.95**
This translation of the first book of the "Lemegton" which is now for the first time made accessible to students of Talismanic Magic was done, after careful collation and edition, from numerous Ancient Manuscripts in Hebrew, Latin, and French...   New Age/Occult Pages 92

☐ **Rubaiyat Of Omar Khayyam** *by Edward Fitzgerald*   ISBN:*1-59462-332-5*   **$13.95**
Edward Fitzgerald, whom the world has already learned, in spite of his own efforts to remain within the shadow of anonymity, to look upon as one of the rarest poets of the century, was born at Bredfield, in Suffolk, on the 31st of March, 1809. He was the third son of John Purcell...   Music Pages 172

☐ **Ancient Law** *by Henry Maine*   ISBN: *1-59462-128-4*   **$29.95**
The chief object of the following pages is to indicate some of the earliest ideas of mankind, as they are reflected in Ancient Law, and to point out the relation of those ideas to modern thought.   Religion/History Pages 452

☐ **Far-Away Stories** *by William J. Locke*   ISBN: *1-59462-129-2*   **$19.45**
"Good wine needs no bush, but a collection of mixed vintages does. And this book is just such a collection. Some of the stories I do not want to remain buried for ever in the museum files of dead magazine-numbers an author's not unpardonable vanity..."   Fiction Pages 272

☐ **Life of David Crockett** *by David Crockett*   ISBN: *1-59462-250-7*   **$27.45**
"Colonel David Crockett was one of the most remarkable men of the times in which he lived. Born in humble life, but gifted with a strong will, an indomitable courage, and unremitting perseverance...   Biographies/New Age Pages 424

☐ **Lip-Reading** *by Edward Nitchie*   ISBN: *1-59462-206-X*   **$25.95**
Edward B. Nitchie, founder of the New York School for the Hard of Hearing, now the Nitchie School of Lip-Reading, Inc, wrote "LIP-READING Principles and Practice". The development and perfecting of this meritorious work on lip-reading was an undertaking...   How-to Pages 400

☐ **A Handbook of Suggestive Therapeutics, Applied Hypnotism, Psychic Science**   ISBN: *1-59462-214-0*   **$24.95**
by Henry Munro   Health/New Age/Health/Self-help Pages 376

☐ **A Doll's House: and Two Other Plays** *by Henrik Ibsen*   ISBN: *1-59462-112-8*   **$19.95**
Henrik Ibsen created this classic when in revolutionary 1848 Rome. Introducing some striking concepts in playwriting for the realist genre, this play has been studied the world over.   Fiction/Classics/Plays 308

☐ **The Light of Asia** *by sir Edwin Arnold*   ISBN: *1-59462-204-3*   **$13.95**
In this poetic masterpiece, Edwin Arnold describes the life and teachings of Buddha. The man who was to become known as Buddha to the world was born as Prince Gautama of India but he rejected the worldly riches and abandoned the reigns of power when...   Religion/History/Biographies Pages 170

☐ **The Complete Works of Guy de Maupassant** *by Guy de Maupassant*   ISBN: *1-59462-157-8*   **$16.95**
"For days and days, nights and nights, I had dreamed of that first kiss which was to consecrate our engagement, and I knew not on what spot I should put my lips..."   Fiction/Classics Pages 240

☐ **The Art of Cross-Examination** *by Francis L. Wellman*   ISBN: *1-59462-309-0*   **$26.95**
Written by a renowned trial lawyer, Wellman imparts his experience and uses case studies to explain how to use psychology to extract desired information through questioning.   How-to/Science/Reference Pages 408

☐ **Answered or Unanswered?** *by Louisa Vaughan*   ISBN: *1-59462-248-5*   **$10.95**
Miracles of Faith in China   Religion Pages 112

☐ **The Edinburgh Lectures on Mental Science (1909)** *by Thomas*   ISBN: *1-59462-008-3*   **$11.95**
This book contains the substance of a course of lectures recently given by the writer in the Queen Street Hall, Edinburgh. Its purpose is to indicate the Natural Principles governing the relation between Mental Action and Material Conditions...   New Age/Psychology Pages 148

☐ **Ayesha** *by H. Rider Haggard*   ISBN: *1-59462-301-5*   **$24.95**
Verily and indeed it is the unexpected that happens! Probably if there was one person upon the earth from whom the Editor of this, and of a certain previous history, did not expect to hear again...   Classics Pages 380

☐ **Ayala's Angel** *by Anthony Trollope*   ISBN: *1-59462-352-X*   **$29.95**
The two girls were both pretty, but Lucy who was twenty-one who supposed to be simple and comparatively unattractive, whereas Ayala was credited, as her Bombwhat romantic name might show, with poetic charm and a taste for romance. Ayala when her father died was nineteen...   Fiction Pages 484

☐ **The American Commonwealth** *by James Bryce*   ISBN: *1-59462-286-8*   **$34.45**
An interpretation of American democratic political theory. It examines political mechanics and society from the perspective of Scotsman James Bryce   Politics Pages 572

☐ **Stories of the Pilgrims** *by Margaret P. Pumphrey*   ISBN: *1-59462-116-0*   **$17.95**
This book explores pilgrims religious oppression in England as well as their escape to Holland and eventual crossing to America on the Mayflower, and their early days in New England...   History Pages 268

QTY

The Fasting Cure *by Sinclair Upton*   ISBN: *1-59462-222-1*   **$13.95**
In the Cosmopolitan Magazine for May, 1910, and in the Contemporary Review (London) for April, 1910, I published an article dealing with my experiences in fasting. I have written a great many magazine articles, but never one which attracted so much attention... New Age/Self Help/Health Pages 164

Hebrew Astrology *by Sepharial*   ISBN: *1-59462-308-2*   **$13.45**
In these days of advanced thinking it is a matter of common observation that we have left many of the old landmarks behind and that we are now pressing forward to greater heights and to a wider horizon than that which represented the mind-content of our progenitors...   Astrology Pages 144

Thought Vibration or The Law of Attraction in the Thought World   ISBN: *1-59462-127-6*   **$12.95**
by William Walker Atkinson   *Psychology/Religion Pages 144*

Optimism *by Helen Keller*   ISBN: *1-59462-108-X*   **$15.95**
Helen Keller was blind, deaf, and mute since 19 months old, yet famously learned how to overcome these handicaps, communicate with the world, and spread her lectures promoting optimism. An inspiring read for everyone...   Biographies/Inspirational Pages 84

Sara Crewe *by Frances Burnett*   ISBN: *1-59462-360-0*   **$9.45**
In the first place, Miss Minchin lived in London. Her home was a large, dull, tall one, in a large, dull square, where all the houses were alike, and all the sparrows were alike, and where all the door-knockers made the same heavy sound...   Childrens/Classic Pages 88

The Autobiography of Benjamin Franklin *by Benjamin Franklin*   ISBN: *1-59462-135-7*   **$24.95**
The Autobiography of Benjamin Franklin has probably been more extensively read than any other American historical work, and no other book of its kind has had such ups and downs of fortune. Franklin lived for many years in England, where he was agent...   Biographies/History Pages 332

Name	
Email	
Telephone	
Address	
City, State ZIP	

☐ **Credit Card**   ☐ **Check / Money Order**

Credit Card Number	
Expiration Date	
Signature	

Please Mail to: Book Jungle
PO Box 2226
Champaign, IL 61825
or Fax to: 630-214-0564

ORDERING INFORMATION

web: *www.bookjungle.com*
email: *sales@bookjungle.com*
fax: *630-214-0564*
mail: *Book Jungle PO Box 2226 Champaign, IL 61825*
or PayPal *to sales@bookjungle.com*

Please contact us for bulk discounts

DIRECT-ORDER TERMS

**20% Discount if You Order
Two or More Books**
Free Domestic Shipping!
Accepted: Master Card, Visa,
Discover, American Express

www.ingramcontent.com/pod-product-compliance
Lightning Source LLC
Chambersburg PA
CBHW080908020726
47502CB00008B/2383